Thomas Hood

The Early Poems and Sketches of Thomas Hood

Including the Odes and Addresses to Great Men, etc.

Thomas Hood

The Early Poems and Sketches of Thomas Hood
Including the Odes and Addresses to Great Men, etc.

ISBN/EAN: 9783744770699

Printed in Europe, USA, Canada, Australia, Japan

Cover: Foto ©Andreas Hilbeck / pixelio.de

More available books at **www.hansebooks.com**

THE EARLY
POEMS AND SKETCHES

OF

THOMAS HOOD,

INCLUDING

" *THE ODES AND ADDRESSES TO GREAT MEN,"*
ETC., ETC., ETC.

EDITED BY

HIS DAUGHTER.

The Bottle Imp.

LONDON:

E. MOXON, SON, & CO., DOVER STREET, W.
1869.

PREFACE.

THE present collection of the Early Poems and Sketches of the late Thomas Hood, has been issued to meet the growing demand for, and appreciation of the writings of a man, now universally acknowledged to be one of the greatest and most genial of modern humorists. Although the contents of the present volume are included in the Complete Edition of Hood's Works, it was believed that a smaller and less expensive series would be acceptable to a wider class of readers. Early Poems, &c., the two series of "Whims and Oddities," and the "Serious and Comic Poems," have been arranged for that purpose, as People's Editions.

There is another reason attaching more especially to the present volume, that may be of interest to the reading public, in the fact that these authorised editions are the only ones edited and revised by his children, and in which they have any substantial interest. The law of Copyright remains in the same state of "Copywrong" as when my father lived and wrote so energetically upon its shortcomings. Consequently, by the lapse of years, some of his works will erelong be at the mercy of those he so aptly called "*Bookanecrs.*" To the grievances and injuries of the Copyright law, so ably and humorously chronicled by my father, he might have added that of his heirs being reduced in protection of their just rights to the level of vendors of quack medicines, in advertising the original as the only genuine article, and as he says, "It must be an ungrateful generation, that in its love for cheap copies, can lose all regard for 'the dear originals!'" *

FRANCES FREELING BRODERIP.

---

* See "Petition of Thomas Hood," Complete Works, vol. v. p. 366.

ADVERTISEMENT BY THE PUBLISHERS.

Several weeks ago the copyright of the First Series of the "Whims and Oddities" lapsed, and a London bookseller issued it in a cheap form, as though it were the entire work, and advertised his copies of the Author's drawings as the original illustrations. As the copyright of the Second Series of the "Whims and Oddities," and many of the pieces in the present volume, does not expire for a considerable period, the Publishers beg to advise the public that no editions of the works of Thomas Hood, save those bearing their imprint, can possibly be complete, or be of any pecuniary value to the family of the Author.

44 Dover Street, W.,
April 1869.

CONTENTS.

HOOD'S EARLY POEMS AND SKETCHES.

ODE TO DR. KITCHENER.

YE Muses nine inspire
And stir up my poetic fire ;
Teach my burning soul to speak
With a bubble and a squeak !
Of Dr. Kitchener I fain would sing,
Till pots, and pans, and mighty kettles ring.

O culinary sage !
(I do not mean the herb in use,
That always goes along with goose)
How have I feasted on thy page :
" When like a lobster boil'd the morn
From black to red began to turn,"
Till midnight, when I went to bed,
And clapt my tewah-diddle* on my head.

Who is there cannot tell,
Thou leadest a life of living well ?

* The Doctor's composition for a nightcap.

"What baron, or squire, or knight of the shire
Lives half so well as a holy Fry—er?"
In doing well thou must be reckon'd
The first,—and Mrs. Fry the second;
And twice a Job,—for, in thy fev'rish toils,
Thou wast all over roasts—as well as boils.

Thou wast indeed no dunce,
To treat thy subjects and thyself at once:
Many a hungry poet eats
  His brains like thee,
  But few there be
Could live so long on their receipts.
  What living soul or sinner
  Would slight thy invitation to a dinner,
Ought with the Danaïdes to dwell,
  Draw gravy in a cullender, and hear
  For ever in his ear
The pleasant tinkling of thy dinner bell.

Immortal Kitchener ! thy fame
  Shall keep itself when Time makes game
Of other men's—yea, it shall keep, all weathers,
And thou shalt be upheld by thy pen feathers.
Yea, by the sauce of Michael Kelly!
  Thy name shall perish never,
  But be magnified for ever—
—By all whose eyes are bigger than their belly.

Yea, till the world is done—
  —To a turn—and Time puts out the sun,
Shall live the endless echo of thy name.
But, as for thy more fleshy frame,

Ah! Death's carnivorous teeth will tittle
    Thee out of breath, and eat it for cold victual;
But still thy fame shall be among the nations
Preserved to the last course of generations.

Ah me, my soul is touch'd with sorrow !
    To think how flesh must pass away—
    So mutton, that is warm to-day,
Is cold, and turn'd to hashes, on the morrow !
    Farewell ! I would say more, but.I
    Have other fish to fry.

TO HOPE.

OH ! take, young seraph, take thy harp,
    And play to me so cheerily ;
For grief is dark, and care is sharp,
    And life wears on so wearily.
      Oh ! take thy harp !
Oh ! sing as thou were wont to do,
    When, all youth's sunny season long,
    I sat and listen'd to thy song,
And yet 'twas ever, ever new,
With magic in its heaven-tuned string—
    The future bliss thy constant theme,
Oh ! then each little woe took wing
    Away, like phantoms of a dream ;
      As if each sound
      That flutter'd round
    Had floated over Lethe's stream !
By all those bright and happy hours
We spent in life's sweet eastern bow'rs,

Where thou wouldst sit and smile, and show,
Ere buds were come, where flowers would
    grow,
And oft anticipate the rise
Of life's warm sun that scaled the skies;
By many a story of love and glory,
And friendships promised oft to me;
By all the faith I lent to thee,—
Oh! take, young seraph, take thy harp,
   And play to me so cheerily;
For grief is dark, and care is sharp,
   And life wears on so wearily.
      Oh! take thy harp!

Perchance the strings will sound less clear,
   That long have lain neglected by
In sorrow's misty atmosphere;
It ne'er may speak as it has spoken
   Such joyous notes so brisk and high;
But are its golden chords all broken?
Are there not some, though weak and low,
To play a lullaby to woe?
But thou canst sing of love no more,
   For Celia show'd that dream was vain;
And many a fancied bliss is o'er,
   That comes not e'en in dreams again.
     Alas! alas!
     How pleasures pass,
And leave thee now no subject, save
The peace and bliss beyond the grave!
Then be thy flight among the skies:
   Take, then, oh! take the skylark's wing,
And leave dull earth, and heavenward rise

O'er all its tearful clouds, and sing
    On skylark's wing !
Another life-spring there adorns
    Another youth, without the dread
Of cruel care, whose crown of thorns
    Is here for manhood's aching head
Oh ! there are realms of welcome day,
A world where tears are wiped away !
Then be thy flight among the skies :
    Take, then, oh ! take the skylark's wing,
And leave dull earth, and heavenward rise
    O'er all its tearful clouds, and sing
        On skylark's wing !

THE COOK'S ORACLE.*

DR. KITCHENER has greatly recognised the genius of his name by taking boldly the path to which it points; disregarding all the usual seductions of life, he has kept his eye steadily on the larder, the *Mecca* of his appetite; and has unravelled all the mysteries and intricacies of *celery soup*, and *beef haricot*, to the eyes of a reading public. He has taken an extensive *kitchen range* over the whole world of stews, and broils, and roasts, and comes home to the fireside (from which, indeed, his body has never departed), boiling over with knowledge—stored with curiosities of bone and sinew—a made-up human dish of cloves, mace, curry, catsup, cayenne, and the like. He has

* The Cook's Oracle; containing Receipts for Plain Cookery, &c.; the whole being the Result of Experiments instituted in the Kitchen of a Physician.

sailed over all the soups, has touched at all quarters
of the lamb, has been, in short, round the stomach
world and returns a second *Captain Cook!* Dr.
Kitchener has written a book; and if he, good easy
man, should think to surprise any friend or acquaintance by slily asking, "What book have I written?"
he would be sure to be astounded with a successful
reply, "A book on Cookery." His name is above
all disguises. In the same way a worthy old gentleman of our acquaintance, who was wont to lead his
visitors around his kitchen garden (the Doctor will
prick up his ears at this) which he had carefully and
cunningly obscured with a laurel hedge, and who
always said, with an exulting tone, "now you would
be puzzled to say where the kitchen garden was
situated," once met with a strong-hearted man who
remorselessly answered, "Not I! over that hedge, to
be sure." The Doctor might expect you, in answer
to his query, to say; "A book, sir! Why, perhaps
you have plunged your whole soul into the ocean of
an epic; or rolled your mind, with the success of a
Sisyphus, up the hills of metaphysics; or played the
sedate game of the mathematics, that Chinese puzzle
to English minds! or gone a tour with Dugald Stuart,
in search of the picturesque, or leaped double sentences and waded through metaphors, in a gram-
matical steeple chase with Colonel Thornton; or
turned literary cuckoo, and gone sucking the eggs of
other people's books, and making the woods of the
world echo with one solitary, complaining, *reviewing*
note." Such might be the Doctor's notion of a reply
to which we fancy we see him *simmering* with delight,
and saying, "No sir! I have not meddled either

with the curry of poetry or the cold meat of prose. I
have not wasted over the slow fire of the metaphysics,
or cut up the mathematics into thin slices—I have
not lost myself amongst the *kick-shaws* of fine scenery,
or pampered myself on the mock turtle of metaphors.
Neither have I dined at the table and the expense of
other men's minds! No, sir, I have written on
cookery, on the kitchen, on the solids—'the substantials, Sir Giles, the substantials'!"

If it were not that critics are proverbial for having
no bowels, we should hesitate at entering the paradise
of pies and puddings which Dr. Kitchener has opened
to us; for the steam of his rich sentences rises about
our senses like the odours of flowers around the imagination of a poet; and larded beef goes nigh to
lord it over our bewildered appetites. But being
steady men, of sober and temperate habits, and used
to privations in the way of food, we shall not scruple
at looking a leg of mutton in the face or shaking
hands with a shoulder of veal. "Minced collops"
nothing daunt us; we brace our nerves, and are not
overwhelmed with "cockle catsup!" When Bags asks
his friend, "How do you do when you write?" it
would seem that he had the Cook's Oracle in his eye
—for to men of any mastication, never was there a
book that required more training for a quiet and
useful perusal. Cod's head rises before you in all its
glory! While the oysters revolve around it, in their
firmament of melted butter, like its well ordered
satellites! Moorgame, mackarel, muscles, fowls,
eggs, and force-meat balls, start up in all directions
and dance the hays in the imagination. We should
recommend those readers with whom dinner is a

habit, not to venture on the Doctor's pages, without
seeing that their hunger, like a ferocious house-dog,
is carefully tied up. To read four pages with an
unchained appetite, would bring on dreadful dreams
of being destroyed with spits, or drowned in mulliga-
tawny soup, or of having your tongue neatly smothered
in your own brains, and, as Matthew says, a lemon
stuck in your mouth. We cannot but conceive that
such reading, in such unprepared minds, would have
strange influences; and that the dreams of persons
should be dished up to suit the various palates. The
school girl would, like the French goose, "be persuaded to roast itself." The indolent man would
"sleep a fortnight" and even then would not be fit
for use. The lover would dream that his heart was
overdone. The author would be roasted alive in his
own quills and basted with cold ink. It were an
endless task to follow this speculation; and indeed
we are keeping our readers too long without the meal
to which we have taken the liberty of inviting them.
The dinner "bell invites" us—we go, and it is *done.*

The book, the Cook's Oracle, opens with a preface,
as other books occasionally do; but "the likeness
ends;" for it continues with a whole bunch of intro-
ductions, treating of cooks, and invitations to dinner,
and refusals, and "friendly advice," and weights and
measures, and then we get fairly launched on the sea
of boiling, broiling, roasting, stewing, and again return
and cast anchor among the vegetables. It is impossible to say where the book begins; it is a heap
of initiatory chapters—a parcel of graces before meat,
—a bunch of heads,—the asparagus of literature.
You are not troubled with "more last words of Mr.

Baxter," but are delighted, and *re*delighted, with more first words of Dr. Kitchener. He makes several starts like a restless race-horse before he fairly gets upon the second course ; or rather, like Lady Macbeth's dinner party, he stands much upon the order of his going. But now, to avoid sinking into the same trick, we will proceed without further preface to conduct our readers through the maze of pots, gridirons and frying pans, which Dr. Kitchener has rendered a very poetical, or we should say, a very palatable amusement.

The *first* preface tells us, *inter alia*, that he has worked all the culinary problems which his book contains, in his own kitchen ; and that, after this warm experience, he did not venture to print a sauce, or a stew, until he had read "two hundred cookery books," which, as he says, "he patiently pioneered through, before he set about recording the results of his own experiments!" We scarcely thought there had been so many volumes written on the Dutchoven.

"The following receipts are not a mere marrowless collection of shreds, and patches, and cuttings, and pastings, but a *bonâ fide* register of practical facts,—accumulated by a perseverance not to be subdued, or evaporated, by the igniferous terrors of a roasting fire in the dog days,—in defiance of the odoriferous and calefacient repellants of roasting,—boiling,—frying,—and broiling ; moreover the author has submitted to a labour no preceding Cookery Book maker, perhaps, ever attempted to encounter,—having *eaten* each receipt before he set it down in his book."

We should like to see the Doctor, we confess, after this extraordinary statement. To have superintended the agitations of the pot,—to have hung affectionately over a revolving calf's heart—to have patiently witnessed the noisy marriage of bubble and squeak,—to have coolly investigated the mystery of a haricot,—appears within the compass of any old lady or gentleman, whose frame could stand the fire and whose soul could rule the roast. But to have eaten the substantials of four hundred and forty closely printed pages is "a thing to read of, not to tell." It calls for a man of iron interior, a man *alieni appetens, sui profusus.* It demands the rival of time; an *edax rerum!* The Doctor does not tell us how he travelled from gridiron to frying-pan—from frying-pan to Dutch-oven —from Dutch-oven to spit—from spit to pot—from pot to fork—he leaves us to guess at his progress. We presume he ate his way, page by page, through fish, flesh, fowl and vegetable; he would have left us dead among the soups and gravies. Had a whole army of martyrs accompanied him on this Russian retreat of the appetite, we should have found *them* strewing the way; and *him* alone, the Napoleon of the task, living and fattening at the end of the journey. The introduction goes on very learnedly, descanting upon Shakspeare, Descartes, Dr. Johnson, Mrs. Glasse, Professor Bradley, Pythagoras, Miss Seward, and other persons equally illustrious. The Doctor's chief aim is to prove, we believe, that cookery is the most laudable pursuit, and the most pleasurable amusement of life. Much depends on the age of your domestics; for we are told that "it is a good maxim to select servants not younger than

THIRTY." Is it so? Youth "thou art shamed!" This first introduction concludes with a long eulogy upon the Doctor's "laborious stove work;" and upon the spirit, temper and ability with which he had *dressed* his book. The Doctor appends to this introduction a chapter called "Culinary Curiosities," in which he gives the following recipe for "persuading a goose to roast itself." We must say it outhorrors all the horrors we ever read of.

"How to roast a Goose alive."

"Take a goose, or a duck, or some such lively creature (but a goose is best of all for such purpose), pull off all her feathers, only the head and neck must be spared, then make a fire round about her, not too close to her, that the smoke do not choke her, and that the fire may not burn her too soon; nor too far off, that she may not escape fire: within the circle of the fire let there be set small cups and pots full of water wherein salt and honey are mingled, and let there be set also chargers full of sodden apples, cut into small pieces in the dish. The goose must be all larded and basted over with butter, to make her the more fit to be eaten, and may roast the better: put then fire about her, but do not make too much haste, when you see her beginning to roast; for by walking about, and flying here and there, being cooped in by the fire that stops her way out, the unwearied goose is kept in;* she will fall to drink the water to quench her

* This cook of a goose, or goose of a cook, whichever it may be, strangely reminds us of the Doctor's own intense and enthusiastic bustle among the butter-boats. We fancy we see him, and not the goose, "walking about, and flying here and there,

thirst, and cool her heart, and all her body, and the apple-sauce will make her dung, and cleanse and empty her. And when she roasteth, and consumes inwardly, always wet her head and heart with a wet sponge; and when you see her giddy with running, and begin to stumble, her heart wants moisture, and she is roasted enough. Take her up, set her before your guests, and she will cry as you cut off any part from her, and will be almost eaten up before she be dead. It is mighty pleasant to behold!!! See *Wecker's Secrets of Nature*, in folio, London, 1660, pp. 148, 309."

The next chapter, or introduction (for we are not within forty spits length of the cookery directions yet), is entitled "Invitations to Dinner;" and commences thus:

"In the affairs of the mouth the strictest punctuality is indispensable;—the gastronomer ought to be as accurate an observer of time as the astronomer— the least delay produces fatal and irreparable misfortunes."

It appearing, therefore, that delay is dangerous, as mammas say to their daughters on certain occasions, the Doctor directs that "the dining-room should be furnished with a good-going clock." He then speaks of food "well done when it is done," which leads to certain learned sentences on indigestion. The sad disregard of dinner-hours generally observed meets with his most serious displeasure and rebuke; but to refuse an invitation to dinner is the capital crime,

being cooped in by the fire." By this time, we should suppose, he must be about "roasted enough."

for which there is apparently no capital punishment. "Nothing can be more disobliging than a refusal which is not grounded on some very strong and unavoidable cause, except not coming at the appointed hour; according to the laws of conviviality, a certificate from a sheriff's officer, a doctor, or an undertaker, are the only pleas which are admissible. The duties which invitation imposes do not fall only on the persons invited, but, like all other social duties, are reciprocal."

If you should, therefore, fortunately happen to be arrested, or have had the good luck to fracture a limb, or, if better than all, you should have taken a box in that awful threatre at which all must be present once and for ever; you may be pardoned refusing the invitation of some tiresome friend to take a chop; but there is no other excuse, no other available excuse, for absenting yourself; no mental inaptitude will save you. Late comers are thus rebuked:

"There are some who seldom keep an appointment; we can assure them they as seldom ''scape without whipping,' and exciting those murmurs which inevitably proceed from the best regulated stomachs —when they are empty and impatient to be filled."

Carving is the next subject of the Doctor's care; but he resolutely and somewhat vehemently protests against your wielding the king of knives at any other table than your own: thus for ever excluding an author from the luxuries of table-anatomy. After giving an erudite passage from the "Almanach des Gourmands," the Doctor wanders into anecdote, and becomes facetious after the following recipe:

"I once heard a gentle hint on this subject given

to a blue mould fancier, who, by looking too long at a Stilton cheese, was at last completely overcome by his eye exciting his appetite, till it became quite ungovernable, and unconscious of everything but the *mity* object of his contemplation, he began to pick out, in no small portions, the primest parts his eye could select from the centre of the cheese."

The good natured founder of the feast, highly amused at the ecstasies each morsel created in its passage over the palate of the enraptured *gourmand*, thus encouraged the perseverance of his guest—"Cut away, my dear sir, use no ceremony, I pray;—I hope you will pick out all the best of my cheese—the rind and the rotten will do very well for my wife and family!"

There is something so serene and simple in the above little story, that we recommend it to persons after dinner in preference to those highly seasoned and spicy jests which Mr. Joseph Miller has potted for the use of posterity. The next introduction contains "Friendly Advice to Cooks and other servants;" but we cannot help thinking that Dr. Swift has in some degree forestalled our own good Doctor in this department of literature, although perhaps Dr. Kitchener is the most sober of counsellors. The following, to be sure, is a little suspicious. "Enter into all their plans of economy, and endeavour to make the most of everything as well for your own honour as your master's profit." This, without the note, would be unexceptionable; but the Doctor quotes from Dr. Trusler (all the Doctor's are *redolent* of servants) as follows:—"I am persuaded that no servant ever *saved* her master sixpence but she found it in the end of her own *pocket.*"—"Have the dust removed," says Dr. Kitchener, "regularly every fortnight!"—What dust?—Not that, we trust, which people are often entreated to come down with. The accumulation of soot has its dire evils: for "many good dinners have been spoiled, and many houses burned down, by the soot falling." Thus the Doctor, very properly, puts the greater evil first. "Give notice to your employers when the contents of your coal cellar are *diminished* to a chaldron." *Diminished!* we should be glad to hear when our cellars had increased to this stock. There is no hope, then, for those chamber-gentlemen who fritter away their lives by sack or bushel! Dr. Kitchener is rather abstruse and particular in another of his directions:—"*The best rule for marketing is to pay ready money for everything.*" This is a good rule with the elect;—but, is there no luxury in a baker's bill? Are butchers' reckonings nothing? Is there no virtue in a milk-tally? We cannot help thinking that *tick* was a great invention, and gives many a man a dinner that would otherwise go unfed.

The chapter on weights and measures is short, but deeply interesting and intense. There is an episode upon *trough nutmeg-graters* that would do the water-gruel generation good to hear.

And now the book begins *to boil.* The reader is told that meat takes twenty minutes to the pound; and that block-tin saucepans are the best. We can fish out little else, except a long and rather skilful calculation of the manner in which meat jockeys itself and reduces its weight in the cooking. Buckle and Sam Chiffney are nothing to "a leg of mutton with the shank bone taken out;" and it perhaps might not be amiss if the Newmarket profession were to consider how far it would be practicable to substitute the *cauldron* for the *blanket*, and thus reduce by *steam.* We should suppose a young gentleman, with half-an-hour's boiling, would ride somewhere about feather-weight.

Baking is dismissed in a page and a half. We are sorry to find that some joints, when fallen into poverty and decay, are quite unworthy of credit. "When baking a joint of *poor* meat I have seen *it* (what?) start from the bone, and shrivel up *scarcely to be believed.*"

Roasting is the next object of Dr. Kitchener's anxious care; and if this chapter be generally read, we shall not be surprised to see people in future roasting their meat before their doors and in their areas: for the Doctor says—

"*Roasting should be done in the open air*, to ventilate the meat from its own fumes, and by the radiant heat of a clear glowing fire,—otherwise it is in fact baked—the machines the economical grate-makers call roasters, are, in plain English, ovens."

The Doctor then proceeds, not being content with telling you how to cook your victuals, to advise carefully as to the best method of cooking the *fire.* "The fire that is but just sufficient to receive the noble sirloin will parch up a lighter joint;" which is plainly a translation into the cook's own particular language of "temper the wind to the shorn lamb." The chapter does not conclude without observing that "everybody knows the advantage of *slow boiling—slow roasting* is equally important." This is an axiom.

Frying is a very graceful and lively species of cooking, though yielding perhaps in its vivacity and music to *boiling*—but of this more anon. We are sorry to find the Doctor endeavouring to take away from the originality of *frying*, classing it unkindly with the inferior sorts of boiling—calling it, in fact, the mere corpulence of boiling.

"A frying-pan should be about four inches deep, with a perfectly flat and thick bottom, twelve inches long, and nine broad, with perpendicular sides, and must be half filled with fat : good frying is, in fact, boiling in fat. To make sure that the pan is quite clean, rub a little fat over it, and then make it warm, and rub it with a clean cloth."

Broiling follows. We really begin to be enacting this sort of cookery ourselves, from the vigour and spirit with which we have rushed along in the company of Dr. Kitchener. *Broiling* is the poetry of cooking. The lyre-like shape of the instrument on which it was performed, and the brisk and pleasant sounds that arise momentarily, are rather musical than culinary. We are transported, at the thought, to that golden gridiron in the Beef Steak Club, which seems to confine the white cook in his burning cage, which generates wit, whim, and song, for hours together, and pleasantly blends the fanciful and the substantial in one laughing and robust harmony.

The Doctor is profound on the subject of vegetables, and when we consider the importance of it, we are not surprised to hear him earnestly exclaim, "I should as soon think of *roasting an animal alive*, as of boiling *a vegetable after it is dead.*" No one will question that the one is quite as pardonable as the

other.   Our readers cannot be too particular in
looking to their brocoli and potatoes.   "This branch
of cookery requires the most vigilant attention.   If
vegetables are a minute or two too long over the
fire, they lose all their beauty and flavour.   If not
thoroughly boiled tender, they are tremendously in-
digestible, and much more troublesome during their
residence in the stomach than underdone meats."

We pass over the rudiments of dressing fish, and
of compounding broths and soups, except with re-
marking, that a turbot is said to be better for *not*
being fresh, and that "lean juicy beef, mutton, or
veal form the *basis of broth*."

Gravies and sauces are not neglected.   The Doctor
writes—"However 'les pompeuses Bagatelles de la
cuisine masquée,' may tickle the fancy of *demi con-
noisseurs*, who, leaving the substance to pursue the
shadow, prefer wonderful and whimsical metamor-
phoses, and things extravagantly expensive, to those
which are intrinsically excellent—in whose mouth,
mutton can hardly hope for a welcome unless accompanied by venison sauce—or a rabbit any chance
for a race down the red lane, without assuming the
form of a frog or spider—or pork without being
either 'goosified' or 'lambified,' and game and
poultry in the shape of crawfish or hedgehogs.

"These travesties rather show the patience than
the science of the cook,—and the bad taste of those
who prefer such baby tricks to old English nourishing
and substantial plain cookery.   *We* could have made
this the biggest book with half the trouble it has
taken *me* to make it the best;—concentration and
perspicuity have been my aim."

We do not know what the Doctor understands as "a big book;" but to our notions (and we are experienced in the weights and measures of printed works) the Cook's Oracle is a tolerably huge and Gog-like production. We should have been glad to have had a calculation of what the manuscript lost in the printing. In truth a comparative scale of the wasting of meat and prose during the cooking would be no uninteresting performance. For our parts, we can only remark from experience, that these our articles in the London Magazine boil up like spinage. We fancy, when written, that we have a heap of leaves fit to feed thirty columns; and they absolutely and alarmingly shrink up to a page or two when dressed by the compositor.

The romantic fancy of cooks is thus restrained :

" The imagination of most cooks is so incessantly on the hunt for a relish, that they seem to think they cannot make sauce sufficiently savoury, without putting into it everything that ever was eaten; and supposing every addition must be an improvement, they frequently overpower the natural flavour of their plain sauces, by overloading them with salt and spices, etc. : —but, remember, these will be deteriorated by any addition, save only just salt enough to awaken the palate—the lover of 'piquance' and compound flavours may have recourse to the 'Magazine of Taste.'"

Again——.

" Why have clove and allspice,—or mace and nutmeg, in the same sauce?—or marjoram,—thyme,—and savory?—or onions,—leeks—eschallots—and garlick? one will very well supply the place of the other, —and the frugal cook may save something considerable by attending to this to the advantage of her employers, and her own time and trouble.—You might as well, to make soup, order one quart of water from the Thames, another from the New River, a third from Hampstead, and a fourth from Chelsea, with a certain portion of spring and rain water."

The Doctor himself, however, in spite of his correction of the cooks, is not entirely free from the fanciful. When you have opened a bottle of catsup, he says, "use only the best superfine *velvet taper* corks." This is *drawing* a cork with the hand of a poet.

And now, will the reader believe it? The work commences afresh! After all our labour,—after all our travelling through boiling, broiling, roasting, etc., we find that we have the whole to go over again. To our utter dismay, p. 142 begins anew with—*boiling!* It is little comfort to us that joints and cuttings come in for their distinct treatment : we seem to have made no way, and sit down with as much despair as a young school-girl, who, after three quarters of a year's dancing, is put back to the Scotch step. Beef has been spoken of before; but we have not at all made up our minds on the following subject :—

"Obs.—In Mrs. Mason's Ladies' Assistant this joint is called haunch-bone; in Henderson's Cookery, edge-bone; in Domestic Management, aitch-bone; in Reynolds' Cookery, ische-bone; in Mrs. Lydia Fisher's Prudent Housewife, ach-bone ; in Mrs. M'Iver's Cookery, hook-bone. We have also seen it spelt each-bone, and ridge-bone, and we have also heard it called natch-bone."

Of "half a calf's head" Dr. Kitchener says, slily

enough, if you like it *full-dressed* score it *superficially;* beat up the yolk of an egg, and rub it over the head with a *feather; powder it*, etc. Such a calf's head as this, so full-dressed, might be company for the best nobleman's ditto in the land.

It is quite impossible for us to accompany Dr. Kitchener regularly through "roasting, frying, vegetables," etc., as we are by no means sure that our readers would sanction the *encore.* We shall pick a bit here and a bit there, from the Doctor's dainty larder; and take care to choose, as the English do with a French bill of fare, from those niceties which are novelties.

"A pig," observes the Doctor, as though he were speaking of any other dull, obstinate personage, "is a very troublesome subject to *roast.* Most persons have them *baked:* send a quarter of a pound of butter, and beg the baker to *baste* it well." The following occurs to us to be as difficult a direction to fulfil as any of Sir Thomas Parkin's wrestling instructions: "Lay your *pig back* to *back* in the dish, with one half of the head on each side, and the ears one at each end, which you must take care to make nice and *crisp*, or you will get scolded, as the good man was who brought his wife a pig with one ear." The point at the end is like the point of a spit. Again: "A sucking pig, like a young child, must not be left for an instant!" Never was such affection manifested before for this little interesting and persecuted tribe.

If Izaak Walton be the greatest of writers on the catching of fish, Dr. Kitchener, is, beyond doubt, triumphant over all who have written upon the *dressing* of them. The Doctor dwells upon "the fine pale red rose colour" of pickled salmon, till you doubt whether he is not admiring a carnation. "Cod's skull" becomes flowery and attractive; and fine "silver eels," when "stewed Wiggig's way," swim in beauty as well as butter. The Doctor points out the best method of killing this perversely living fish, observing, very justly, "that the human executioner does certain criminals the favour to *hang* them before he breaks them on the wheel."

Of salmon the Doctor rather quaintly and *posingly* observes, "the *thinnest* part of the fish is the *fattest. If you have any left*, put it into a pie-dish, and cover it," etc. The direction is conditional, we perceive.

"Remember to choose your lobsters '*heavy and lively.*'"—"Motion," says the Doctor, "is the index of their freshness."

Upon Oysters, Dr. Kitchener is eloquent indeed. He is, as it were, "native here, and to the manner born."

"The true lover of an oyster will have some regard for the feelings of his little favourite, and will never abandon it to the mercy of a bungling operator,— but will open it himself, and contrive to detach the fish from the shell so dexterously, that the oyster is hardly conscious he has been ejected from his lodging, till he feels the teeth of the piscivorous gourmand tickling him to death."

Who would not be an oyster to be thus surprised, to be thus pleasingly ejected from its tenement of mother of pearl, to be thus tickled to death? When we are placed in our shell, we should have no objection to be astonished with a similar delicate and titillating opening!   •

Giblet soup requires to be eaten with the fingers. We were not aware that these handy instruments could be used successfully in the devouring of gravies and soups.

"N.B. This is rather a family dish than a company one; the bones cannot be well picked without the help of a live pincers. Since Tom Coryat introduced forks, A.D. 1642, it has not been the fashion to put 'pickers and stealers' into soup."

After giving a most elaborate recipe for mock-turtle soup, he proceeds—

"This soup was eaten by the committee of taste with unanimous applause, and they pronounced it a very satisfactory substitute for 'the far fetcht and dear bought' turtle; which itself is indebted for its title of 'sovereign of savouriness' to the rich soup with which it is surrounded; without its paraphernalia of double relishes, a 'starved turtle' has not more intrinsic sapidity than a FATTED CALF."

And a little further on he observes—

"Obs.—This is a delicious soup, within the reach of those 'who eat to live;' but if it had been composed expressly for those 'who only live to eat,' I do not know how it could have been made more agreeable; as it is, the lover of good eating will 'wish his throat a mile long, and every inch of it palate.'"

Our readers will pant to have "Mr. Michael Kelly's sauce for boiled tripe, calf's-head, or cow-heel." It is this:—

"Garlick vinegar, a tablespoonful; of mustard, brown sugar, and black pepper, a teaspoonful each; stirred into half a pint of oiled melted butter."

Gad-a-mercy, what a gullet must be in possession of Mr. Michael Kelly! .

We think the following almost a superfluous direction to cooks :—"Take your chops out of the frying-pan," p. 324; but then he tells you in another place, "to put your tongue into plenty of cold water;" p. 156, which makes all even again.

After giving ample directions for the making of essence of anchovy, the Doctor rather damps our ardour for entering upon it, by the following observations : "Mem.— *You cannot make essence of anchovy half so cheap as you can buy it.*"

. The following passage is rather too close an imitation of one of the puff directions in the "Critic :"

"To a pint of the cleanest and strongest rectified spirit, (sold by Rickards, Piccadilly,) add two drachms and a half of the sweet oil of orange peel, (sold by Stewart, No. 11, Old Broad-street, near the Bank,) shake it up, etc."

"Obs.—We do not offer this receipt as a rival to Mr. Johnson's curaçoa; it is only proposed as an humble substitute for that incomparable liqueur."

The Doctor proceeds to luxuriate upon made dishes, etc.; in the course of which he says, "The sirloin of beef I divide into three parts : I first have it nicely *boned !*" This is rather a suspicious way of having it at all. Mrs. Philip's Irish stew has all the fascination of her country-women. In treating of shin of beef, the Doctor gives us a proverb which we never remember to have heard before.

"Of all the fowls of the air, commend me to the shin of beef : for there's marrow for the master, meat for the mistress, gristles for. the servants, and bones for the dogs."

On pounded cheese the Doctor writes, " the

piquance of this *buttery-caseous* relish," etc. Is not this a little *overdone?* The passage, however, on the frying of eggs makes up for all.

"Be sure the frying-pan is quite clean; when the fat is hot, break two or three eggs into it; do not turn them, but, while they are frying, keep pouring some of the fat over them with a spoon: when the yolk just begins to look white, which it will be in about a couple of minutes, they are done enough; if they are done nicely, they will look as white and delicate as if they had been poached; take them up with a tin slice, drain the fat from them, trim them neatly, and send them up with the bacon round them."

"The beauty of a poached egg is for the yolk to be seen *blushing* through the white, which should only be just sufficiently hardened to form a transparent veil for the egg."

So much for the Cook's Oracle. The style is a piquant sauce to the solid food of the instructions; and we never recollect reading sentences that relished so savourily. The Doctor appears to have written his work upon the back of a dripping-pan, with the point of his spit, so very cooklike does he dish up his remarks. If we were to be cast away upon a desert island, and could only carry one book ashore, we should take care to secure the Cook's Oracle; for let victuals be ever so scarce, there are pages in that erudite book that are, as Congreve's Jeremy says, "a feast for an emperor." Who could starve with such a larder of reading?

C

THE DEPARTURE OF SUMMER.

SUMMER is gone on swallows' wings,
And Earth has buried all her flowers :
No more the lark,—the linnet—sings,
But Silence sits in faded bowers.
There is a shadow on the plain
Of Winter ere he comes again,—
There is in woods a solemn sound
Of hollow warnings whisper'd round,
As Echo in her deep recess
For once had turn'd a prophetess.
Shuddering Autumn stops to list,
And breathes his fear in sudden sighs,
With clouded face, and hazel eyes
That quench themselves, and hide in mist.

Yes, Summer's gone like pageant bright :
Its glorious days of golden light
Are gone—the mimic suns that quiver,
Then melt in Time's dark-flowing river.
Gone the sweetly-scented breeze
That spoke in music to the trees ;
Gone—for damp and chilly breath,
As if fresh blown o'er marble seas,
Or newly from the lungs of Death.
Gone its virgin roses' blushes,
Warm as when Aurora rushes
Freshly from the god's embrace,
With all her shame upon her face.
Old Time hath laid them in the mould ;
Sure he is blind as well as old,

Whose hand relentless never spares
Young cheeks so beauty-bright as theirs!
Gone are the flame-eyed lovers now
From where so blushing-blest they tarried
Under the hawthorn's blossom-bough,
Gone; for Day and Night are married.
All the light of love is fled :—
Alas! that negro breasts should hide
The lips that were so rosy red,
At morning and at even-tide !

Delightful Summer! then adieu
Till thou shalt visit us anew :
But who without regretful sigh
Can say, adieu, and see thee fly?
Not he that e'er hath felt thy pow'r,
His joy expanding like a flow'r,
That cometh after rain and snow,
Looks up at heaven, and learns to glow :—
Not he that fled from Babel-strife
To the green sabbath-land of life,
To dodge dull Care 'mid cluster'd trees,
And cool his forehead in the breeze,—
Whose spirit, weary-worn perchance,
Shook from its wings a weight of grief,
And perch'd upon an aspen leaf,
For every breath to make it dance.

Farewell !—on wings of sombre stain,
That blacken in the last blue skies,
Thou fly'st; but thou wilt come again
On the gay wings of butterflies.
Spring at thy approach will sprout

Her new Corinthian beauties out,
Leaf-woven homes, where twitter-words
Will grow to songs, and eggs to birds;
Ambitious buds shall swell to flowers,
And April smiles to sunny hours.
Bright days shall be, and gentle nights
Full of soft breath and echo-lights,
As if the god of sun-time kept
His eyes half-open while he slept.
Roses shall be where roses were,
Not shadows, but reality;
As if they never perish'd there,
But slept in immortality:
Nature shall thrill with new delight,
And Time's relumined river run
Warm as young blood, and dazzling bright,
As if its source were in the sun!

But say, hath Winter then no charms?
Is there no joy, no gladness warms
His aged heart? no happy wiles
To cheat the hoary one to smiles?
Onward he comes—the cruel North
Pours his furious whirlwind forth
Before him—and we breathe the breath
Of famish'd bears that howl to death.
Onward he comes from rocks that blanch
O'er solid streams that never flow:
His tears all ice, his locks all snow,
Just crept from some huge avalanche—
A thing half-breathing and half-warm,
As if one spark began to glow
Within some statue's marble form,

Or pilgrim stiffen'd in the storm.
Oh ! will not Mirth's light arrows fail
To pierce that frozen coat of mail !
Oh ! will not joy but strive in vain
To light up those glazed eyes again ?

No ! take him in, and blaze the oak,
And pour the wine, and warm the ale ;
His sides shall shake to many a joke,
His tongue shall thaw in many a tale,
His eyes grow bright, his heart be gay,
And even his palsy charm'd away.
What heeds he then the boisterous shout
Of angry winds that scold without,
Like shrewish wives at tavern door ?
What heeds he then the wild uproar
Of billows bursting on the shore ?
In dashing waves, in howling breeze,
There is a music that can charm him ;
When safe, and shelter'd, and at ease,
He hears the storm that cannot harm him.

But hark ! those shouts ! that sudden din
Of little hearts that laugh within.
Oh ! take him where the youngsters play,
And he will grow as young as they !
They come ! they come ! each blue-eyed Sport,
The Twelfth-Night King and all his court—
'Tis Mirth fresh crown'd with misletoe !
Music with her merry fiddles,
Joy " on light fantastic toe,"
Wit with all his jests and riddles,
Singing and dancing as they go.

And Love, young Love, among the rest,
A welcome—nor unbidden guest.

But still for Summer dost thou grieve?
Then read our Poets—they shall weave
A garden of green fancies still,
Where thy wish may rove at will.
They have kept for after-treats
The essences of summer sweets,
And echoes of its songs that wind
In endless music through the mind :
They have stamp'd in visible traces
The "thoughts that breathe," in words that
    shine—
The flights of soul in sunny places—
To greet and company with thine.
These shall wing thee on to flow'rs—
The past or future, that shall seem
All the brighter in thy dream
For blowing in such desert hours.
The summer never shines so bright
As thought-of in a winter's night;
And the sweetest loveliest rose
Is in the bud before it blows;
The dear one of the lover's heart
Is painted to his longing eyes,
In charms she ne'er can realise—
But when she turns again to part.
Dream thou then, and bind thy brow
With wreath of fancy roses now,
And drink of Summer in the cup
Where the Muse hath mix'd it up;
The " dance, and song, and sun-burnt mirth,"

With the warm nectar of the earth :
Drink ! 'twill glow in every vein,
And thou shalt dream the winter through :
Then waken to the sun again,
And find thy Summer Vision true !

TO A CRITIC.

O CRUEL One ! How littel dost thou knowe
How manye poetes with Unhappyenesse
Thou mayest have slaine ; are they beganne to blowe
Like to yonge Buddes in theyre firste sappyenesse !
Even as Pinkes from littel Pipinges growe
Great Poetes yet maye come of singinges smalle,
Which, if an hungrede Worme doth gnawe belowe,
Fold up theyre strypëd leaves, and dye withalle.
Alake, that pleasaunt Flowre must fayde and falle
Because a Grubbe hath ete into yts Hede,—
That els had growne soe fayre and eke soe talle
To-wardes the Heaven, and opened forthe and sprede
Its blossomes to the Sunne for Menne to rede
In soe brighte hues of Lovelinesse indeede !

TO CELIA.

OLD fictions say that Love hath eyes,
Yet sees, unhappy boy ! with none ;
Blind as the night ! but fiction lies,
For Love doth always see with one.

To one our graces all unveil,
To one our flaws are all exposed ;
But when with tenderness we hail,
He smiles, and keeps the critic closed.

But when he's scorn'd, abused, estranged,
He opes the eye of evil ken,
And all his angel friends are changed
To demons—and are hated then !

Yet once it happ'd that, semi-blind,
He met thee on a summer day,
And took thee for his mother kind,   .
And frown'd as he was push'd away.

But still he saw the shine the same,
Though he had oped his evil eye,
And found that nothing but her shame
Was left to know his mother by !

And ever since that morning sun
He thinks of thee, and blesses Fate
That he can look with both on one
Who hath no ugliness to hate.

PRESENTIMENT.

A FRAGMENT.

IF a man has a little child to whom he bows his
heart and stretches forth his arms—if he has an only
son, or a little daughter, with her sweet face and
innocent hands, with her mother's voice, only louder
—and her mother's eyes, only brighter,—let him go
and caress them while they are his, for the dead
possess nothing.   Let him put fondness in his breath
while it is with him, and caress his babes as if they
would be fatherless, and blend his fingers with their

glossy hair as if it were a frail, frail gossamer. And if he be away, let him hasten homeward with his impatient spirit before him, plotting kisses for their lips; but if he be far distant, let him read my story, and weep and utter fond breath, kissing the words before they go, wishing that they could reach his children's ear. And yet let him be glad; for though he is beyond seas, he is still near them while Death is behind him—for the greater distance swallows the less. And the wings of angels may waft his love to their far-away thoughts, silently, like the whisperings of their own spirits while they weep for their father.

It was in the days of my bitterness, when care had bewildered me, and the feverish strife of this world had vexed me till I was mad, that I went into a little land of graves, and there wept; for my sorrow was deep into darkness, and I could not win friendship by friendship, nor love (though it still loved me) but in heaven—for it was purer than the pure air, and had floated up to God. And I sat down upon a tombstone with my unburied grief, and wondered what that earth contained of joy, and misery and triumph long past, and pride lower than nettles, and how old love was joined to love again, and hate was gone to hate. For there were many monuments with sunshine on one side and shade on the other, like life and death, with black frowning letters upon their white, bright faces; and through those letters one might hear the dead speaking silently and slow, for there was much meaning in those words, and mysteries which long thought could not fathom. And there was dust upon those flat dwellings, which I kissed, for lips like it were there, and eyes where much love had been, and cheeks that had warmed the sunshine. But the dust was gone in a breath, and so were they; and the wind brought shadows that passed and passed incessantly over that land of graves, which you might strive to stay, but could not, even as the dead had passed away and been missed in the after brightness.

Thus I buried my thoughts with the dead; and as I sat, unconsciously, I heard the sound of young sweet voices, and, looking up, I saw two little children coming up the path. The lambs lifted up their heads as they passed and gazed, but fed again without stirring, for there was nothing to fear from such innocent looks and so gentle voices; there was even a melancholy in their tone which does not belong to childhood. The eldest was a young boy, very fair and gentle, with a little hand linked to his; for, by his talk, it seemed that he had brought his sister to show her where her poor father lay, and to speak about Death. Their lips seemed too rosy and tender to utter his dreadful name—but the word was empty to them, and unmeaning as the sound of a shell—for they knew him not, that he had kissed them before they were born or breathed, and would again when the time came. So they approached, dew-dabbled, and struggling through the long-tangled weeds to a new grave, and stood before it, and gazed on its record, like the ignorant sheep, without reading. They did not see their father, but only a little mound of earth, with strange grass and weeds; and they looked and looked again, and at each other, with whisperings in their eyes, and listened, till the flowers dropped from their forgotten hands. And

when I saw how rosy they were in that black, which
only made them the more rosy, and their bright curly
hair, that had no proud hand to part it, I thought of
the yearnings of disembodied love and invisible
agony that had no voice, till methought their father's
spirit passed into mine, and burned, and gazed
through my eyes upon his children. They had not
yet seemed to notice me, but only that silent grave;
and, looking more and more sadly, their eyes filled
with large tears, and their lips dropped, and their
heads sank so mournfully and so comfortless, that my
own grief rushed into my eyes and hid them from me.
And I said inwardly, I will be their father, and dry
their blue eyes, and win their sorrowful cheeks into
dimples, for they are very fair and young—too young
for this stormy life. I will watch them through the
wide world, for it is a cruel place, where the tenderest
are most torn because they are tenderest, and the
most beautiful are most blighted. Therefore this
little one shall be my daughter, that I may gather her
for heaven as my best deed upon earth; and this
young boy shall be my son, to share my blessing
when I die, that God in that time may so deal with
my own offspring. For I feel a misgiving that I shall
soon die, and that my own little ones will come to
my grave and weep over me, even as these poor
orphans. Oh! how shall I leave them to the care of
the careless—to the advice of the winds—to the
home of the wide world? And as I thought of this,
the full tears dropped from my eyes, and I saw again
the two children. They were still there and weeping;
but as I looked at them more earnestly, I perceived
that they were altered, or my sight changed, so that

I knew their faces. I knew them—for I had seen them in very infancy, and through all their growth—in sickness when I prayed over them—and in slumber when I had watched over them till I almost wept.

They were so beautiful! I had kissed, how often! those very cheeks, blushing my own blood, and had breathed blessings upon their glossy brows, and had pressed their little hands in ecstasies of anxious love. They also knew me; but there was an older grief in their looks than had ever been:—and why had they come to me in that place, and in black, so sad and so speechless, and with flowers so withering? but they only shook their heads and wept. Then I trembled exceedingly, and stretched out my arms to embrace them, but there was nothing between me and the tombstone where they had seemed: yet they still gazed at me from behind it, and further and still further as I followed, till they stood upon the verge of the churchyard. Then I saw, in the sunshine, that they were shadowless; and, as they raised their hands in the light, that no blood was in them; and as I moved still closer, they slowly turned into trees, and hills, and pale blue sky, that had been in the distance. Still I gazed where they had been, and the sky seemed full of them; but they were only clouds, and the shadows, and the rustling was the rustling of the sheep. I saw them no more. They were gone from me, as if for ever; but I knew that this was my warning, and wept, for it came to me through my own children in all its bitterness. I felt that I should leave them—as I had foretold—their hearts, and lips, and sweet voices, to one another, to be their own comfort; for I knew that such grief is prophetic of grief, and that angels so minister to man, and that Death thus converses in spirit with his elect. So I spread my arms to the world in farewell, and weaned my eyes from all things that had been pleasant on the Earth, and would be so after me, and prepared myself for her ready bosom. And I said now I will go home and kiss my children before I die, and put a life's love into my last hour; for I must hasten while my last thoughts are with me, lest I madden, and perhaps wrong them in my delirium, and spurn their sorrowful love, and curse them, instead of blessing, with a fierce, strange voice. Thus I hurried towards them faster and faster till I ran; but as my desire increased, my strength failed me, so that I wished for my deathbed, and threw myself down on a green hill, under the shade of trees that almost hid the sky with their intricate branches. And as I lay, the thought of death, with a deep gloom like the shade of a darkened chamber, blinded me to the trees, and the sky, and the grass, that were round me. But a pale light came, as I thought, through the pierced shutters, and I saw by it strange and familiar faces full of grief, and eyes that watched mine for the last look, and tiptoe figures gliding silently with clasped hands—and a woman that chafed my feet; and as she seemed to chafe them, she turned to shake her head, and tears gushed into all eyes as if they had been one, so that I seemed drowned, and could see nothing except their shadows in the light of my own spirit. In that moment I heard the cries of my own children, calling to me fainter and fainter, as if they died and I could not save them; and I tried to stay them, but my tongue was lifeless in my mouth, and breath seemed locked up in my bosom : and I thought, 'surely I now die, and the last of my soul is in my ears, for I still hear, though I see not;' but the voices were soon drowned in a noise like the rushing of waters, for the blood was struggling through my heart, slower and slower, till it stopped, and I turned so cold, that I felt the burning of the air upon me, and the scalding of unknown tears. Yet for a moment the light returned to me, with those mourners—for they were already in black, even their faces ; but they turned darker and darker, and whirled round into one shade till it was utterly dark : and as my breath went forth, the air pressed heavy upon me, so that I seemed buried, and in my deep grave, and suffering the pain of worms till I was all consumed and no more conscious. Thus I lay for unknown time, and without thought ; and again awakening, I saw a dark figure bending over me, and felt him grasp me till I ached in all my bones. Then I asked him if he was Death or an angel, and if he had brought me wings, for I could not see plainly ; but as my senses returned, I knew an intimate friend and neighbour, and recognised the sound of his voice. He had thus found me, he said, in passing, and had seen me faint, and had recovered me ; but not till he had almost wrung the blood from my fingers ; and he inquired the cause of my distress. So I thanked him, and told him of my vision, and he tried to comfort me : but I knew that the angels of my children had told me truly, and the more so for this shadow of Death that I had passed ; and feeling that my hour was near, and recollecting my home, I endeavoured to rise. But my strength was gone, and I fell backwards; till fear, which had first taken away my strength, restored it tenfold, and I descended the hill, and hurried onwards before my friend, who could not keep up with me.

When I had gone a little way, however, the road was of deep sand, so that I grew impatient of my steps, and wished for the speed of a horse that I heard galloping before me. Even as I heard it, the horse suddenly turned an angle of the road, and came running with all the madness of fright, plunging and scattering the loose sand from his fiery heels. As he came nearer, I thought I saw a rider upon his back—it was only fancy; but he looked like Death, and very terrible, for I knew that he was coming to tear me and trample me under his horse's hoofs, and carry me away for ever, so that I should never see my children again. At that thought my soul fainted within me without his touch, and my breath went from me, so that I could not stir even from Death, though he came nearer and nearer, and I could see him frown through the black tossing mane. In a moment he was close; the wild foaming horse struck at me with his furious heels—so that the loose sand flew up in my bosom—reared his head disdainfully, and flew past me with the rush of a whirlwind. The fiend grinned upon me as he passed, and tossed his arms in an ecstasy of triumph; but he left me untouched, and the noise soon died away behind me. Then a warm joy trembled over my limbs, and I hurried forward again with an hour's hope of life. My heart's beat quickened my feet, and I soon reached the corner where I had first seen the horse; but there I stopped—it was only a low moan—but my heart stopped with it. In another throb I was with my children, and in another they were with God. I saw their eyes before they closed—but my son's——

How it happened I have never asked, or have forgotten. I only knew that I had children, and that they are dead. Now I have only their angels. They still visit me in the churchyard; but their eyes are closed, and their little locks drop blood—they still shrink, and faint, and fade away—but still I die not!

THE SEA OF DEATH.

A FRAGMENT.

——Methought I saw
Life swiftly treading over endless space;
And, at her foot-print, but a bygone pace,
The ocean Past, which, with increasing wave,
Swallow'd her steps like a pursuing grave.

Sad were my thoughts that anchor'd silently
On the dead waters of that passionless sea,
Unstirr'd by any touch of living breath:
Silence hung over it, and drowsy Death,
Like a gorged sea-bird, slept with folded wings
On crowded carcases—sad passive things
That wore the thin grey surface, like a veil
Over the calmness of their features pale.

And there were spring-faced cherubs that did sleep
Like water-lilies on that motionless deep,
How beautiful! with bright unruffled hair
On sleek unfretted brows, and eyes that were

Buried in marble tombs, a pale eclipse!
And smile-bedimpled cheeks, and pleasant lips,
Meekly apart, as if the soul intense
Spake out in dreams of its own innocence:
And so they lay in loveliness, and kept
The birth-night of their peace, that Life e'en wept
With very envy of their happy fronts;
For there were neighbour brows scarr'd by the brunts
Of strife and sorrowing—where Care had set
His crooked autograph, and marr'd the jet
Of glossy locks, with hollow eyes forlorn,
And lips that curl'd in bitterness and scorn—
Wretched,—as they had breathed of this world's pain,
And so bequeathed it to the world again,
Through the beholder's heart in heavy sighs.
So lay they garmented in torpid light,
Under the pall of a transparent night,
Like solemn apparitions lull'd sublime
To everlasting rest,—and with them Time
Slept, as he sleeps upon the silent face
Of a dark dial in a sunless place.

TO AN ABSENTEE.

O'ER hill, and dale, and distant sea,
Through all the miles that stretch between,
My thought must fly to rest on thee,
And would,—though worlds should intervene.

Nay, thou art now so dear, methinks
The farther we are forced apart,
Affection's firm elastic links
But bind thee closer round the heart.

D

For now we sever each from each,
I learn what I have lost in thee;
Alas, that nothing else could teach
How great indeed my love should be!

Farewell! I did not know thy worth;
But thou art gone, and now 'tis prized:
So angels walk'd unknown on earth,
But when they flew were recognised!

LYCUS THE CENTAUR.*

FROM AN UNROLLED MANUSCRIPT OF APOLLONIUS CURIUS.

THE ARGUMENT.

Lycus, detained by Circe in her magical dominion is beloved bv a Water
Nymph, who, desiring to render him immortal, has recourse to the
Sorceress. Circe gives her an incantation to pronounce. which should
turn Lycus into a horse; but the horrible effect of the charm causing
her to break off in the midst, he becomes a Centaur.

WHO hath ever been lured and bound by a spell
To wander, fore-damn'd, in that circle of hell
Where Witchery works with her will like a god,
Works more than the wonders of time at a nod,—
At a word,—at a touch,—at a flash of the eye,
But each form is a cheat, and each sound is a lie,

* When this poem was republished in "The Plea of the Midsummer
Fairies," the following dedication was added to it:—

TO J. II. REYNOLDS, ESQ.

My dear Reynolds,
      You will remember "Lycus."—It was written in the pleasant
spring-time of our friendship, and I am glad to maintain that association
by connecting your name with the poem. It will gratify me to find that
you regard it with the old partiality for the writings of each other, which
prevailed with us in those days. For my own sake, I must regret that your
pen goes now into far other records than those which used to delight me.
Your true triend and brother,
T. HOOD.

Things born of a wish—to endure for a thought,
Or last for long ages—to vanish to nought,
Or put on new semblance?   O Jove, I had given
The throne of a kingdom to know if that heaven,
And the earth and its streams were of Circe, or whether
They kept the world's birthday and brighten'd together! `
For I loved them in terror, and constantly dreaded
That the earth where I trod, and the cave where I
     ·bedded,
The face I might dote on, should live out the lease
Of the charm that created, and suddenly cease :
And I gave me to slumber, as if from one dream
To another—each horrid,—and drank of the stream
Like a first taste of blood, lest as water I quaff'd
Swift poison, and never should breathe from the
     draught,—
Such drink as her own monarch husband drain'd up
When he pledged her, and Fate closed his eyes in
     the cup.
And I pluck'd of the fruit with held breath, and a fear
That the branch would start back and scream out in
     my ear;
For once, at my suppering, I pluck'd in the dusk
An apple, juice-gushing and fragrant of musk ;
But by daylight my fingers were crimson'd with gore,
And the half-eaten fragment was flesh at the core ;
And once—only once—for the love of its blush,
I broke a bloom bough, but there came such a gush
On my hand, that it fainted away in weak fright,
While the leaf-hidden woodpecker shriek'd at the
     sight ;   ˏ
And oh ! such an agony thrill'd in that note,
That my soul, startling up, beat its wings in my throat,

As it long'd to be free of a body whose hand
Was doom'd to work torments a Fury had plann'd!

There I stood without stir, yet how willing to flee,
As if rooted and horror-turn'd into a tree,—
Oh! for innocent death,—and to suddenly win it,
I drank of the stream, but no poison was in it;
I plunged in its waters, but ere I could sink,
Some invisible fate pull'd me back to the brink;
I sprang from the rock, from its pinnacle height,
But fell on the grass with a grasshopper's flight;
I ran at my fears—they were fears and no more,
For the bear would not mangle my limbs, nor the boar,
But moan'd—all their brutalised flesh could not
    smother
The horrible truth,—we were kin to each other!

They were mournfully gentle, and group'd for relief,
All foes in their skin, but all friends in their grief:
The leopard was there,—baby-mild in its feature;
And the tiger, black-barr'd, with the gaze of a creature
That knew gentle pity; the bristle-back'd boar,
His innocent tusks stain'd with mulberry gore;
And the laughing hyena—but laughing no more;
And the snake, not with magical orbs to devise
Strange death, but with woman's attraction of eyes;
The tall ugly ape, that still bore a dim shine
Through his hairy eclipse of a manhood divine;
And the elephant stately, with more than its reason,
How thoughtful in sadness! but this is no season
To reckon them up from the lag-bellied toad
To the mammoth, whose sobs shook his ponderous
    load.

There were woes of all shapes, wretched forms, when
    I came,
That hung down their heads with a human-like shame;
The elephant hid in the boughs, and the bear
Shed over his eyes the dark veil of his hair;
And the womanly soul turning sick with disgust,
Tried to vomit herself from her serpentine crust;
While all groan'd their groans into one at their lot,
As I brought them the image of what they were not.

    Then rose a wild sound of the human voice choking
Through vile brutal organs—low tremulous croaking;
Cries swallow'd abruptly—deep animal tones
Attuned to strange passion, and full-utter'd groans;
All shuddering weaker, till hush'd in a pause
Of tongues in mute motion and wide-yawning jaws;
And I guess'd that those horrors were meant to tell
    o'er
The tale of their woes; but the silence told more,
That writhed on their tongues; and I knelt on the
    sod,
And pray'd with my voice to the cloud-stirring god,
For the sad congregation of suppliants there,
That upturn'd to his heaven brute faces of prayer;
And I ceased, and they utter'd a moaning so deep,
That I wept for my heart-ease,—but they could not
    weep,
And gazed with red eyeballs, all wistfully dry,
At the comfort of tears in a stag's human eye.
Then I motion'd them round, and, to soothe their
    distress,
I caress'd, and they bent them to meet my caress,
Their necks to my arm, and their heads to my palm,

And with poor grateful eyes suffer'd meekly and calm
Those tokens of kindness, withheld by hard fate
From returns that might chill the warm pity to hate;
So they passively bow'd—save the serpent, that leapt
To my breast like a sister, and pressingly crept
In embrace of my neck, and with close kisses blister'd
My lips in rash love,—then drew backward, and
glister'd
Her eyes in my face, and loud hissing affright,
Dropt down, and swift started away from my sight!

This sorrow was theirs, but thrice wretched my lot,
Turn'd brute in my soul, though my body was not,
When I fled from the sorrow of womanly faces,
That shrouded their woe in the shade of lone places,
And dashed off bright tears, till their fingers were wet,
And then wiped their lids with long tresses of jet:
But I fled—though they stretch'd out their hands,
all entangled
With hair, and blood-stain'd of the breasts they had
mangled,—
Though they call'd—and perchance but to ask, had I
seen   .
Their loves, or to tell the vile wrongs that had been:
But I stay'd not to hear, lest the story should hold
Some hell-form of words, some enchantment, once
told,
Might translate me in flesh to a brute; and I dreaded
To gaze on their charms, lest my faith should be
wedded
With some pity,—and love in that pity perchance—
To a thing not all lovely; for once at a glance,
Methought, where one sat, I descried a bright wonder

That flow'd like a long silver rivulet under
The long fenny grass,—with so lovely a breast,
Could it be a snake-tail made the charm of the rest?

   So I roam'd in that circle of horrors, and Fear
Walk'd with me, by hills, and in valleys, and near
Cluster'd trees for their gloom—not to shelter from
     heat—
But lest a brute-shadow should grow at my feet;
And besides that full oft in the sunshiny place
Dark shadows would gather like clouds on its face,
In the horrible likeness of demons (that none
Could see, like invisible flames in the sun);
But grew to one monster that seized on the light,
Like the dragon that strangles the moon in the night;
Fierce sphinxes, long serpents, and asps of the south;
Wild birds of huge beak, and all horrors that drouth
Engenders of slime in the land of the pest,
Vile shapes without shape, and foul bats of the West,
Bringing Night on their wings; and the bodies
     wherein
Great Brahma imprisons the spirits of sin,
Many-handed, that blent in one phantom of fight
Like a Titan, and threatfully warr'd with the light;
I have heard the wild shriek that gave signal to close,
When they rush'd on that shadowy Python of foes,
That met with sharp beaks and wide gaping of jaws,
With flappings of wings, and fierce grasping of claws,
And whirls of long tails:—I have seen the quick
     flutter
Of fragments dissever'd,—and necks stretched to
     utter
Long screamings of pain,—the swift motion of blows,

And wrestling of arms—to the flight at the close,
When the dust of the earth startled upward in rings,
And flew on the whirlwind that follow'd their wings.

Thus they fled—not forgotten—but often to grow
Like fears in my eyes, when I walk'd to and fro
In the shadows, and felt from some beings unseen
The warm touch of kisses, but clean or unclean,
I knew not, nor whether the love I had won
Was of heaven or hell—till one day in the sun,
In its very noon-blaze, I could fancy a thing
Of beauty, but faint as the cloud-mirrors fling
On the gaze of the shepherd that watches the sky,
Half-seen and half-dream'd in the soul of his eye.
And when in my musings I gazed on the stream,
In motionless trances of thought, there would seem
A face like that face, looking upward through mine;
With its eyes full of love, and the dim-drownëd shine
Of limbs and fair garments, like clouds in that blue
Serene :—there I stood for long hours but to view
Those fond earnest eyes that were ever uplifted
Towards me, and wink'd as the water-weed drifted
Between; but the fish knew that presence, and plied
Their long curvy tails, and swift darted aside.

There I gazed for lost time, and forgot all the
    things
That once had been wonders—the fishes with wings,
And the glimmer of magnified eyes that look'd up
From the glooms of the bottom like pearls in a cup,
And the huge endless serpent of silvery gleam,
Slow winding along like a tide in the stream.
Some maid of the waters, some Naiad, methought,

Held me dear in the pearl of her eye—and I brought
My wish to that fancy; and often I dash'd
My limbs in the water, and suddenly splash'd
The cool drops around me, yet clung to the brink,
Chill'd by watery fears, how that beauty might sink
With my life in her arms to her garden, and bind me
With its long tangled grasses, or cruelly wind me
In some eddy to hum out my life in her ear,
Like a spider-caught bee,—and in aid of that fear
Came the tardy remembrance—Oh falsest of men!
Why was not that beauty remember'd till then?
My love, my safe love, whose glad life would have run
Into mine—like a drop—that our fate might be one,
That now, even now,—may-be—clasp'd in a dream,
That form which I gave to some jilt of the stream,
And gazed with fond eyes that her tears tried to
    smother
On a mock of those eyes that I gave to another!

   Then I rose from the stream, but the eyes of my
      mind,
Still full of the tempter, kept gazing behind
On her crystalline face, while I painfully leapt
To the bank, and shook off the curst waters, and wept
With my brow in the reeds; and the reeds to my ear
Bow'd, bent by no wind, and in whispers of fear,
Growing small with large secrets, foretold me of one
That loved me,—but oh to fly from her, and shun
Her love like a pest—though her love was as true
To mine as her stream to the heavenly blue;
For why should I love her with love that would bring
All misfortune, like hate, on so joyous a thing?
Because of her rival,—even Her whose witch-face

I had slighted, and therefore was doom'd in that place
To roam, and had roam'd, where all horrors grew rank,
Nine days ere I wept with my brow on that bank;
Her name be not named, but her spite would not fail
To our love like a blight ; and they told me the tale
Of Scylla,—and Picus, imprison'd to speak
His shrill-screaming woe through a woodpecker's beak.

Then they ceased—I had heard as the voice of my
          star
That told me the truth of my fortunes—thus far
I had read of my sorrow, and lay in the hush
Of deep meditation,—when lo ! a light crush
Of the reeds, and I turn'd and look'd round in the night
Of new sunshine, and saw, as I sipp'd of the light
Narrow-winking, the realised nymph of the stream,
Rising up from the wave with the bend and the gleam
Of a fountain, and o'er her white arms she kept throwing
Bright torrents of hair, that went flowing and flowing
In falls to her feet, and the blue waters roll'd
Down her limbs like a garment, in many a fold,
Sun-spangled, gold-broider'd, and fled far behind,
Like an infinite train.   So she came and reclined
In the reeds, and I hunger'd to see her unseal
The buds of her eyes that would ope and reveal
The blue that was in them;—they oped and she raised
Two orbs of pure crystal, and timidly gazed
With her eyes on my eyes; but their colour and shine
Was of that which they look'd on, and mostly of mine—
For she loved me,—except when she blush'd, and they
          sank,
Shame-humbled, to number the stones on the bank,
Or her play-idle fingers, while lisping she told me

How she put on her veil, and in love to behold me
Would wing through the sun till she fainted away
Like a mist, and then flew to her waters and lay
In love-patience long hours, and sore dazzled her eyes
In watching for mine 'gainst the midsummer skies.
But now they were heal'd,—O my heart, it still dances
When I think of the charm of her changeable glances,
And my image how small when it sank in the deep
Of her eyes where her soul was,—Alas! now they weep,
And none knoweth where.   In what stream do her
    eyes
Shed invisible tears?   Who beholds where her sighs
Flow in eddies, or sees the ascent of the leaf
She has pluck'd with her tresses?   Who listens her grief
Like a far fall of waters, or hears where her feet
Grow emphatic among the loose pebbles, and beat
Them together?   Ah ! surely her flowers float adown
To the sea unaccepted, and little ones drown
For need of her mercy,—even he whose twin-brother
Will miss him for ever ; and the sorrowful mother
Imploreth in vain for his body to kiss
And cling to, all dripping and cold as it is,   ,
Because that soft pity is lost in hard pain !
We loved,—how we loved !—for I thought not again
Of the woes that were whisper'd like fears in that place
If I gave me to beauty.   Her face was the face
Far away, and her eyes were the eyes that were drown'd
For my absence, — her arms were the arms that
    sought round
And claspt me to nought ; for I gazed and became
Only true to my falsehood, and had but one name
For two loves, and called ever on Ægle, sweet maid
Of the sky-loving waters,—and was not afraid

Of the sight of her skin ;—for it never could be,
Her beauty and love were misfortunes to me !

Thus our bliss had endured for a time-shorten'd
   space,
Like a day made of three, and the smile of her face
Had been with me for joy,—when she told me indeed
Her love was self-task'd with a work that would need'
Some short hours, for in truth 'twas the veriest pity
Our love should not last, and then sang me a ditty,
Of one with warm lips that should love her, and love her
When suns were burnt dim and long ages past over.
So she fled with her voice, and I patiently nested
My limbs in the reeds, in still quiet, and rested
Till my thoughts grew extinct, and I sank in a sleep
Of dreams,—but their meaning was hidden too deep
To be read what their woe was ;—but still it was woe
That was writ on all faces that swam to and fro
In that river of night ;—and the gaze of their eyes
Was sad,—and the bend of their brows,—and their cries
Were seen, but I heard not. The warm touch of tears
Travell'd down my cold cheeks, and I shook till my fears
Awaked me, and lo ! I was couch'd in a bower,
The growth of long summers rear'd up in an hour !
Then I said, in the fear of my dream, I will fly
From this magic, but could not, because that my eye
Grew love-idle among the rich blooms ; and the earth
Held me down with its coolness of touch, and the mirth
Of some bird was above me,—who, even in fear,
Would startle the thrush ? and methought there drew
   near
A form as of Ægle,—but it was not the face
Hope made, and I knew the witch-Queen of that place,

Even Circe the Cruel, that came like a Death
Which I fear'd, and yet fled not, for want of my breath.
There was thought in her face, and her eyes were not
    raised
From the grass at her foot, but I saw, as I gazed,
Her spite—and her countenance changed with her
    mind
As she plann'd how to thrall me with beauty, and bind
My soul to her charms,—and her long tresses play'd
From shade into shine and from shine into shade,
Like a day in mid-autumn,—first fair, O how fair !
With long snaky locks of the adder-black hair
That clung round her neck,—those dark locks that I
    prize,
For the sake of a maid that once loved me with eyes
Of that fathomless hue,—but they changed as they
    roll'd,
And brighten'd, and suddenly blazed into gold
That she comb'd into flames, and the locks that fell
    down
Turn'd dark as they fell, but I slighted their brown,
Nor loved, till I saw the light ringlets shed wild,
That innocence wears when she is but a child ;
And her eyes,—Oh I ne'er had been witch'd with
    their shine,
Had they been any other, my Ægle, than thine !

Then I gave me to magic, and gazed till I madden'd
In the full of their light,—but I sadden'd and sadden'd
The deeper I look'd,—till I sank on the snow
Of her bosom, a thing made of terror and woe,
And answer'd its throb with the shudder of fears,
And hid my cold eyes from her eyes with my tears,

And strain'd her white arms with the still languid
    weight
Of a fainting distress.   There she sat like the Fate
That is nurse unto Death, and bent over in shame
To hide me from her—the true Ægle—that came
With the words on her lips the false witch had fore-
    given
To make me immortal—for now I was even
At the portals of Death, who but waited the hush
Of world-sounds in my ear to cry welcome, and rush
With my soul to the banks of his black-flowing river.
Oh, would it had flown from my body for ever,
Ere I listen'd those words, when I felt with a start,
The life-blood rush back in one throb to my heart,
And saw the pale lips where the rest of that spell
Had perish'd in horror—and heard the farewell
Of that voice that was drown'd in the dash of the
    stream !
How fain had I follow'd, and plunged with that scream
Into death, but my being indignantly lagg'd
Through the brutalised flesh that I painfully dragg'd
Behind me :—" O Circe ! O mother of spite !
Speak the last of that curse ! and imprison me quite
In the husk of a brute,—that no pity may name
The man that I was,—that no kindred may claim
The monster I am !   Let me utterly be
Brute-buried, and Nature's dishonour with me
Uninscribed !"—But she listen'd my prayer, that was
    praise
To her malice, with smiles, and advised me to gaze
On the river for love,—and perchance she would make
In pity a maid without eyes for my sake,
And she left me like Scorn.   Then I ask'd of the wave,

What monster I was, and it trembled and gave
The true shape of my grief, and I turn'd with my face
From all waters for ever, and fled through that place,
'Till with horror more strong than all magic I pass'd
Its bounds, and the world was before me at last.

There I wander'd in sorrow, and shunn'd the abodes
Of men, that stood up in the likeness of Gods,
But I saw from afar the warm shine of the sun
On their cities, where man was a million, not one;
And I saw the white smoke of their altars ascending,
That show'd where the hearts of the many were
    blending,
And the wind in my face brought shrill voices that
    came
From the trumpets that gather'd whole bands in one
    fame
As a chorus of man,—and they stream'd from the gates
Like a dusky libation pour'd out to the Fates.
But at times there were gentler processions of peace
That I watch'd with my soul in my eyes till their cease,
There were women! there men! but to me a third sex
I saw them all dots—yet I loved them as specks:
And oft to assuage a sad yearning of eyes
I stole near the city, but stole covert-wise
Like a wild beast of love, and perchance to be smitten
By some hand that I rather had wept on than bitten!
Oh, I once had a haunt near a cot where a mother
Daily sat in the shade with her child, and would
    smother
Its eyelids in kisses, and then in its sleep
Sang dreams in its ear of its manhood, while deep
In a thicket of willows I gazed o'er the brooks

That murmur'd between us and kiss'd them with looks;
But the willows unbosom'd their secret, and never
I return'd to a spot I had startled for ever,
Though I oft long'd to know, but could ask it of none,
Was the mother still fair, and how big was her son?

　　For the haunters of fields they all shunn'd me by
　　　　flight,
The men in their horror, the women in fright;
None ever remain'd save a child once that sported
Among the wild bluebells, and playfully courted
The breeze; and beside him a speckled snake lay
Tight strangled, because it had hiss'd him away
From the flower at his finger; he rose and drew near
Like a Son of Immortals, one born to no fear,
But with strength of black locks and with eyes azure
　　　　bright
To grow to large manhood of merciful might.
He came, with his face of bold wonder, to feel,
The hair of my side, and to lift up my heel,
And question'd my face with wide eyes; but when
　　　under
My lids he saw tears,—for I wept at his wonder,
He stroked me, and utter'd such kindliness then,
That the once love of women, the friendship of men
In past sorrow, no kindness e'er came like a kiss
On my heart in its desolate day such as this!
And I yearn'd at his cheeks in my love, and down
　　　bent, 　.
And lifted him up in my arms with intent
To kiss him,—but he cruel-kindly, alas!
Held out to my lips a pluck'd handful of grass!
Then I dropt him in horror, but felt as I fled

The stone he indignantly hurl'd at my head,
That dissever'd my ear,—but I felt not, whose fate
Was to meet more distress in his love than his hate !

　　Thus I wander'd, companion'd of grief and forlorn
Till I wish'd for that land where my being was born,
But what was that land with its love, where my home
Was self-shut against me ; for why should I come.
Like an after-distress to my grey-bearded father,
With a blight to the last of his sight ?—let him rather
Lament for me dead, and shed tears in the urn
Where I was not, and still in fond memory turn
To his son even such as he left him.   Oh, how
Could I walk with the youth once my fellows, but now
Like Gods to my humbled estate ?—or how bear
The steeds once the pride of my eyes and the care
Of my hands ?   Then I turn'd me self-banish'd, and
　　came
Into Thessaly here, where I met with the same
As myself.   I have heard how they met by a stream
In games, and were suddenly changed by a scream
That made wretches of many, as she roll'd her wild eyes
Against heaven, and so vanish'd.—The gentle and wise
Lose their thoughts in deep studies, and others their ill
In the mirth of mankind where they mingle them still.*

---

* Although "Lycus" has never met with very warm admirers, owing,
perhaps, to its classical origin and style (indeed, in a letter I have of his,
simple John Clare confesses he does not understand a word of it), I incline
to hold with the following opinion from a letter written to my father by
Hartley Coleridge, in 1831.

"I wish you would write a little more in the style of 'Lycus the Centaur,
or 'Eugene Aram's Dream.' In whatever you attempt you excel. Then
why not exert your best and noblest talent, as well as that wit, which I
would never wish to be dormant? I am not a graduate in the Academy of
Compliment, but I think 'Lycus' a work absolutely unique in its line, such
as no man has written, or could have written, but yourself."

E

THE TWO PEACOCKS OF BEDFONT.

ALAS! That breathing Vanity should go
　　Where Pride is buried,—like its very ghost,
Uprisen from the naked bones below,
　　In novel flesh, clad in the silent boast
Of gaudy silk that flutters to and fro,
　　Shedding its chilling superstition most
On young and ignorant natures—as it wont
To haunt the peaceful churchyard of Bedfont!

Each Sabbath morning, at the hour of prayer,
　　Behold two maidens, up the quiet green
Shining, far distant, in the summer air
　　That flaunts their dewy robes and breathes between
Their downy plumes,—sailing as if they were
　　Two far-off ships,—until they brush between
The churchyard's humble walls, and watch and wait
On either side of the wide open'd gate.

And there they stand—with haughty necks before
　　God's holy house, that points towards the skies—
Frowning reluctant duty from the poor,
　　And tempting homage from unthoughtful eyes :
And Youth looks lingering from the temple door,
　　Breathing its wishes in unfruitful sighs,
With pouting lips,—forgetful of the grace,
Of health, and smiles, on the heart-conscious face ;—

Because that Wealth, which has no bliss beside,
　　May wear the happiness of rich attire ;
And those two sisters, in their silly pride,
　　May change the soul's warm glances for the fire

Of lifeless diamonds;—and for health denied,—
  With art, that blushes at itself, inspire
Their languid cheeks—and flourish in a glory
That has no life in life, nor after-story.

The aged priest goes shaking his grey hair
  In meekest censuring, and turns his eye
Earthward in grief, and heavenward in pray'r,
  And sighs, and clasps his hands, and passes by,
Good-hearted man! what sullen soul would wear
  Thy sorrow for a garb, and constantly
Put on thy censure, that might win the praise
Of one so grey in goodness and in days?

Also the solemn clerk partakes the shame
  Of this ungodly shine of human pride,
And sadly blends his reverence and blame
  In one grave bow, and passes with a stride
Impatient:—many a red-hooded dame
  Turns her pain'd head, but not her glance, aside
From wanton dress, and marvels o'er again,
That heaven hath no wet judgments for the vain.

"I have a lily in the bloom at home,"
  Quoth one, "and by the blessed Sabbath day
I'll pluck my lily in its pride, and come
  And read a lesson upon vain array;—
And when stiff silks are rustling up, and some
  Give place, I'll shake it in proud eyes and say—
Making my reverence,—'Ladies, an you please,
King Solomon's not half so fine as these.'"

Then her meek partner, who has nearly run
  His earthly course,—"Nay, Goody, let your text

Grow in the garden.—We have only one—
　Who knows that these dim eyes may see the next?
Summer will come again, and summer sun,
　And lilies too,—but I were sorely vext
To mar my garden, and cut short the blow
Of the last lily I may live to grow."

" The last !" quoth she, "and though the last it were—
　Lo ! those two wantons, where they stand so proud
With waving plumes, and jewels in their hair,
　And painted cheeks, like Dagons to be bow'd
And curtsey'd to !—last Sabbath after pray'r,
　I heard the little Tomkins ask aloud
If they were angels—but I made him know
God's bright ones better, with a bitter blow !"

So speaking, they pursue the pebbly walk
　That leads to the white porch the Sunday throng,
Hand-coupled urchins in restrainëd talk,
　And anxious pedagogue that chastens wrong,
And posied churchwarden with solemn stalk,
　And gold-bedizen'd beadle flames along,
And gentle peasant clad in buff and green,
Like a meek cowslip in the spring serene;

And blushing maiden—modestly array'd
　In spotless white,—still conscious of the glass;
And she, the lonely widow, that hath made
　A sable covenant with grief,—alas !
She veils her tears under the deep, deep shade,
　While the poor kindly-hearted, as they pass,
Bend to unclouded childhood, and caress
Her boy,—so rosy !—and so fatherless !

Thus, as good Christians ought, they all draw near
  The fair white temple, to the timely call
Of pleasant bells that tremble in the ear.—
  Now the last frock, and scarlet hood, and shawl
Fade into dusk, in the dim atmosphere
  Of the low porch, and heav'n has won them all,
—Saving those two, that turn aside and pass,
In velvet blossom, where all flesh is grass.

Ah me ! to see their silken manors trail'd
  In purple luxuries—with restless gold,—
Flaunting the grass where widowhood has wail'd
  In blotted black,—over the heapy mould
Panting wave-wantonly ! They never quail'd
  How the warm vanity abused the cold ;
Nor saw the solemn faces of the gone
Sadly uplooking through transparent stone :

But swept their dwellings with unquiet light,
  Shocking the awful presence of the dead ;
Where gracious natures would their eyes benight
  Nor wear their being with a lip too red,
Nor move too rudely in the summer bright
  Of sun, but put staid sorrow in their tread,
Meting it into steps, with inward breath,
In very pity to bereaved death.

Now in the church, time-sober'd minds resign
  To solemn pray'r, and the loud chaunted hymn,—
With glowing picturings of joys divine
  Painting the mist-light where the roof is dim
But youth looks upward to the window shine,
  Warming with rose and purple and the swim

Of gold, as if thought-tinted by the stains
Of gorgeous light through many-colour'd panes:

Soiling the virgin snow wherein God hath
    Enrobed his angels,—and with absent eyes
Hearing of Heav'n, and its directed path,
    Thoughtful of slippers,—and the glorious skies
Clouding with satin,—till the preacher's wrath
    Consumes his pity, and he glows, and cries
With a deep voice that trembles in its might,
    And earnest eyes grown eloquent in light:

"Oh, that the vacant eye would learn to look
    On very beauty, and the heart embrace
True loveliness, and from this holy book
    Drink the warm-breathing tenderness and grace,
Of love indeed! Oh, that the young soul took
    Its virgin passion from the glorious face
Of fair religion, and address'd its strife,
To win the riches of eternal life!

"Doth the vain heart love glory that is none,
    And the poor excellence of vain attire?
Oh go, and drown your eyes against the sun,
    The visible ruler of the starry quire,
Till boiling gold in giddy eddies run,
    Dazzling the brain with orbs of living fire;
And the faint soul down-darkens into night,
And dies a burning martyrdom to light.

"Oh go, and gaze,—when the low winds of ev'n
    Breathe hymns, and Nature's many forests nod
Their gold-crown'd heads; and the rich blooms of
        heav'n

Sun-ripen'd give their blushes up to God;
And mountain-rocks and cloudy steeps are riv'n
   By founts of fire, as smitten by the rod
Of heavenly Moses,—that your thirsty sense
May quench its longings of magnificence!

"Yet suns shall perish—stars shall fade away—
   Day into darkness—darkness into death—
Death into silence; the warm light of day,
   The blooms of summer, the rich glowing breath
Of even—all shall wither and decay,
   Like the frail furniture of dreams beneath
The touch of morn—or bubbles of rich dyes
That break and vanish in the aching eyes."

They hear, soul-blushing, and repentant shed
   Unwholesome thoughts in wholesome tears, and
      pour
Their sin to earth,—and with low drooping head
   Receive the solemn blessing, and implore
Its grace—then soberly with chasten'd tread,
   They meekly press towards the gusty door,
With humbled eyes that go to graze upon
The lowly grass—like him of Babylon.

The lowly grass!—O water-constant mind!
   Fast-ebbing holiness!—soon-fading grace
Of serious thought, as if the gushing wind
   Through the low porch had wash'd it from the face
For ever!—How they lift their eyes to find
   Old vanities!—Pride wins the very place
Of meekness, like a bird, and flutters now
With idle wings on the curl-conscious brow!

And lo ! with eager looks they seek the way
    Of old temptation at the lowly gate;
To feast on feathers, and on vain array,
    And painted cheeks, and the rich glistering state
Of jewel-sprinkled locks.—But where are they,
    The graceless haughty ones that used to wait
With lofty neck, and nods, and stiffen'd eye?—
None challenge the old homage bending by.

In vain they look for the ungracious bloom
    Of rich apparel where it glow'd before,—
For Vanity has faded all to gloom,
    And lofty Pride has stiffen'd to the core,
For impious Life to tremble at its doom,—
    Set for a warning token evermore,
Whereon, as now, the giddy and the wise
Shall gaze with lifted hands and wond'ring eyes.

The aged priest goes on each Sabbath morn,
    But shakes not sorrow under his grey hair;
The solemn clerk goes lavender'd and shorn
    Nor stoops his back to the ungodly pair;—
And ancient lips that pucker'd up in scorn,
    Go smoothly breathing to the house of pray'r;
And in the garden plot, from day to day,
The lily blooms its long white life away.

And where two haughty maidens used to be,
    In pride of plume, where plumy Death had trod,
Trailing their gorgeous velvets wantonly,
    Most unmeet pall, over the holy sod;—
There, gentle stranger, thou may'st only see
    Two sombre Peacocks.——Age, with sapient nod

Marking the spot, still tarries to declare
How they once lived, and wherefore they are there.

HYMN TO THE SUN.

GIVER of glowing light!
Though but a god of other days,
    The kings and sages
    Of wiser ages
Still live and gladden in thy genial rays!

King of the tuneful lyre,
Still poets' hymns to thee belong
    Though lips are cold
    Whereon of old
Thy beams all turn'd to worshipping and song!

Lord of the dreadful bow,
None triumph now for Python's death;
    But thou dost save
    From hungry grave
The life that hangs upon a summer breath.

Father of rosy day,
No more thy clouds of incense rise;
    But waking flow'rs
    At morning hours,
Give out their sweets to meet thee in the skies.

God of the Delphic fane,
No more thou listenest to hymns sublime;
    But they will leave
    On winds at eve,
A solemn echo to the end of time.

MIDNIGHT.

UNFATHOMABLE Night ! how dost thou sweep
  Over the flooded earth, and darkly hide
  The mighty city under thy full tide ;
Making a silent palace for old Sleep,
Like his own temple under the hush'd deep,
  Where all the busy day he doth abide,
  And forth at the late dark, outspreadeth wide
His dusky wings, whence the cold water sweep !
How peacefully the living millions lie !
  Lull'd unto death beneath his poppy spells ;
There is no breath—no living stir—no cry—
No tread of foot—no song—no music-call—
  Only the sound of melancholy bells—
The voice of Time—survivor of them all !

TO A SLEEPING CHILD.*

I.

OH, 'tis a touching thing, to make one weep,—
A tender infant with its curtain'd eye,
Breathing as it would neither live nor die
With that unchanging countenance of sleep !
As if its silent dream, serene and deep,
Had lined its slumber with a still blue sky
So that the passive cheeks unconscious lie
With no more life than roses—just to keep
The blushes warm, and the mild, odorous breath.
O blossom boy ! so calm is thy repose,

---

* This and the following sonnet were written to the infant son of the late
Rev. Edward Rice, Master of Christ's Hospital.

So sweet a compromise of life and death,
'Tis pity those fair buds should e'er unclose
For memory to stain their inward leaf,
Tinging thy dreams with unacquainted grief.

TO A SLEEPING CHILD.

II.

THINE eyelids slept so beauteously, I deem'd
No eyes could wake so beautiful as they :
Thy rosy cheeks in such still slumbers lay,
I loved their peacefulness, nor ever dream'd
Of dimples :—for those parted lips so seem'd,
I never thought a smile could sweetlier play,
Nor that so graceful life could chase away
Thy graceful death,—till those blue eyes upbeam'd.
Now slumber lies in dimpled eddies drown'd,
And roses bloom more rosily for joy,
And odorous silence ripens into sound,
And fingers move to sound.—All-beauteous boy !
How thou dost waken into smiles, and prove,
If not more lovely, thou art more like Love !

TO FANCY.

MOST delicate Ariel ! submissive thing,
Won by the mind's high magic to its hest,—
Invisible embassy, or secret guest,—
Weighing the light air on a lighter wing ;—
Whether into the midnight moon, to bring
Illuminate visions to the eye of rest,—
Or rich romances from the florid West,—

Or to the sea, for mystic whispering,—
Still by thy charm'd allegiance to the will,
The fruitful wishes prosper in the brain,
As by the fingering of fairy skill,—
Moonlight, and waters, and soft music's strain,
Odours, and blooms, and *my* Miranda's smile,
Making this dull world an enchanted isle.

MR. MARTIN'S PICTURES AND THE BONASSUS.

A LETTER FROM MRS. WINIFRED LLOYD TO HER FRIEND MRS. PRICE, AT THE PARSONAGE HOUSE AT ——, IN MON-MOUTHSHIRE.

MY DEAR MRS. PRICE,

This is to let you know that me and Becky and little Humphry are safe arrived in London, where we have been since Monday. My darter is quite inchanted with the metropalus and longs to be intraduced to it satiety, which please God she shall be as soon as things are ready to make her debutt in. It is high time now she should be brought into the world being twenty years old come Midsummer & very big for her size. You knows, Mrs. Price, that with her figure and accomplishments she was quite berried in Wales, but I hopes when the country is scowered off she will shine as bright as the best & make rare havock among the mail sects. She has learned the pinaforte and to draw, and does flowers and shells, as Mr. Owen says, to a mirrikle, for I spares no munny on her to make her fit for any gentleman's wife, when he shall please to ax her. I took her the other day to the Bullock's Museum to see Mr.

Martin's expedition of picters—because she has such
a pretty notion of painting herself—and a very nice
site it was thof it cost half-a-crown. I tried to get the
children in for half-price but the man said that Becky
was a full-grown lady, and so she is sure enuff, so I
could only beat him down to take a sixpence off little
Humphry.

The picters are hung in a parler up-stairs (Becky
calls it a drawing room) and you see about a dozen
for your munny which brings it to about a penny a
piece, & that is not dear. The first on the left hand
as you go in—and on the right coming out—is called
Revenge. It represents a man and woman with a
fire breaking out at their backs—Becky thought it
was the fire of London—but the show gentleman said
it was Troy that was burned out of revenge, so that
was a very good thought to paint. Then there was
Bell Shazzar's Feast as you read of it in the Bible,
with Daniel interrupting the handwriting on the wall
—with the cunning men & the king & all the nobility.
Becky said she never saw such bewtiful painting—and
sure enuff they were the finest cullers I ever set eyes
on, blews, & pinks and purples & greens, all as bright
as fresh sattin and velvet, and no doubt they had
court sutes all span new for the Banket. As for
Humphry there was no getting him from a picter of
the Welsh Bard because he knew the ballad about it
& saw the whole core of Captain Edwards's sodgers
coming down the hill, with their waggin' train and all,
quite nateral. To be sure their cullers were very
bewtiful, but there was so many mountings piled atop
of one another and some going out of sight into
heaven that it made my neck ake to look after them.

Next to that there was a storm in Babylon,* but not
half so well painted Becky said as the rest.   There
was none hardly of those smart bright cullers only a
bunch of flowers in a garden, that Becky said would
look bewtiful on a chaney teacup.   Howsomever
some gentlemen looked at it a long while and called
it clever and said they preferred his architecter work
to his painting & he makes very handsum bildings
for sartin.   They said too that this picter was quieter
than all the rest—but how that can be, God he knows,
for I could not hear a pin's difference betwixt them—
and besides that it was in better keeping which I suppose means it is sold to a Lord.   The next was only
a lady very well dressed and walking in a landskip.
But oh, Mrs. Price, how shall I tell you about the
burning of Herculeum!   Becky said it put her in
mind of what is written in the Revelations about the
sky being turned to blood, and indeed it seemed to
take all the culler out of her face when she looked at
it.   It looked as if all the world was going to be
burnt to death with a shower of live coals!   Oh dear
to see the pore things running about in sich an
earthquack as threw the pillers off their legs—and all
the men of war in distress, beating their bottoms, &
going to rack and ruin in the arber.   It is a shocking
site to see only in a picter, with so many people in
silks and sattins and velvets having their things so
scorched & burnt into holes!   O Mrs. Price! what a
mercy we was not born in Vesuvus & there is no
burning mountings in Wales!—only think to be hold-
ing our sheelds over our heads to keep off the hot

---

* The storming of Babylon: Mrs Lloyd must have got her catalogue by
hearsay.

sinders, and almost suffercated to death with brimstun.
It puts one in a shiver to think of it.

There is another picture of a burning mounting
with Zadok* hanging upon a rock—Becky knows the
story & shall tell it you—but it looked nothing after the
other, though the criketal gentleman, you knows of,
said it was a much better painting. But there is no
saying for people's tastes—as Mr. Owen says, the
world does not dine upon one dinner—but I have
forgot one more & that is Mac Beth and the three
Whiches, with such a ridgment of Hilanders that I
wonder how they got into one picter. Becky said the
band ought to be playing bag Pipes instead of Kittle
drums, but no doubt Mr. Martin knows better than
Becky, and I am sure from what I heard in the North
that either Kittles or Drums would sound better than
bag Pipes.

We are going to-morrow to the play, and any other
sites we may see you shall hear. Till then give my
respective complements to Mr. Price with a kiss from
Beck & Humphry and remane,

Your faithful humble servant
WINIFRED LLOYD.

P.S. I forgot to say that after we had seen Mr.
Martin's expedition, we went from the Bullock's to
the Bonassus—as it is but a step from wan to the
other. The man says it is a perfect picter, & so it is
for sartin, and ought to be painted. It is like a bull
only quite different, and comes from the Appellation
Mountings. My Humphry thought it must have
been catched in a pound, and I wundered the child

---

* Mrs. Lloyd means Zadak, in the "Tales of the Genii."

could make sich a nateral idear, but he is a sweet
boy and very foreward in his larning. He was eyely
delited at the site you may be sure, but Becky being
timersome shut her eyes all the time she was seeing
it. But saving his pushing now & then the anymil is
no ways veracious & eats nothing but vegeatables.
The man showed us some outlandish sort of pees
that it lives upon but he gave it two hole pales of
rare carruts besides. It must be a handsum cus-
tomer to the green Grocer and a pretty penny I
warrant it costs for vittles. But it is a wonderful
work of Natur, and ought to make man look to his
ways as Mr. Lloyd says. Which of our infiddles
could make a Bonassus? let them tell me that, Mrs.
Price. I would have carried him home in my eye to
describe to you & Mr. Price, but we met Mrs. Striker
the butcher's lady & she drove him quite out of my
head. Howsomever as you likes carosities I shall
send his playbill that knows more about him than I
do, though there's nothing like seeing him with wan's
one eye's. I think if the man would take him down
to Monmouth in a Carry Wan he would get a good
many hapence by showing him. Till then I remane
once more   Your faithful humble sarvent

Winifred Lloyd.

PRESENCE OF MIND IN A GHOST.

It has been much questioned amongst the curious
if there be such things (or nothings) as Ghosts; but
whether or not, and leaving this Argument to the
Learned,—the following may be relied upon as a wonderful instance of presence of mind in an apparition.

In the year 1421, the widow of Ralph Cranfield, of Dipmore End, in the parish of Sandhurst, Berkshire, was one midnight alarmed by a noise in her bed-chamber, and looking up she saw at her bed-foot the appearance of a skeleton (which she verily believed was her husband) nodding and talking to her on its fingers, or finger-bones, after the manner of a dumb person. [And the moonlight shone through the ribs as if through a trellis, making a barred shadow upon the counterpane.]* Whereupon she was so smitten with fear that after striving to scream aloud, which she could not by reason of her fright, she fell backward as in a swoon : yet not so insensible but she could see that the figure was greatly agitated and distressed, and would have clasped her, but on seeing her loathing, it desisted—only moving its jaw upward and downward, as if it would cry for help but could not for want of its parts of speech.

At last, she growing more and more faint and likely to die of fright, the skeleton suddenly, and as if at a thought, began to swing round its hand (which was loose at the wrist) with a brisk motion ; and the finger-bones, being hard and long, and striking sharply against each other, made a loud noise like the springing of a watchman's rattle ; at which alarm the neighbours running hastily in, and stoutly armed as against thieves and murderers, the Spectre suddenly departed.†

* This sentence is barely legible, having been scratched through on second thoughts.

† I cannot discover wnetber this ingenious ghost was the offspring of my father's brain, or the hero of some legend of Sandhurst, where my father resided, as a young man, for some period with his uncle, the late Mr. Sands.

F

THOUGHTS ON SCULPTURE.

THERE is something sublime in the pale repose of fine sculpture : colour is as noise and motion.—Harlequin is motley and active—but a Statue is a thing only of light and shade; and stillness and silence are its proper attributes, and the first inspiration of its presence.

On entering the repository of the Elgin Marbles, the voice is instantly subdued to a whisper, and the foot is restrained in its tread; there is no occasion for the written request of the students to preserve silence—it will keep itself, the best peace-officer of the place. We seem to be, not among imitations, but petrifactions of life,—feel as if noise, or mirth, or ungentle motion, were an insult to their constrained quietness. The most impassioned, the most ruffled, are as mute as Niobe when she turned to stone : even that snorting horse, wild and fiery as he may once have been, distends only a breathless nostril to the air, and is fixed for ever. If he move not now, he will never move more, so much has he the look of fierce intent. Theseus sits too, as if he would never rise again; but in him you might fancy it merely the fault of his will. This repose seems the proper mood of a statue. It should be pale in act, as pale in substance—either above or beneath all violence—too rock-like to be rudely acted on, or too delicate and aerial, too sylph-like for touch—too pure even (as it seems) to be stained by the light. I remember a female figure of this nature, which might have been a personification of silence,—a marble metaphor of peace. Alone, and still, and hushed, it stood in the dark of a long passage, like an embodied twilight,—not dead, but with such a breathless life as we conceive in a solemn midnight apparition ;—passionless, yet not incapable of passion, as if only there was no cause mighty enough in this world to disturb her divine rest. There she stood, with her blank eyes,* gazing no one knew whither—not asleep,—but as in one of those dreams which make up the life of gods, blissful, serene, and eternal—herself almost a dream, she seemed so pale, and shadowy, and unreal—as unreal as if only framed out of moonlight, or (what is quite possible) only the fanciful creation of my own theory.

FAIR INES.

O saw ye not fair Ines?
She's gone into the West,
To dazzle when the sun is down,
And rob the world of rest :
She took our daylight with her,
The smiles that we love best,
With morning blushes on her cheek,
And pearls upon her breast.

O turn again, fair Ines,
Before the fall of night,
For fear the moon should shine alone,
And stars unrivall'd bright ;

* These blank eyes (wherein there is no indication of the pupil) are the true eyes in sculpture. They seem to hold no communion with your own, but to gaze, not on points, but on all space, like the eyes of gods, or of prophets looking into the futur

And blessed will the lover be
That walks beneath their light,
And breathes the love against thy cheek
I dare not even write !

Would I had been, fair Ines,
That gallant cavalier,
Who rode so gaily by thy side,
And whisper'd thee so near !
Were there no bonny dames at home,
Or no true lovers here,
That he should cross the seas to win
The dearest of the dear?

I saw thee, lovely Ines,
Descend along the shore,
With bands of noble gentlemen,
And banners waved before ;
And gentle youth and maidens gay,
And snowy plumes they wore ;
It would have been a beauteous dream,
—If it had been no more !

Alas, alas, fair Ines,
She went away with song,
With Music waiting on her steps,
And shoutings of the throng ;
But some were sad and felt no mirth,
But only Music's wrong,
In sounds that sang Farewell, Farewell,
To her you've loved so long.

Farewell, farewell, fair Ines,
That vessel never bore

So fair a lady on its deck,
Nor danced so light before,—
Alas, for pleasure on the sea,
And sorrow on the shore!
The smile that blest one lover's heart
Has broken many more!

TO A FALSE FRIEND.

OUR hands have met, but not our hearts;
Our hands will never meet again.
Friends, if we have ever been,
Friends we cannot now remain:
I only know I loved you once,
I only know I loved in vain;
Our hands have met, but not our hearts;
Our hands will never meet again!

Then farewell to heart and hand!
I would our hands had never met:
Even the outward form of love
Must be resign'd with some regret.
Friends, we still might seem to be,
If I my wrong could e'er forget
Our hands have join'd, but not our hearts;
I would our hands had never met!

ODE.

AUTUMN.

I SAW old Autumn in the misty morn
Stand shadowless like Silence, listening

To silence, for no lonely bird would sing
Into his hollow ear from woods forlorn,
Nor lowly hedge nor solitary thorn;
Shaking his languid locks all dewy bright
With tangled gossamer that fell by night,
      Pearling his coronet of golden corn.

Where are the songs of Summer?—With the sun,
Oping the dusky eyelids of the south,
Till shade and silence waken up as one,
And Morning sings with a warm odorous mouth.
Where are the merry birds?—Away, away,
On panting wings through the inclement skies,
      Lest owls should prey
      Undazzled at noon-day,
And tear with horny beak their lustrous eyes.

Where are the blooms of Summer?—In the west,
Blushing their last to the last sunny hours,
When the mild Eve by sudden Night is prest
Like tearful Proserpine, snatch'd from her flow'rs
      To a most gloomy breast.
Where is the pride of Summer,—the green prime,—
The many, many leaves all twinkling?—Three
On the moss'd elm; three on the naked lime
Trembling,—and one upon the old oak tree!
    Where is the Dryad's immortality?—
Gone into mournful cypress and dark yew,
Or wearing the long gloomy Winter through
    In the smooth holly's green eternity.

The squirrel gloats o'er his accomplish'd hoard,
The ants have brimm'd their garners with ripe grain,
      And honey bees have stored

The sweets of summer in their luscious cells;
The swallows all have wing'd across the main;
But here the Autumn melancholy dwells,
    And sighs her tearful spells
Amongst the sunless shadows of the plain.
      Alone, alone,
      Upon a mossy stone,
She sits and reckons up the dead and gone,
With the last leaves for a love-rosary;
Whilst all the wither'd world looks drearily,
Like a dim picture of the drownëd past
In the hush'd mind's mysterious far-away,
Doubtful what ghostly thing will steal the last
Into that distance, grey upon the grey.

O go and sit with her, and be o'ershaded
Under the languid downfall of her hair;
She wears a coronal of flowers faded
Upon her forehead, and a face of care;—
There is enough of wither'd everywhere
To make her bower,—and enough of gloom;
There is enough of sadness to invite,
If only for the rose that died, whose doom
Is Beauty's,—she that with the living bloom
Of conscious cheeks most beautifies the light;
There is enough of sorrowing, and quite
Enough of bitter fruits the earth doth bear,—
Enough of chilly droppings from her bowl;
Enough of fear and shadowy despair,
To frame her cloudy prison for the soul!

SONNET.

DEATH.

IT is not death, that—sometime—in a sigh
This eloquent breath shall take its speechless flight;
That—sometime—these bright stars, that now reply
In sunlight to the sun, shall set in night;
That this warm conscious flesh shall perish quite,
And all life's ruddy springs forget to flow;
That thoughts shall cease, and the immortal sprite
Be lapp'd in alien clay and laid below;
It is not death to know this,—but to know
That pious thoughts, which visit at new graves
In tender pilgrimage, will cease to go
So duly and so oft,—and when grass waves
Over the past-away, there may be then
No resurrection in the minds of men.

SONNET.

SILENCE.

THERE is a silence where hath been no sound,
There is a silence where no sound may be,
In the cold grave—under the deep deep sea,
Or in wide desert where no life is found,
Which hath been mute, and still must sleep profound;
No voice is hush'd—no life treads silently,
But clouds and cloudy shadows wander free,
That never spoke, over the idle ground:
But in green ruins, in the desolate walls
Of antique palaces, where Man hath been,

Though the dun fox, or wild hyæna, calls,
And owls, that flit continually between,
Shriek to the echo, and the low winds moan,——
There the true Silence is, self-conscious and alone.

SONNET.

WRITTEN IN KEATS' " ENDYMION."

I saw pale Dian, sitting by the brink
Of silver falls, the overflow of fountains
From cloudy steeps ; and I grew sad to think
Endymion's foot was silent on those mountains
And he but a hush'd name, that Silence keeps
In dear remembrance,—lonely, and forlorn,
Singing it to herself until she weeps
Tears, that perchance still glisten in the morn :—
And as I mused, in dull imaginings,
There came a flash of garments, and I knew
The awful Muse by her harmonious wings
Charming the air to music as she flew—
Anon there rose an echo through the vale
Gave back Endymion in a dreamlike tale.

SONNET.

TO AN ENTHUSIAST.

Young ardent soul, graced with fair Nature's truth,
Spring warmth of heart, and fervency of mind,
And still a large late love of all thy kind,
Spite of the world's cold practice and Time's tooth,—
For all these gifts, I know not, in fair sooth,

Whether to give thee joy, or bid thee blind
Thine eyes with tears,—that thou hast not resign'd
The passionate fire and fierceness of thy youth :
For as the current of thy life shall flow,
Gilded by shine of sun or shadow-stain'd,
Through flow'ry valley or unwholesome fen,
Thrice blessed in thy joy, or in thy woe
Thrice cursed of thy race,—thou art ordain'd
To share beyond the lot of common men.

TO A COLD BEAUTY.

LADY, wouldst thou heiress be
    To Winter's cold and cruel part ?
When he sets the rivers free,
    Thou dost still lock up thy heart ;—
Thou that shouldst outlast the snow,
But in the whiteness of thy brow.

Scorn and cold neglect are made
    For winter gloom and winter wind,
But thou wilt wrong the summer air,
    Breathing it to words unkind,—
Breath which only should belong
To love, to sunlight, and to song !

When the little buds unclose,
    Red, and white, and pied, and blue,
And that virgin flow'r, the rose,
    Opes her heart to hold the dew,
Wilt thou lock thy bosom up
With no jewel in its cup ?

Let not cold December sit
   Thus in Love's peculiar throne :
Brooklets are not prison'd now,
   But crystal frosts are all agone,
And that which hangs upon the spray,
It is no snow, but flow'r of May !

SERENADE.

AH, sweet, thou little knowest how
   I wake and passionate watches keep ;
And yet while I address thee now,
   Methinks thou smilest in thy sleep.
'Tis sweet enough to make me weep,
   That tender thought of love and thee,
That while the world is hush'd so deep,
   Thy soul's perhaps awake to me !

Sleep on, sleep on, sweet bride of sleep !
   With golden visions for thy dower,
While I this midnight vigil keep,
   And bless thee in thy silent bower ;
To me 'tis sweeter than the power
   Of sleep, and fairy dreams unfurl'd,
That I alone, at this still hour,
   In patient love outwatch the world.

OLD BALLAD.

Air—"There was a King in the North Countree."

THERE was a Fairy lived in a well,
And she pronounced a magical spell ;
" Whoever looks in this wave," she said,
" Shall see the lady that he's to wed !"

A King came by with his hunting-spear
And stoop'd to look in the waters clear;
He laid by the brim his signet of gold,
And gave his Brother his crown to hold.

But while he knelt and was looking down,
His Brother stood and tried-on the crown;
The pearls were bright, and the rubies brave,
So he tumbled his brother into the wave.

"Oh Brother, oh Brother, you've got my ring
And the lawful crown that made me king;
But your heart shall fail, and your hand shall quake,
And the head that wears my jewels shall ache!"

The murderer stood and look'd from the brink
"The sun is so hot, I should like to drink!"
But lo! as he stoop'd with a silver cup,
His head went down, and his heels flew up!

"Oh! Brother, oh! Brother,—I've got your crown,
But the weight of the jewels has pull'd me down,
You shall be crowned in the skies again,—
But I shall be mark'd on the brow like Cain!"

Down he sank in the dismal wave,
As cold as death, and dark as the grave;
But when he came to the stones at last,
The Fairy caught him, and held him fast.

She took him into her crystal hall
And there he saw his face in the wall;
She look'd rosy, but he look'd white,
And all the tapers were burning bright.

The King leap'd down from his Fairy throne,
With eyes that brighter than diamonds shone;
His left hand balanced a golden globe,
But his right hand lifted his purple robe.

"Oh Brother! oh Brother! bend down your knee,
But kneel to Heaven, and not to me,
For God may frown on your grievous sin,
But I'm too happy you push'd me in.

Come hither, come hither, you're welcome now,
To my crown of gold that decks your brow;
There's smiles worth heav'n on my true-love's face,
And she has made me King of this place!"

LINES SUGGESTED BY A BUNCH OF ENGLISH GRAPES.

WE did not wear a leafy crown,
And darkly glance to darker glance,
Under the green leaf and the brown,
Wooing the eyes of maids of France,
With very bloomy down:
We stain'd not hands with purple blood
In golden Arno's pleasant vale,
Where the proud Brothers quench'd the stain,
And saw two murderers in the flood
With faces guilty-pale:
Nor on the sunny hills of Spain
We used to drink the sun and twine
Long amorous tendrils to entrap
The careless finger of maid to linger
And pluck us from the trembling vine
To brim her dimpled lap.

SONNET.

Love, I am jealous of a worthless man
Whom—for his merits—thou dost hold too dear:
No better than myself, he lies as near
And precious to thy bosom.   He may span
Thy sacred waist and with thy sweet breath fan
His happy cheek, and thy most willing ear
Invade with words and call his love sincere
And true as mine, and prove it—if he can :—
Not that I hate him for such deeds as this—
He were a devil to adore thee less,
Who wears thy favour,—I am ill at ease
Rather lest he should e'er too coldly press
Thy gentle hand :—This is my jealousy
Making myself suspect but never thee !

SONNET.

Love, see thy lover humbled at thy feet,
Not in servility, but homage sweet,
Gladly inclined :—and with my bended knee
Think that my inward spirit bows to thee—
More proud indeed than when I stand or climb
Elsewhere :—there is no statue so sublime
As Love's in all the world, and e'en to kiss
The pedestal is still a better bliss
Than all ambitions.   O ! Love's lowest base
Is far above the reaching of disgrace
To shame this posture.   Let me then draw nigh
Feet that have fared so nearly to the sky,
And when this duteous homage has been given
I will rise up and clasp the heart in Heaven.

THE FORSAKEN.

THE dead are in their silent graves,
And the dew is cold above,
And the living weep and sigh,
Over dust that once was love.

Once I only wept the dead,
But now the living cause my pain :
How couldst thou steal me from my tears,
To leave me to my tears again ?

My Mother rests beneath the sod,—
Her rest is calm and very deep :
I wish'd that she could see our loves,—
But now I gladden in her sleep.

Last night unbound my raven locks,
The morning saw them turn'd to grey,
Once they were black and well beloved,
But thou art changed,—and so are they !

The useless lock I gave thee once,
To gaze upon and think of me,
Was ta'en with smiles,—but this was torn
In sorrow that I send to thee !

SONG.

THE stars are with the voyager
    Wherever he may sail ;
The moon is constant to her time ;
    The sun will never fail ;

But follow, follow round the world,
   The green earth and the sea,
So love is with the lover's heart,
   Wherever he may be.

Wherever he may be, the stars
   Must daily lose their light;
The moon will veil her in the shade;
   The sun will set at night.
The sun may set, but constant love
   Will shine when he's away;
So that dull night is never night,
   And day is brighter day.

SONG.

O LADY, leave thy silken thread
   And flowery tapestrie :
There's living roses on the bush,
   And blossoms on the tree;
Stoop where thou wilt, thy careless hand
   Some random bud will meet;
Thou canst not tread, but thou wilt find
   The daisy at thy feet.

'Tis like the birthday of the world,
   When earth was born in bloom;
The light is made of many dyes,
   The air is all perfume;
There's crimson buds, and white and blue—
   The very rainbow showers
Have turn'd to blossoms where they fell,
   And sown the earth with flowers.

There's fairy tulips in the east,
    The garden of the sun;
The very streams reflect the hues,
    And blossoms as they run:
While Morn opes like a crimson rose,
    Still wet with pearly showers;
Then, lady, leave the silken thread
    Thou twinest into flowers!

BIRTHDAY VERSES.

Good morrow to the golden morning
    Good morrow to the world's delight—
I've come to bless thy life's beginning,
    Since it makes my own so bright!

I have brought no roses, sweetest,
    I could find no flowers, dear,—
It was when all sweets were over
    Thou wert born to bless the year.*

But I've brought thee jewels, dearest,
    In thy bonny locks to shine,—
And if love shows in their glances,
    They have learned that look of mine!

I LOVE THEE.

I love thee—I love thee!
    'Tis all that I can say;—
It is my vision in the night,
    My dreaming in the day;

* My mothers's birthday was the 6th November.

G

The very echo of my heart,
　The blessing when I pray:
I love thee—I love thee!
　Is all that I can say.

I love thee—I love thee!
　Is ever on my tongue;
In all my proudest poesy
　That chorus still is sung;
It is the verdict of my eyes,
　Amidst the gay and young:
I love thee—I love thee!
　A thousand maids among.

I love thee—I love thee!
　Thy bright and hazel glance,
The mellow lute upon those lips,
　Whose tender tones entrance;
But most, dear heart of hearts, thy proofs
　That still these words enhance.
I love thee—I love thee!
　Whatever be thy chance.

LINES.

Let us make a leap, my dear,
In our love, of many a year
And date it very far away,
On a bright clear summer day,
When the heart was like a sun
To itself, and falsehood none;
And the rosy lips a part
Of the very loving heart,

And the shining of the eye
But a sign to know it by;—
When my faults were all forgiven,
And my life deserved of Heaven.
Dearest, let us reckon so,
And love for all that long ago;
Each absence count a year complete,
And keep a birthday when we meet.

FALSE POETS AND TRUE.

TO WORDSWORTH.

Look how the lark soars upward and is gone,
Turning a spirit as he nears the sky!
His voice is heard, but body there is none *
To fix the vague excursions of the eye.
So, poets' songs are with us, tho' they die
Obscured, and hid by death's oblivious shroud,
And Earth inherits the rich melody
Like raining music from the morning cloud.
Yet, few there be who pipe so sweet and loud
Their voices reach us through the lapse of space:
The noisy day is deafen'd by a crowd
Of undistinguish'd birds, a twittering race;
But only lark and nightingale forlorn
Fill up the silences of night and morn.

FRAGMENT.

" Farewell—Farewell "—it is an awful word
When that the quick do speak it to the dead;

* These lines are repeated in the fourth verse of " Hero and Leander."

For though 'tis brief upon the speaker's lips,
'Tis more than death can answer to, and hath
No living echo on the living ear

    *   *   *   *

'Tis awful to behold the midnight stars
They say do rule the destinies of men,
Gazing upon us from that point of space,
Where they were set even from their lustrous birth,
With a most sure foreknowledge of our doom
Watching its consummation.

    *   *   *   *

GUIDO AND MARINA.

A DRAMATIC SKETCH.

[Guido, having given himself up to the pernicious study of magic and astrology, casts his nativity, and resolves that at a certain hour of a certain day he is to die. MARINA, to wean him from this fatal delusion, which hath gradually wasted him away, even to the verge of death, advances the hour-hand of the clock. He is supposed to be seated beside her in the garden of his palace at Venice.]

Guido. Clasp me again!   My soul is very sad;
And hold thy lips in readiness near mine,
Lest I die suddenly.   Clasp me again!
'Tis such a gloomy day!
    Mar.   Nay, sweet, it shines.
    Guido. Nay, then, these mortal clouds are in mine
        eyes.
Clasp me again!—ay, with thy fondest force,
Give me one last embrace.
    Mar.   Love, I do clasp thee!
    Guido. Then closer—closer—for I feel thee not;
Unless thou art this pain around my heart
Thy lips at such a time should never leave me.

Mar. What pain—what time, love? Art thou ill?
    Alas!
I see it in thy cheek. Come, let me nurse thee.
Here, rest upon my heart.
    Guido.   Stay, stay, Marina.
Look!—when I raise my hand against the sun,
Is it red with blood?
    Mar.   Alas! my love, what wilt thou?
Thy hand is red—and so is mine—all hands
Show thus against the sun.
    Guido.   All living men's,
Marina, but not mine. Hast never heard
How death first seizes on the feet and hands,
And thence goes freezing to the very heart?
    Mar. Yea, love, I know it; but what then?—the
        hand
I hold is glowing.
    Guido.   But my eyes!—my eyes!—
Look *there*, Marina—there is death's own sign.
I have seen a corpse,
E'en when its clay was cold, would still have seem'd
Alive, but for the eyes—such deadly eyes!
So dull and dim! Marina, look in mine!
    Mar. Ay, they are dull. No, no—not dull, but
        bright:
I see myself within them. Now, dear love,
Discard these horrid fears that make me weep.
    Guido. Marina, Marina—where thy image lies,
There must be brightness—or perchance they glance
And glimmer like the lamp before it dies.
Oh, do not vex my soul with hopes impossible!
My hours are ending.   [*Clock strikes.*
    Mar.   Nay, they shall not! Hark!

The hour—four—five—hark !—six !—the very time !
And, lo ! thou art alive !   My love—dear love—
Now cast this cruel phantasm from thy brain—
This wilful, wild delusion—cast it off !
The hour is come—and *gone !*   What ! not a word !
What, not a smile, even, that thou livest for me *!*
Come, laugh and clap your hands as I do—come
Or kneel with me, and thank th' eternal God
For this blest passover !   Still sad ! still mute !—
Oh, why art thou not glad, as I am glad,
That death forbears thee ?   Nay, hath all my love
Been spent in vain, that thou art sick of life ?

   Guido. Marina, I am no more attach'd to death
Than Fate hath doomed me.   I am his elect,
That even now forestalls thy little light,
And steals with cold infringement on my breath :
Already he bedims my spiritual lamp,
Not yet his due—not yet—quite yet, though Time,
Perchance, to warn me, speaks before his wont :
Some minutes' space my blood has still to flow—
Some scanty breath is left me still to spend
In very bitter sighs.
But there's a point, true measured by my pulse,
Beyond or short of which it may not live
By one poor throb.   Marina, it is near.

   Mar. Oh, God of heaven !

   Guido.　　　　　　　　Ay, it is *very* near.
Therefore, cling now to me, and say farewell
While I can answer it.   Marina, speak !
Why tear thine helpless hair ? it will not save
Thy heart from breaking, nor pluck out the thought
That stings thy brain.   Oh, surely thou hast known
This truth too long to look so like Despair ?

Mar. O, no, no, no!—a hope—a little hope—
I had erewhile—but I have heard its knell.
Oh, would my life were measured out with thine—
All my years number'd—all my days, my hours,
My utmost minutes, all summ'd up with thine?
   Guido. Marina—
   Mar.   Let me weep—no, let me kneel
To God—but rather thee—to spare this end
That is so wilful. Oh, for pity's sake!
Pluck back thy precious spirit from these clouds
That smother it with death. Oh! turn from death,
And do not woo it with such dark resolve,
To make me widow'd.
   Guido.   I have lived my term.
   Mar. No—not thy term—no! not the natural term
Of one so young. Oh! thou hast spent thy years
In sinful waste upon unholy—
   Guido.   Hush!
Marina.
   Mar. Nay, I must. Oh! cursed lore,
That hath supplied this spell against thy life.
Unholy learning—devilish and dark—
Study! O, God! O, God!—how can thy stars
Be bright with such black knowledge? Oh, that men
Should ask more light of them than guides their steps
At evening to love!
   Guido.   Hush, hush, oh hush!
Thy words have pain'd me in the midst of pain.
True, if I had not read, I should not die;
For, if I had not read, I had not been.
All our acts of life are pre-ordain'd,
And each pre-acted, in our several spheres,
By ghostly duplicates. They sway our deeds

By their performance.   What if mine hath been
To be a prophet and foreknow my doom ?
If I had closed my eyes, the thunder then
Had roar'd it in my ears ; my own mute brain
Had told it with a tongue.   What must be, must.
Therefore I knew when my full time would fall ;
And now—to save thy widowhood of tears—
To spare the very breaking of thy heart,
I may not gain even a brief hour's reprieve !
What seest thou yonder ?

  Mar.   Where ?—a tree—the sun
Sinking behind a tree.

  Guido.   It is no tree,
Marina, but a shape—the awful shape
That comes to claim me.   Seest thou not his shade
Darken before his steps?   Ah me ! how cold
It comes against my feet !   Cold, icy cold !
And blacker than a pall.

  Mar.   My love !

  Guido.   -   Oh heaven
And earth, where are ye ?   Marina— [Guido *dies.*

  Mar.   I am here !
What wilt thou ?   dost thou speak ?—Methought I
  heard thee
Just whispering.   He is dead ?—O God ! he's dead !

THE TWO SWANS.

A FAIRY TALE.

IMMORTAL Imogen, crown'd queen above
The lilies of thy sex, vouchsafe to hear
A fairy dream in honour of true love—
True above ills, and frailty, and all fear—

Perchance a shadow of his own career
Whose youth was darkly prison'd and long-twined
By serpent-sorrow, till white Love drew near,
And sweetly sang him free, and round his mind
A bright horizon threw, wherein no grief may wind.

I saw a tower builded on a lake,
Mock'd by its inverse shadow, dark and deep—
That seem'd a still intenser night to make,
Wherein the quiet waters sank to sleep,—
And, whatsoe'er was prison'd in that keep,
A monstrous Snake was warden :—round and round
In sable ringlets I beheld him creep,
Blackest amid black shadows, to the ground
Whilst his enormous head the topmast turret crown'd.

From whence he shot fierce light against the stars,
Making the pale moon paler with affright;
And with his ruby eye out-threaten'd Mars—
That blazed in the mid-heavens, hot and bright—
Nor slept, nor wink'd, but with a steadfast spite
Watch'd their wan looks and tremblings in the skies;
And that he might not slumber in the night,
The curtain-lids were pluck'd from his large eyes,
So he might never drowse, but watch his secret prize.

Prince or princess in dismal durance pent,
Victims of old Enchantment's love or hate,
Their lives must all in painful sighs be spent,
Watching the lonely waters soon and late,
And clouds that pass and leave them to their fate,
Or company their grief with heavy tears :—
Meanwhile that Hope can spy no golden gate

For sweet escapement, but in darksome fears
They weep and pine away as if immortal years.

No gentle bird with gold upon its wing
Will perch upon the grate—the gentle bird
Is safe in leafy dell, and will not bring
Freedom's sweet key-note and commission-word
Learn'd of a fairy's lips, for pity stirr'd—
Lest while he trembling sings, untimely guest!
Watch'd by that cruel Snake and darkly heard,
He leave a widow on her lonely nest,
To press in silent grief the darlings of her breast.

No gallant knight, adventurous, in his bark,
Will seek the fruitful perils of the place,
To rouse with dipping oar the waters dark
That bear that serpent-image on their face.
And Love, brave Love! though he attempt the
　　base,
Nerved to his loyal death, he may not win
His captive lady from the strict embrace
Of that foul Serpent, clasping her within
His sable folds—like Eve enthrall'd by the old Sin.

But there is none—no knight in panoply,
Nor Love, intrench'd in his strong steely coat:
No little speck—no sail—no helper nigh,
No sign—no whispering—no plash of boat :—
The distant shores show dimly and remote,
Made of a deeper mist,—serene and grey,—
And slow and mute the cloudy shadows float
Over the gloomy wave, and pass away,
Chased by the silver beams that on their marges play.

And bright and silvery the willows sleep
Over the shady verge—no mad winds tease
Their hoary heads ; but quietly they weep
Their sprinkling leaves—half fountains and half trees:
There lilies be—and fairer than all these,
A solitary Swan her breast of snow
Launches against the wave that seems to freeze
Into a chaste reflection, still below
Twin-shadow of herself wherever she may go.

And forth she paddles in the very noon
Of solemn midnight like an elfin thing,
Charm'd into being by the argent moon—
Whose silver light for love of her fair wing
Goes with her in the shade, still worshipping
Her dainty plumage :—all around her grew
A radiant circlet, like a fairy ring ;
And all behind, a tiny little clue
Of light, to guide her back across the waters blue.

And sure she is no meaner than a fay
Redeem'd from sleepy death, for beauty's sake,
By old ordainment :—silent as she lay,
Touch'd by a moonlight wand I saw her wake,
And cut her leafy slough, and so forsake
The verdant prison of her lily peers,
That slept amidst the stars upon the lake—
A breathing shape—restored to human fears,
And new-born love and grief—self-conscious of her
    tears.

And now she clasps her wings around her heart,
And near that lonely isle begins to glide,

Pale as her fears, and oft-times with a start
Turns her impatient head from side to side
In universal terrors—all too wide
To watch ; and often to that marble keep
Upturns her pearly eyes, as if she spied
Some foe, and crouches in the shadows steep
That in the gloomy wave go diving fathoms deep.

And well she may, to spy that fearful thing
All down the dusky walls in circlets wound
Alas ! for what rare prize, with many a ring
Girding the marble casket round and round?
His folded tail, lost in the gloom profound,
Terribly darkeneth the rocky base ;
But on the top his monstrous head is crown'd
With prickly spears, and on his doubtful face ·
Gleam his unwearied eyes, red watchers of the place.

Alas ! of the hot fires that nightly fall,
No one will scorch him in those orbs of spite,
So he may never see beneath the wall
That timid little creature, all too bright,
That stretches her fair neck, slender and white,
Invoking the pale moon, and vainly tries
Her throbbing throat, as if to charm the night
With song—but, hush—it perishes in sighs,
And there will be no dirge sad-swelling, though she
    dies !

She droops—she sinks—she leans upon the lake,
Fainting again into a lifeless flower
But soon the chilly springs anoint and wake
Her spirit from its death, and with new power

She sheds her stifled sorrows in a shower
Of tender song, timed to her falling tears—
That wins the shady summit of that tower,
And, trembling all the sweeter for its fears,
Fills with imploring moan that cruel monster's ears.

And, lo ! the scaly beast is all deprest,
Subdued like Argus by the might of sound—
What time Apollo his sweet lute addrest
To magic converse with the air, and bound
The many monster eyes, all slumber-drown'd :—
So on the turret-top that watchful Snake
Pillows his giant head, and lists profound,
As if his wrathful spite would never wake,
Charm'd into sudden sleep for Love and Beauty's sake

His prickly crest lies prone upon his crown,
And thirsty lip from lip disparted flies,
To drink that dainty flood of music down—
His scaly throat is big with pent-up sighs—
And whilst his hollow ear entrancëd lies,
His looks for envy of the charmed sense
Are fain to listen, till his steadfast eyes,
Stung into pain by their own impotence,
Distil enormous tears into the lake immense.

Oh, tuneful Swan ! oh, melancholy bird !
Sweet was that midnight miracle of song,
Rich with ripe sorrow, needful of no word
To tell of pain, and love, and love's deep wrong—
Hinting a piteous tale—perchance how long
Thy unknown tears were mingled with the lake,
What time disguised thy leafy mates among—

And no eye knew what human love and ache
Dwelt in those dewy leaves, and heart so nigh to
    break.

Therefore no poet will ungently touch
The water-lily, on whose eyelids dew
Trembles like tears ; but ever hold it such
As human pain may wander through and through,
Turning the pale leaf paler in its hue—
Wherein life dwells, transfigured, not entomb'd,
By magic spells.   Alas ! who ever knew
Sorrow in all its shapes, leafy and plumed,
Or in gross husks of brutes eternally inhumed ?

And now the winged song has scaled the height
Of that dark dwelling, builded for despair,
And soon a little casement flashing bright
Widens self-open'd into the cool air—
That music like a bird may enter there
And soothe the captive in his stony cage ;
For there is nought of grief, or painful care,
But plaintive song may happily engage
From sense of its own ill, and tenderly assuage.

And forth into the light, small and remote,
A creature, like the fair son of a king,
Draws to the lattice in his jewell'd coat
Against the silver moonlight glistening,
And leans upon his white hand listening
To that sweet music that with tenderer tone
Salutes him, wondering what kindly thing
Is come to soothe him with so tuneful moan,
Singing beneath the walls as if for him alone.

And while he listens, the mysterious song,
Woven with timid particles of speech,
Twines into passionate words that grieve along
The melancholy notes, and softly teach
The secrets of true love,—that trembling reach
. His earnest ear, and through the shadows dun
He missions like replies, and each to each
Their silver voices mingle into one,
Like blended streams that make one music as they run.

" Ah ! Love, my hope is swooning in my heart,—"
" Ay, sweet, my cage is strong and hung full high—"
" Alas ! our lips are held so far apart,
Thy words come faint,—they have so far to fly !—"
" If I may only shun that serpent-eye,—"
" Ah me ! that serpent eye doth never sleep ;—"
" Then, nearer thee, Love's martyr, I will die !—"
" Alas, alas ! that word has made me weep !
For pity's sake remain safe in thy marble keep !"

" My marble keep ! it is my marble tomb—"
" Nay, sweet! but thou hast there thy living breath—'
" Aye to expend in sighs for this hard doom ;—"
" But I will come to thee and sing beneath,
And nightly so beguile this serpent wreath ;—"
' Nay, I will find a path from these despairs.'
' Ah, needs then thou must tread the back of death,
Making his stony ribs thy stony stairs.—
Behold his ruby eye, how tearfully it glares !"

Full sudden at these words, the princely youth
Leaps on the scaly back that slumbers, still
Unconscious of his foot. yet not for ruth,

But numb'd to dulness by the fairy skill
Of that sweet music (all more wild and shrill
For intense fear) that charm'd him as he lay—
Meanwhile the lover nerves his desperate will,
Held some short throbs by natural dismay,
Then down the serpent-track begins his darksome way

Now dimly seen—now toiling out of sight,
Eclipsed and cover'd by the envious wall;
Now fair and spangled in the sudden light,
And clinging with wide arms for fear of fall;
Now dark and shelter'd by a kindly pall
Of dusky shadow from his wakeful foe;
Slowly he winds adown—dimly and small,
Watch'd by the gentle Swan that sings below,
Her hope increasing, still, the larger he doth grow.

But nine times nine the serpent folds embrace
The marble walls about—which he must tread
Before his anxious foot may touch the base:
Long is the dreary path, and must be sped!
But Love, that holds the mastery of dread,
Braces his spirit, and with constant toil
He wins his way, and now, with arms outspread
Impatient plunges from the last long coil:
So may all gentle Love ungentle Malice foil!

The song is hush'd, the charm is all complete,
And two fair Swans are swimming on the lake:
But scarce their tender bills have time to meet,
When fiercely drops adown that cruel Snake—
His steely scales a fearful rustling make,
Like autumn leaves that tremble and foretell

The sable storm ;—the plumy lovers quake—
And feel the troubled waters pant and swell,
Heaved by the giant bulk of their pursuer fell.

His jaws, wide yawning like the gates of Death,
Hiss horrible pursuit—his red eyes glare
The waters into blood—his eager breath
Grows hot upon their plumes:—now, minstrel fair !
She drops her ring into the waves, and there
It widens all around, a fairy ring
Wrought of the silver light—the fearful pair
Swim in the very midst, and pant and cling
The closer for their fears, and tremble wing to wing.

Bending their course over the pale grey lake,
Against the pallid East, wherein light play'd
In tender flushes, still the baffled Snake
Circled them round continually, and bay'd
Hoarsely and loud, forbidden to invade
The sanctuary ring—his sable mail
Roll'd darkly through the flood, and writhed and made
A shining track over the waters pale,
Lash'd into boiling foam by his enormous tail.

And so they sail'd into the distance dim,
Into the very distance—small and white,
Like snowy blossoms of the spring that swim
Over the brooklets—follow'd by the spite
Of that huge Serpent, that with wild affright
Worried them on their course, and sore annoy,
Till on the grassy marge I saw them 'light,
And change, anon, a gentle girl and boy,
Lock'd in embrace of sweet unutterable joy !

H

Then came the Morn, and with her pearly showers
Wept on them, like a mother, in whose eyes
Tears are no grief; and from his rosy bowers
The Oriental sun began to rise,
Chasing the darksome shadows from the skies;
Wherewith that sable Serpent far away
Fled, like a part of night—delicious sighs
From waking blossoms purified the day,
And little birds were singing sweetly from each spray.

ODE ON A DISTANT PROSPECT OF CLAPHAM ACADEMY.*

AH me! those old familiar bounds!
That classic house, those classic grounds
   My pensive thought recalls!
What tender urchins now confine,
What little captives now repine,
   Within yon irksome walls?

Ay, that's the very house! I know
Its ugly windows, ten a-row!
   Its chimneys in the rear!
And there's the iron rod so high,
That drew the thunder from the
   And turn'd our table-beer!

There I was birch'd! there I was bred!
There like a little Adam fed
   From Learning's woeful tree!
The weary tasks I used to con!—
The hopeless leaves I wept upon!—
   Most fruitless leaves to me!—

* No connexion with any other Ode.

The summon'd class!—the awful bow!—
I wonder who is master now
   And wholesome anguish sheds!
How many ushers now employs,
How many maids to see the boys
   Have nothing in their heads!

And Mrs. S * * *?—Doth she abet
(Like Pallas in the parlour) yet
   Some favour'd two or three,—
The little Crichtons of the hour,
Her muffin-medals that devour,
   And swill her prize—bohea?

Ay, there's the playground! there's the lime,
Beneath whose shade in summer's prime
   So wildly I have read!—
Who sits there *now*, and skims the cream
Of young Romance, and weaves a dream
   Of Love and Cottage-bread?

Who struts the Randall of the walk?
Who models tiny heads in chalk?
   Who scoops the light canoe?
What early genius buds apace?
Where's Poynter? Harris? Bowers? Chase?
   Hal Baylis? blithe Carew?

Alack! they're gone—a thousand ways!.
And some are serving in "the Greys,"
   And some have perish'd young!—
Jack Harris weds his second wife;
Hal Baylis drives the *wane* of life;
   And blithe Carew—is hung!

Grave Bowers teaches A B C
To savages at Owhyee
   Poor Chase is with the worms !—
All, all are gone—the olden breed !—
New crops of mushroom boys succeed,
   " And push us from our *forms !*"

Lo ! where they scramble forth, and shout,
And leap, and skip, and mob about,
   At play where we have play'd !
Some hop, some run, (some fall,) some twine
Their crony arms ; some in the shine,—
   And some are in the shade !

Lo there what mix'd conditions run !
The orphan lad ; the widow's son ;
   And Fortune's favour'd care—
The wealthy-born, for whom she hath
Mac-Adamised the future path—
   The Nabob's pamper'd heir !

Some brightly starr'd—some evil born,—
For honour some, and some for scorn,—
   For fair or foul renown !
Good, bad, indiff'rent—none may lack !
Look, here's a White, and there's a Black !
   And there's a Creole brown !

Some laugh and sing, some mope and weep,
And wish *their* ' frugal sires would keep
   Their only sons at home ;'—
Some tease the future tense, and plan
The full-grown doings of the man,
   And pant for years to come !

A foolish wish! There's one at hoop;
And four at *fives!* and five who stoop
   The marble taw to speed!
And one that curvets in and out,
Reining his fellow Cob about,—
   Would I were in his *stead!*

Yet he would gladly halt and drop
That boyish harness off, to swop
   With this world's heavy van—
To toil, to tug. O little fool!
While thou canst be a horse at school,
   To wish to be a man!

Perchance thou deem'st it were a thing
To wear a crown,—to be a king!
   And sleep on regal down!
Alas! thou know'st not kingly cares;
Far happier is thy head that wears
   That hat without a crown!

And dost thou think that years acquire
New added joys? Dost think thy sire
   More happy than his son?
That manhood's mirth?—Oh, go thy ways
To Drury-lane when ———* *plays,*
   And she how *forced* our fun!

Thy taws are brave!—thy tops are rare!— ·
Our tops are spun with coils of care,
   Our *dumps* are no delight!—
The Elgin marbles are but tame,
And 'tis at best a sorry game
   To fly the Muse's kite!

    * This blank exists in the original.

Our hearts are dough, our heels are lead,
Our topmost joys fall dull and dead
   Like balls with no rebound !
And often with a faded eye
We look behind, and send a sigh
   Towards that merry ground !

Then be contented. Thou hast got
The most of heaven in thy young lot ;
   There's sky-blue in thy cup !
Thou'lt find thy Manhood all too fast—
Soon come, soon gone ! and Age at last
   A sorry *breaking-up !*

ODES AND ADDRESSES TO GREAT PEOPLE.

"Catching all the oddities, the whimsies, the absurdities, and the littleness
of conscious greatness by the way."—*Citizen of the World.*

ADDRESS.

THE present being the first appearance of this little
Work, some sort of Address seems to be called for
from the Author, Editor, and Compiler,—and we
come forward in prose, totally overcome, like a
flurried manager in his every-day clothes, to solicit
public indulgence—protest an indelible feeling of
reverence — bow, beseech, promise,—and "all that."

To the persons addressed in the Poems nothing
need be said, as it would be only swelling the book,
(a custom which we detest,) to recapitulate in prose
what we have said in verse. To those unaddressed
an apology is due ;—and to them it is very respect-
fully offered. Mr. Hunt, for his Permanent Ink,
deserves to have his name recorded in his own

composition—Mr. Colman, the amiable King's Jester, and Oath-blaster of the modern Stage, merits a line— Mr. Accum, whose fame is potted—Mr. Bridgman, the maker of Patent Safety Coffins—Mr. Kean, the great Lustre of the Boxes—Sir Humphry Davy, the great Lamplighter of the Pits—Sir William Congreve, one of the proprietors of the Portsmouth Rocket— yea, several others call for the Muse's approbation; —but our little Volume, like the Adelphi House, is easily filled, and those who are disappointed of places are requested to wait until the next performance.

Having said these few words to the uninitiated, we leave our Odes and Addresses, like Gentlemen of the Green Isle, to hunt their own fortunes;—and, by a modest assurance, to make their way to the hearts of those to whom they have addressed themselves.

ADVERTISEMENT TO THE SECOND EDITION.

A SECOND Edition being called for, the Author takes the opportunity of expressing his grateful thanks to his Readers and Reviewers, for the kind way in which they have generally received his little Book. Many of those who have been *be-Oded* in the following pages have taken the verse-offerings in good part; and the Author has been given to understand that certain "Great People," who have been kept "out of situations," have, like Bob Acres, looked upon themselves as very ill-used Gentlemen. It is rather hard that there should not be room for all the Great;— but this little conveyance,—a sort of light coach to Fame,—like other conveyances, while it has only four *in*, labours under the disadvantage of having twelve *out.* The Proprietor apprehends he must meet the wants of the Public by starting an extra coach: in which case Mr. Colman (an anxious Licenser) and Mr. Hunt (the best maker of speeches and blacking in the City and Liberty of Westminster) shall certainly be *booked* for places. To the latter Gentleman, the Author gratefully acknowledges the compliment of a bottle of his permanent ink: it will be, indeed, pleasant to write an Address to Mr. Wilberforce in the liquid of a beautiful jet Black, which the Author now meditates doing. Odes, written in permanent ink, will doubtless stand a chance of running a good race with Gray's!

A few objections have been made to the present Volume, which the Author regrets he cannot attend to, without serious damage to the whole production. The Address to Maria Darlington is said by several ingenious and judicious persons to be *namby-pamby.* —This is a sad disappointment to the Writer, as he was in hopes he had accomplished a bit of the right *Shenstonian.* The verses to the Champion of England are declared irreverent,—and those to Dr. Ireland, and his Partners in the Stone Trade, are held out as an improper interference with sacred things; these Addresses are certainly calumniated: the one was really written as an affectionate inquiry after a great and reverend Warrior, now in rural retirement; and the other was intended as a kindly advertisement of an exhibition, which, although cheaper than the Tower, and nearly as cheap as Mrs. Salmon's Wax-work, the modesty of the Proprietors will not permit them sufficiently to puff.

To the universal objection,—that the Book is overrun with puns,—the Author can only say, he has searched every page without being able to detect a thing of the kind. He can only promise, therefore, that if any respectable Reviewer will point the *vermin* out, they shall be carefully trapped and thankfully destroyed.

PREFACE TO THE THIRD EDITION.

FROM the kindness with which this little volume has been received, the Authors have determined upon presenting to the Public " more last Baxterish words;" and the Reader will be pleased therefore to consider this rather as a Preface or Advertisement to the volume to come, than a third Address in prose, explanatory or recommendatory of the present portion of the Work. It is against etiquette to introduce one gentleman to another thrice ; and it must be confessed, that if these few sentences were to be billeted upon the first volume, the Public might overlook the Odes, but would have great reason to complain of the Addresses.

So many Great Men stand over, like the correspondents to a periodical, that they must be " continued in our next." These are certainly bad times for paying debts ; but all persons having any claims upon the Authors, may rest assured that they will ultimately be paid in full.

No material alterations have been made in this third Edition,—with the exception of the introduction of a few new commas, which the lovers of punctuation will immediately detect and duly appreciate ;—and

the omission of the three puns,* which, in the opinion
of all friends and reviewers, were detrimental to the
correct humour of the publication.

ODE TO MR. GRAHAM,

THE AERONAUT.

"Up with me !—up with me into the sky !"
Wordsworth—on a Lark!

DEAR GRAHAM, whilst the busy crowd,
The vain, the wealthy, and the proud,
   Their meaner flights pursue,
Let us cast off the foolish ties
That bind us to the earth, and rise
   And take a bird's-eye view !—

'A few more whiffs of my cigar
And then, in Fancy's airy car,
   Have with thee for the skies :—
How oft this fragrant smoke upcurl'd
Hath borne me from this little world,
   And all that in it lies !—

Away !—away !—the bubble fills—
Farewell to earth and all its hills !—
   We seem to cut the wind !—
So high we mount, so swift we go,
The chimney tops are far below,
   The Eagle's left behind !—

---

* I have read, and had the two editions read repeatedly, but have failed
to detect any of these omissions, unless one of them is the elision of the
word "washing" in Bridget Jones's letter, as pointed out in a note there.

Ah me ! my brain begins to swim !—
The world is growing rather dim ·
   The steeples and the trees—
My wife is getting very small !
I cannot see my babe at all !—
   The Dollond if you please !—

Do, Graham, let me have a quiz,
Lord ! what a Lilliput it is,
   That little world of Mogg's !—
Are those the London Docks ?—that channel,
The mighty Thames ?—a proper kennel
   For that small Isle of Dogs !—

What is that seeming tea-urn there ?
That fairy dome, St. Paul's !—I swear,
   Wren must have been a Wren !—
And that small stripe ?—it cannot be
The City Road !—Good lack ! to see
   The little ways of men !

Little, indeed !—my eyeballs ache
To find a turnpike.—I must take
   Their tolls upon my trust !—
And where is mortal labour gone ?
Look, Graham, for a little stone
   Mac Adamized to dust !

Look at the horses !—less than flies !—
Oh, what a waste it was of sighs
   To wish to be a Mayor !
What is the honour ?—none at all,
One's honour must be very small
   For such a civic chair !—

And there's Guildhall !—'tis far aloof—
Methinks, I fancy through the roof
   Its little guardian Gogs
Like penny dolls—a tiny show !—
Well,—I must say they're ruled below
   By very little logs !—

Oh ! Graham, how the upper air
Alters the standards of compare ;
   One of our silken flags
Would cover London all about—
Nay then—let's even empty out
   Another brace of bags !

Now for a glass of bright champagne
Above the clouds ! Come, let us drain
   A bumper as we go !—
But hold !—for God's sake do not cant
The cork away—unless you want
   To brain your friends below.

Think ! what a mob of little men
Are crawling just within our ken,
   Like mites upon a cheese !—
Pshaw !—how the foolish sight rebukes
Ambitious thoughts !—can there be *Dukes*
   Of *Gloster* such as these !—

Oh ! what is glory?—what is fame?
Hark to the little mob's acclaim,
   'Tis nothing but a hum !—
A few near gnats would trump as loud
As all the shouting of a crowd
   That has so far to come !—

Well—they are wise that choose the near,
A few small buzzards in the ear,
  To organs ages hence !—
Ah me, how distance touches all ;
It makes the true look rather small,
  But murders poor pretence.

" The world recedes !—it disappears !
Heav'n opens on my eyes—my ears
  With buzzing noises ring !"—
A fig for Southey's Laureat lore !—
What's Rogers here ?—Who cares for Moore
  That hears the Angels sing !—

A fig for earth, and all its minions !—
We are above the world's opinions,
  Graham ! we'll have our own !—
Look what a vantage height we've got !—
Now——*do* you think Sir Walter Scott
  Is such a Great Unknown ?

Speak up,—or hath he hid his name
To crawl through " subways " unto fame,
  Like Williams of Cornhill ?—
Speak up, my lad !—when men run small
We'll show what's little in them all,
  Receive it how they will !—

Think now of Irving !—shall he preach
The princes down,—shall he impeach
  The potent and the rich,
Merely on ethic stilts,—and I
Not moralize at two miles high
  The true didactic pitch !

Come :—what d'ye think of Jeffrey, sir?
Is Gifford such a Gulliver
   In Lilliput's Review,
That like Colossus he should stride
Certain small brazen inches wide
   For poets to pass through?

Look down ! the world is but a spot.
Now say—Is Blackwood's *low* or not,
   For all the Scottish tone?
It shall not weigh us here—not where
The sandy burden's lost in air—
   Our lading—where is't flown?

Now,—like you Croly's verse indeed—
In heaven—where one cannot read
   The " Warren " on a wall?
What think you here of that man's fame?
Though Jerdan magnified his name,
   To me 'tis very small !

And, truly, is there such a spell
In those three letters, L. E. L.,
   To witch a world with song?
On clouds the Byron did not sit,
Yet dared on Shakspeare's head to spit,
   And say the world was wrong !

And shall not we?   Let's think aloud '
Thus being couch'd upon a cloud,
   Graham, we'll have our eyes !
We felt the great when we were less,
But we'll retort on littleness
   Now we are in the skies.

O Graham, Graham, how I blame ,
The bastard blush,—the petty shame,
   That used to fret me quite,—
The little sores I cover'd then,
No sores on earth, nor sorrows when
   The world is out of sight !

My name is Tims.—I am the man
That North's unseen diminish'd clan
   So scurvily abused !
I am the very P. A. Z.
The London's Lion's small pin's head
   So often hath refused !

Campbell—(you cannot see him here)—
Hath scorn'd my *lays :*—do his appear
   Such great eggs from the sky ?—
And Longman, and his lengthy Co.
Long only in a little Row,
   Have thrust my poems by !

What else ?—I'm poor, and much beset
With damn'd small duns—that is—in debt
   Some grains of golden dust !
But only worth above, is worth.—
What's all the credit of the earth ?
   An inch of cloth on trust !

What's Rothschild here, that wealthy man !
Nay, worlds of wealth ?—Oh, if you can
   Spy out,—the *Golden Ball !*
Sure as we rose, all money sank :
What's gold or silver now ?—the Bank
   Is gone—the 'Change and all !

What's all the ground-rent of the globe?—
Oh, Graham, it would worry Job
    To hear its landlords prate!
But after this survey, I think
I'll ne'er be bullied more, nor shrink
    From men of large estate!

And less, still less, will I submit
To poor mean acres' worth of wit—
    I that have heaven's span—
I that like Shakspeare's self may dream
Beyond the very clouds, and seem
    An Universal Man!

Mark, Graham, mark those gorgeous crowds!
Like Birds of Paradise the clouds
    Are winging on the wind!
But what is grander than their range?
More lovely than their sun-set change?—
    The free creative mind!

Well! the Adults' School's in the air!
The greatest men are lesson'd there
    As well as the Lessee!
Oh could Earth's Ellistons thus small
Behold the greatest stage of all,
    How humbled they would be!

"Oh would some Power the giftie gie em
To see themselves as others see 'em,"
    'Twould much abate their fuss!
If they could think that from the skies
They are as little in our eyes
    As they can think of us!

Of us! are *we* gone out of sight?
Lessen'd! diminish'd! vanish'd quite!
   Lost to the tiny town!
Beyond the Eagle's ken—the grope
Of Dollond's longest telescope!
   Graham! we're going down!

Ah me! I've touch'd a string that opes
The airy valve!—the gas elopes—
   Down goes our bright Balloon!—
Farewell the skies! the clouds! I smell
The lower world! Graham, farewell,
   Man of the silken moon!

The earth is close! the City nears—
Like a burnt paper it appears,
   Studded with tiny sparks!
Methinks I hear the distant rout
Of coaches rumbling all about—
   We're close above the Parks!

I hear the watchmen on their beats,
Hawking the hour about the streets.
   Lord! what a cruel jar
It is upon the earth to light!
Well—there's the finish of our flight!
   I've smoked my last cigar!

ODE TO MR. M'ADAM.

" Let us take to the road !"—Beggar's Opera.

M'ADAM, hail!
Hail, Roadian! hail, Colossus! who dost stand
Striding ten thousand turnpikes on the land!

I

Oh universal Leveller! all hail!
To thee, a good, yet stony-hearted man,
   The kindest one, and yet the flintiest going,—
To thee,—how much for thy commodious plan,
   Lanark Reformer of the Ruts, is Owing!
      The Bristol mail
Gliding o'er ways, hitherto deem'd invincible,
   When carrying Patriots, now shall never fail
Those of the most "*unshaken* public principle."
     Hail to thee, Scot of Scots!
Thou northern light, amid those heavy men!
Foe to Stonehenge, yet friend to all beside,
Thou scatter'st flints and favours far and wide,
      From palaces to cots;—
    Dispenser of coagulated good!
    Distributor of granite and of food!
Long may thy fame its even path march on,
   E'en when thy sons are dead!
Best benefactor! though thou giv'st a stone
   To those who ask for bread!

Thy first great trial in this mighty town
Was, if I rightly recollect, upon
   That gentle hill which goeth
Down from "the County" to the Palace gate,
   And, like a river, thanks to thee, now floweth
Past the Old Horticultural Society,—
The chemist Cobb's, the house of Howell and James,
Where ladies play high shawl and satin games—
    A little *Hell* of lace!
And past the Athenæum, made of late,
    Severs a sweet variety
Of milliners and booksellers who grace
    Waterloo Place,

Making division, the Muse fears and guesses,
'Twixt Mr. Rivington's and Mr. Hessey's.
Thou stood'st thy trial, Mac! and shaved the road
From Barber Beaumont's to the King's abode
So well, that paviors threw their rammers by,
Let down their tuck'd shirt sleeves, and with a sigh
Prepared themselves, poor souls, to chip or die!

Next, from the palace to the prison, thou
 Didst go, the highway's watchman, to thy beat,—
 Preventing though the *rattling* in the street,
   Yet kicking up a row,
Upon the stones—ah! truly watchman-like,
Encouraging thy victims all to strike,
 To further thy own purpose, Adam, daily;—
Thou hast smooth'd, alas, the path to the Old Bailey!
  And to the stony bowers
Of Newgate, to encourage the approach,
  By caravan or coach,—
Hast strew'd the way with flints as soft as flowers.

   Who shall dispute thy name!
  Insculpt in stone in every street,
   We soon shall greet
  Thy trodden down, yet all unconquer'd fame!
Where'er we take, even at this time, our way,
Nought see we, but mankind in open air,
Hammering thy fame, as Chantrey would not dare;—
  And with a patient care
Chipping thy immortality all day!
Demosthenes, of old,—that rare old man,—
Prophetically *follow'd*, Mac! thy plan:—
   For he, we know,
   (History says so,)

Put *pebbles* in his mouth when he would speak
   The *smoothest* Greek!
  It is "impossible, and cannot be,"
   But that thy genius hath,
   Besides the turnpike, many another path
  Trod, to arrive at popularity.
O'er Pegasus, perchance, thou hast thrown a thigh,
Nor ridden a roadster only;—mighty Mac!
And 'faith I'd swear, when on that wingèd hack,
Thou hast observed the highways in the sky!
Is the path up Parnassus rough and steep,
  And "hard to climb," as Dr. B. would say?
Dost think it best for Sons of Song to keep
  The noiseless *tenor* of their way? (see Gray.)
What line of road *should* poets take to bring
  Themselves unto those waters, loved the first!—
Those waters which can wet a man to sing!
  Which, like thy fame, "from *granite* basins burst,
  Leap into life, and, sparkling, woo the thirst?"

That thou'rt a proser, even thy birthplace might
  Vouchsafe;—and Mr. Cadell *may*, God wot,
  Have paid thee many a pound for many a blot,—
   Cadell's a wayward wight!
Although no Walter, still thou art a Scot,
And I can throw, I think, a little light
Upon some works thou hast written for the town,—
And publish'd, like a Lilliput Unknown!
  "Highways and Byeways" is thy book, no doubt,
   (One whole edition's out,)
    And next, for it is fair
     That Fame,
  Seeing her children, should confess she had 'em;—

"Some *Passages* from the life of Adam Blair,"—
 (Blair is a Scottish name,)
What are they, but thy own good roads M'Adam?

  O! indefatigable labourer
In the paths of men! when thou shalt die, 'twill be
A mark of thy surpassing industry,
 That of the monument, which men shall rear
Over thy most inestimable bone,
Thou didst thy very self lay the first stone!—
Of a right ancient line thou comest,—through
Each crook and turn we trace the unbroken clue,
Until we see thy sire before our eyes,—
Rolling his gravel walks in Paradise!
But he, our great Mac Parent, err'd, and ne'er
  Have our walks since been fair!
Yet Time, who, like the merchant, lives on 'Change,
For ever varying, through his varying range,
  Time maketh all things even!'
In this strange world, turning beneath high heaven,
 He hath redeem'd the Adams, and contrived,—
  (How are Time's wonders hived!)
In pity to mankind, and to befriend 'em,—
  (Time is above all praise,)
That he, who first did make our evil ways,
Reborn in Scotland, should be first to mend 'em!

A *FRIENDLY* EPISTLE TO MRS. FRY,
IN NEWGATE.

"Sermons in stones."—*As you like It.*
"Out! out! damned spot!"—*Macbeth.*

I LIKE you, Mrs. Fry! I like your name!
It speaks the very warmth you feel in pressing

In daily act round Charity's great flame—
I like the crisp Browne way you have of dressing,
Good Mrs. Fry ! I like the placid claim
You make to Christianity,—professing
Love, and good *works*—of course you buy of Barton
Beside the young *fry's* bookseller, Friend Darton !

I like, good Mrs. Fry, your brethren mute—
Those serious, solemn gentlemen that sport—
I should have said, that *wear*, the sober suit
Shaped like a court dress—but for heaven's court.
I like your sisters too,—sweet Rachel's fruit—
Protestant nuns ! I like their stiff support
Of virtue—and I like to see them clad
With such a difference—just like good from bad !

I like the sober colours—not the wet;
Those gaudy manufactures of the rainbow—
Green, orange, crimson, purple, violet—
In which the fair, the flirting, and the vain, go—
The others are a chaste, severer set,
In which the good, the pious, and the plain, go—
They're moral *standards*, to know Christians by—
In short, they are your *colours*, Mrs. Fry !

As for the naughty tinges of the prism—
Crimson's the cruel uniform of war—
Blue—hue of brimstone ! minds no catechism;
And green is young and gay—not noted for
Goodness, or gravity, or quietism,
Till it is sadden'd down to tea-green, or
Olive—and purple's giv'n to wine, I guess ;
And yellow is a convict by its dress !

They're all the devil's liveries, that men
And women wear in servitude to sin—
But how will they come off, poor motleys, when
Sin's wages are paid down, and they stand in
The Evil presence? You and I know, then
How all the party colours will begin
To part—the *Pit*tite hues will sadden there,
Whereas the *Foxite* shades will all show fair!

Witness their goodly labours one by one!
Russet makes garments for the needy poor—
Dove-colour preaches love to all—and *dun*
Calls every day at Charity's street-door—
Brown studies scripture, and bids woman shun
All gaudy furnishing—*olive* doth pour
Oil into wounds : and *drab* and *slate* supply
Scholar and book in Newgate, Mrs. Fry!

Well! Heaven forbid that I should discommend
The gratis, charitable, jail-endeavour!
When all persuasions in your praises blend—
The Methodist's creed and cry are, *Fry* for ever!
No—I will be your friend—and, like a friend,
Point out your very worst defect—Nay, never
Start at that word!—But I *must* ask you why
You keep your school *in* Newgate, Mrs. Fry?

Too well I know the price our mother Eve
Paid for *her* schooling : but must all her daughters
Commit a petty larceny, and thieve—
Pay down a crime for "*entrance*" to your "*quarters?*"
Your classes may increase, but I must grieve
Over your pupils at their bread-and-waters!

Oh, tho' it cost you rent—(and rooms run high !)
Keep your school *out* of Newgate, Mrs. Fry !

O save the vulgar soul before it's spoil'd !
Set up your mounted sign *without* the gate—
And there inform the mind before 'tis soil'd !
'Tis sorry writing on a greasy slate !
Nay, if you would not have your labours foil'd,
Take it *inclining* tow'rds a virtuous state,
Not prostrate and laid flat—else, woman meek !
The *upright* pencil will but hop and shriek !

Ah, who can tell how hard it is to drain
The evil spirit from the heart it preys in,—
To bring sobriety to life again,
Choked with the vile Anacreontic raisin,—
To wash Black Betty when her black's ingrain,—
To stick a moral lacquer on Moll Brazen,
Of Suky Tawdry's habits to deprive her ;
To tame the wild-fowl-ways of Jenny Diver !

Ah, who can tell how hard it is to teach
Miss Nancy Dawson on her bed of straw—
To make Long Sal sew up the endless breach
She made in manners—to write heaven's own law
On hearts of granite.—Nay, how hard to preach,
In cells, that are not memory's—to draw
The moral thread, thro' the immortal eye
Of blunt Whitechapel natures, Mrs. Fry !

In vain you teach them baby-work within :
'Tis but a clumsy botchery of crime ;
'Tis but a tedious darning of old sin—

Come out yourself, and stitch up souls in time—
It is too late for scouring to begin
When virtue's ravell'd out, when all the prime
Is worn away, and nothing sound remains;
You'll fret the fabric out before the stains!

I like your chocolate, good Mistress Fry!
I like your cookery in every way;
I like your shrove-tide service and supply;
I like to hear your sweet *Pandeans* play;
I like the pity in your full-brimm'd eye;
I like your carriage, and your silken grey,
Your dove-like habits, and your silent preaching;
But I don't like your Newgatory teaching.

Come out of Newgate, Mrs. Fry! Repair
Abroad, and find your pupils in the streets.
O, come abroad into the wholesome air,
And take your moral place, before Sin seats
Her wicked self in the Professor's chair.
Suppose some morals raw! the true receipt's
To dress them in the pan, but do not try
To cook them in the fire, good Mrs. Fry!

Put on your decent bonnet, and come out!
Good lack! the ancients did not set up schools
In jail—but at the *Porch* / hinting, no doubt,
That Vice should have a lesson in the rules
Before 'twas whipt by law.—O come about,
Good Mrs. Fry! and set up forms and ʼstools
All down the Old Bailey, and thro' Newgate-street,
But not in Mr. Wontner's proper seat!

Teach Lady Barrymore, if, teaching, you
That peerless Peeress can absolve from dolour;

Teach her it is not virtue to pursue
Ruin of blue, or any other colour
Teach her it is not Virtue's crown to rue,
Month after month, the unpaid drunken dollar;
Teach her that " flooring Charleys" is a game
Unworthy one that bears a Christian name.

O come and teach our children—that ar'n't *ours*—
That heaven's straight pathway is a narrow way,
Not Broad St. Giles's, where fierce Sin devours
Children, like Time—or rather they both prey
On youth together—meanwhile Newgate low'rs
Ev'n like a black cloud at the close of day,
To shut them out from any more blue sky:
Think of these hopeless wretches, Mrs. Fry!

You are not nice—go into their retreats,
And make them Quakers, if you will.—'Twere best
They wore straight collars, and their shirts sans *pleats;*
That they had hats *with* brims,—that they were drest
In garbs without *lappels*—than shame the streets
With so much raggedness.—You may invest
Much cash this way—but it will cost its price,
To give a good, round, real *cheque* to Vice!

In brief,—Oh teach the child its moral rote,
Not *in* the way from which 'twill not depart,—
But *out*—out—out!   Oh, bid it walk remote!
And if the skies are closed against the smart,
Ev'n let him wear the single-breasted coat,
For that ensureth singleness of heart.—
Do what you will, his every want supply,
Keep him—but *out* of Newgate, Mrs. Fry!

ODE TO RICHARD MARTIN, ESQ.,

M.P. FOR GALWAY.

"Martin in this has proved himself a very good man!"—*Boxiana.*

How many sing of wars,
Of Greek and Trojan jars—
The butcheries of men!
The Muse hath a " Perpetual Ruby Pen!"
Dabbling with heroes and the blood they spill;
But no one sings the man
That, like a pelican,
Nourishes Pity with his tender *Bill.*
Thou Wilberforce of hacks!
Of whites as well as blacks,
Pyebald and dapple gray,
Chesnut and bay—
No poet's eulogy thy name adorns!
But oxen, from the fens,
Sheep—in their pens,
Praise thee, and red cows with their winding horns!
Thou art sung on brutal pipes!
Drovers may curse thee,
Knackers asperse thee,
And sly M.P.'s bestow their cruel wipes;
But the old horse neighs thee,
And zebras praise thee,—
Asses, I mean—that have as many stripes!

Hast thou not taught the Drover to forbear,
In Smithfield's muddy, murderous, vile environ,—
Staying his lifted bludgeon in the air!
Bullocks don't wear
Oxide of iron!

The cruel Jarvy thou hast summon o oft,
Enforcing mercy on the course Yahoo,
That thought his horse the *courser* of the two—
    Whilst Swift smiled down aloft!—
O worthy pair! for this, when he inhabit
Bodies of birds—(if so the spirit shifts
From flesh to feather)—when the clown uplifts
His hand against the sparrow's nest, to *grab* it,—
He shall not harm the MARTINS and the *Swifts!*

Ah! when Dean Swift was *quick*, how he enhanced
The horse!—and humbled biped man like Plato!
But now he's dead, the charger is mischanced—
Gone backward in the world—and not advanced,—
            Remember Cato!
Swift was the horse's champion—not the King's
            Whom Southey sings
Mounted on Pegasus—would he were thrown!
He'll wear that ancient hackney to the bone,
Like a mere clothes-horse airing royal things!
Ah well-a-day! the ancients did not use
Their steeds so cruelly!—let it debar men
From wanton rowelling and whip's abuse—
        Look at the ancients' *Muse!*
        Look at their *Carmen!*

    O, Martin! how thine eye—
        That one would think had put aside his lashes,—
            That can't bear gashes
Thro' any horse's side, must ache to spy
That horrid window fronting Fetter-lane,—
    For there's a nag the crows have pick'd for victual,
        Or some man painted in a bloody vein—

Gods ! is there no *Horse-spital !*
That such raw shows must sicken the humane !
Sure Mr. Whittle
Loves thee but little,
To let that poor horse linger in his *pane !*

O build a Brookes's Theatre for horses !
O wipe away the national reproach—
And find a decent Vulture for their corses !
And in thy funeral track
Four sorry steeds shall follow in each coach !
Steeds that confess " the luxury of *wo !*"
True mourning steeds, in no extempore black,
And many a wretched hack
Shall sorrow for thee,—sore with kick and blow
And bloody gash—it is the Indian knack—
(Save that the savage is his own tormentor)—
Banting shall weep too in his sable scarf—
The biped woe the quadruped shall enter,
And Man and Horse go half and half,
As if their griefs met in a common *Centaur !*

ODE TO THE GREAT UNKNOWN.

"O breathe not his name !"—*Moore.*

THOU Great Unknown !
I do not mean Eternity nor Death,
That vast incog !
For I suppose thou hast a living breath,
Howbeit we know not from whose lungs 'tis blown,
Thou man of fog !
Parent of many children—child of none !
Nobody's son !

Nobody's daughter—but a parent still!
Still but an ostrich parent of a batch
Of orphan eggs,—left to the world to hatch.
      Superlative Nil!
A vox and nothing more,—yet not Vauxhall;
A head in papers, yet without a curl!
      Not the Invisible Girl!
No hand—but a hand-writing on a wall—
      A popular nonentity,
Still call'd the same,—without identity
      A lark, heard out of sight,—
A nothing shined upon,—invisibly bright,
      "Dark with excess of light!"
Constable's literary John-a-Nokes—
The real Scottish wizard—and not which,
      Nobody—in a niche;
      Every one's hoax!
     Maybe Sir Walter Scott—
      Perhaps not!
Why dost thou so conceal, and puzzle curious folks?

Thou,—whom the second-sighted never saw,
The Master Fiction of fictitious history!
      Chief Nong-tong-paw!
No mister in the world—and yet all mystery!
The "tricksy spirit" of a Scotch Cock Lane—
A *novel* Junius puzzling the world's brain—
A man of magic—yet no talisman!
A man of clair obscure—not he o' the moon!
      A star—at noon.
A non-descriptus in a caravan,
A private—of no corps—a nothern light
    In a dark lantern,—Bogie in a crape—

A figure—but no shape;
A vizor—and no knight;
The real abstract hero of the age;
The staple Stranger of the stage;
A Some One made in every man's presumption,
Frankenstein's monster—but instinct with gumption
Another strange state captive in the north,
Constable-guarded in an iron mask—
Still let me ask,
Hast thou no silver platter,
No door-plate, or no card—or some such matter,
To scrawl a name upon, and then cast forth?

Thou Scottish Barmecide, feeding the hunger
Of Curiosity with airy gammon!
Thou mystery-monger,
Dealing it out like middle cut of salmon,
That people buy, and can't make head or tail of it;
(Howbeit that puzzle never hurts the sale of it;)
Thou chief of authors mystic and abstractical,
That lay their proper bodies on the shelf—
Keeping thyself so truly to thyself,
Thou Zimmerman made practical!
Thou secret fountain of a Scottish style,
That, like the Nile
Hideth its source wherever it is bred,
But still keeps disemboguing
(Not disembroguing)
Thro' such broad sandy mouths without a head
Thou disembodied author—not yet dead,—
The whole world's literary Absentee!
Ah! wherefore hast thou fled,
Thou learned Nemo—wise to a degree,
Anonymous L. L. D.!

Thou nameless captain of the nameless gang
That do—and inquests cannot say who did it!
    Wert thou at Mrs. Donatty's death-pang?
Hast thou made gravy of Weare's watch—or hid it?
Hast thou a Blue-Beard chamber? Heaven forbid it!
    I should be very loth to see thee hang!
I hope thou hast an alibi well plann'd,
An innocent, altho' an ink-black hand.
    Tho' thou hast newly turn'd thy private bolt on
        The curiosity of all invaders—
I hope thou art merely closeted with Colton,
Who knows a little of the *Holy Land*,
    Writing thy next new novel—The Crusaders

        Perhaps thou wert even born
To be Unknown.—Perhaps hung, some foggy morn,
At Captain Coram's charitable wicket,
        Pinn'd to a ticket
That Fate had made illegible, foreseeing
The future great unmentionable being.—
        Perhaps thou hast ridden
A scholar poor on St. Augustine's Back,
Like Chatterton, and found a dusty pack
    Of Rowley novels in an old chest hidden;
A little hoard of clever simulation,
    That took the town—and Constable has bidden
Some hundred pounds for a continuation—
To keep and clothe thee in genteel starvation.

I liked thy Waverley—first of thy breeding;
    I like its modest "sixty years ago,"
As if it was not meant for ages' reading.
        I don't like Ivanhoe,
Tho' Dymoke does—it makes him think of clattering

In iron overalls before the king,
Secure from battering, to ladies flattering,
  Tuning his challenge to the gauntlets' ring—
Oh better far than all that anvil clang
  It was to hear thee touch the famous string
Of Robin Hood's tough bow and make it twang,
  Rousing him up, all verdant, with his clan,
      Like Sagittarian Pan!

I like Guy Mannering—but not that sham son
Of Brown.—I like that literary Sampson,
Nine-tenths a Dyer, with a smack of Porson. .
I like Dick Hatteraick, that rough sea Orson
      That slew the Gauger;
And Dandie Dinmont, like old Ursa Major;
And Merrilies, young Bertram's old defender,
      That Scottish Witch of Endor,
That doom'd thy fame.   She was the Witch, I take it,
To tell a great man's fortune—or to make it!

I like thy Antiquary.   With his fit on,
  He makes me think of Mr. Britton,
Who has—or had—within his garden wall,
A *miniature Stone Henge*, so very small
    The sparrows find it difficult to sit on;
And Dousterswivel, like Poyais' M'Gregor;
And Edie Ochiltree, that old *Blue Beggar*,
      Painted so cleverly,
I think thou surely knowest Mrs. Beverly!
I like thy Barber—him that fired the *Beacon*—
But that's a tender subject now to speak on!

  I like long-arm'd Rob Roy.—His very charms
Fashion'd him for renown!—In sad sincerity,

                           K

The man that robs or writes must have long arms,
If he's to hand his deeds down to posterity!
Witness Miss Biffin's posthumous prosperity,
Her poor brown crumpled mummy (nothing more)
  Bearing the name she bore,
A thing Time's tooth is tempted to destroy!
But Roys can never die—why else, in verity,
Is Paris echoing with "Vive le *Roy!*"
 Aye, Rob shall live again, and deathless Di—
(Vernon, of course) shall often live again—
Whilst there's a stone in Newgate, or a chain,
  Who can pass by
Nor feel the Thief's in prison and at hand?
There be Old Bailey Jarvies on the stand!

 I like thy Landlord's Tales!—I like that Idol
Of love and Lammermoor—the blue-eyed maid
That led to church the mounted cavalcade,
 And then pull'd up with such a bloody bridal!
Throwing equestrian Hymen on his haunches—
I like the family—(not silver) branches
  That hold the tapers
 To light the serious legend of Montrose.—
I like M'Aulay's second-sighted vapours,
As if he could not walk or talk alone,
Without the devil—or the Great Unknown,—
 Dalgetty is the nearest of Ducrows!

I like St. Leonard's Lily—drench'd with dew!
I like thy Vision of the Covenanters,
That bloody-minded Graham shot and slew.
  I like the battle lost and won,
  The hurly burly's bravely done,

The warlike gallops and the warlike *canters*!
I like that girded chieftain of the ranters,
Ready to preach down heathens, or to grapple,
    With one eye on his sword
    And one upon the Word,—
How *he* would cram the Caledonian Chapel!
I like stern Claverhouse, though he doth dapple
  His raven steed with blood of many a corse—
I like dear Mrs. Headrigg, that unravels
  Her texts of scripture on a trotting horse—
She is so like Rae Wilson when he travels!

I like thy Kenilworth—but I'm not going
  To take a Retrospective Re-Review
Of all thy dainty novels—merely showing
  The old familiar faces of a few,
    The question to renew,
How thou canst leave such deeds without a name,
Forego the unclaim'd dividends of fame,
Forego the smiles of literary houris—
Mid Lothian's trump, and Fife's shrill note of praise,
    And all the Carse of Gowrie's,
When thou might'st have thy statue in Cromarty—
  Or see thy image on Italian trays,
Betwixt Queen Caroline and Buonaparté,
  Be painted by the Titian of R.A.'s,
Or vie in sign-boards with the Royal Guelph
  Perhaps have thy bust set cheek by jowl with
    Homer's,
Perhaps send out plaster proxies of thyself
  To other Englands with Australian roamers—
    Mayhap, in Literary Owhyhee
    Displace the native wooden gods, or be
The China-Lar of a Canadian shelf!

It is not modesty that bids thee hide—
She never wastes her blushes out of sight:
　　　　It is not to invite
The world's decision, for thy fame is tried,—
　　And thy fair deeds are scatter'd far and wide,
Even royal heads are with thy readers reckon'd,—
　　From men in trencher caps to trencher scholars
　　　　In crimson collars,
And learned serjeants in the forty-second!
Whither by land or sea art thou not beckon'd?
Mayhap exported from the Frith of Forth,
Defying distance and its dim control;
　　Perhaps read about Stromness, and reckon'd
　　　worth
A brace of Miltons for capacious soul—
　　Perhaps studied in the whalers, further north,
And set above ten Shakspeares near the pole!

Oh, when thou writest by Aladdin's lamp,
With such a giant genius at command,
　　　　For ever at thy stamp,
To fill thy treasury from Fairy Land,
When haply thou might'st ask the pearly hand
Of some great British Vizier's eldest daughter,
　　　　Tho' princes sought her,
And lead her in procession hymeneal,
Oh, why dost thou remain a Beau Ideal!
Why stay, a ghost, on the Lethean Wharf,
Envelop'd in Scotch mist and gloomy fogs?
Why, but because thou art some puny Dwarf,
Some hopeless Imp, like Riquet with the Tuft,
Fearing, for all thy wit, to be rebuff'd,
Or bullied by our great reviewing Gogs?

What in this masquing age
Maketh Unknowns so many and so shy?
What but the critic's page?
One hath a cast, he hides from the world's eye;
Another hath a wen,—he won't show where;
A third has sandy hair,
A hunch upon his back, or legs awry,
Things for a vile reviewer to espy!
Another hath a mangel-wurzel nose,—
Finally, this is dimpled,
Like a pale crumpet face, or that is pimpled,
Things for a monthly critic to expose—
Nay, what is thy own case—that being small,
Thou choosest to be nobody at all !

Well, thou art prudent, with such puny bones—
E'en like Elshender, the mysterious elf,
That shadowy revelation of thyself—
To build thee a small hut of haunted stones—
For certainly the first pernicious man
That ever saw thee, would quickly draw thee
In some vile literary caravan—
Shown for a shilling
Would be thy killing,
Think of Crachami's miserable span :
No tinier frame the tiny spark could dwell in
Than there it fell in—
But when she felt herselt a show—she tried
To shrink from the world's eye, poor dwarf! and died!

O since it was thy fortune to be born
A dwarf on some Scotch *Inch*, and then to flinch
From all the Gog-like jostle of great men,

Still with thy small crow pen
Amuse and charm thy lonely hours forlorn—
Still Scottish story daintily adorn,
    Be still a shade—and when this age is fled,
When we poor sons and daughters of reality
    Are in our graves forgotten and quite dead,
And Time destroys our mottoes of morality—
The lithographic hand of Old Mortality
Shall still restore thy emblem on the stone,
    A featureless death's head,
And rob Oblivion ev'n of the Unknown!

ADDRESS TO MR. DYMOKE,

THE CHAMPION OF ENGLAND.

"—— Arma Virumque cano!"—*Virgil.*

Mr. Dymoke! Sir Knight! if I may be so bold—
    (I'm a poor simple gentleman just come to town,)
Is your armour put by, like the sheep in a fold?—
    Is your gauntlet ta'en up, which you lately flung
      down?

Are you—who *that* day rode so mail'd and admired,
    Now sitting at ease in a library chair?
Have you sent back to Astley the war-horse you hired,
    With a cheque upon Chambers to settle the fare?

What's become of the cup? Great tin-plate worker!
    say!
    Cup and ball is a game which some people deem
      fun!
Oh; *three golden balls* haven't lured you to play
    Rather false, Mr. D., to all pledges but one?

How defunct is the show that was chivalry's mimic !
  The breastplate—the feathers—the gallant array !
So fades, so grows dim, and so dies, Mr. Dymoke !
  The day of brass breeches ! as Wordsworth would say !

Perchance in some village remote, with a cot,
  And a cow, and a pig, and a barndoor, and all ;—
You show to the parish that peace is your lot,
  And plenty,—though absent from Westminster Hall !

And of course you turn every accoutrement now
  To its separate use, that your wants may be well-
    met ;—
You toss in your breastplate your pancakes, and grow
  A salad of mustard and cress in your helmet.

And you delve the fresh earth with your falchion, less
    bright
  Since hung up in sloth from its Westminster task ;—
And you bake your own bread in your tin ; and, Sir
    Knight,
  Instead of your brow, put your beer in the casque !

How delightful to sit by your beans and your peas,
  With a goblet of gooseberry gallantly clutch'd,
And chat of the blood that had deluged the Pleas,
  And drench'd the King's Bench,—if the glove had
    been touch'd !

If Sir Columbine Daniel, with knightly pretensions,
  Had snatch'd your " best doe,"—he'd have flooded
    the floor ;—
Nor would even the best of his crafty inventions,
  " Life Preservers," have floated him out of his gore !

Oh, you and your horse ! what a couple was there !
 The man and his *backer*,—to win a great fight !
Though the trumpet was loud,—you'd an undisturb'd
  air !
 And the nag snuff'd the feast and the fray *sans*
  affright !

Yet strange was the course which the good Cato bore
 When he waddled tail-wise with the cup to his stall ;—
For though his departure was at the front door,
 Still he went the back way out of Westminster Hall.

He went,—and 'twould puzzle historians to say,
 When they trust Time's conveyance to carry your
  mail,—
Whether caution or courage inspired him that day,
 For though he retreated, he never turn'd tail.

By my life, he's a wonderful charger !—The best !
 Though not for a Parthian corps !—yet for you !—
Distinguish'd alike at a fray and a feast,
 What a horse for a grand Retrospective Review !

What a creature to keep a hot warrior cool
 When the sun's in the face, and the shade's far
  aloof !—
What a *tailpiece* for Bewick !—or piebald for Poole,
 To bear him in safety from Elliston's hoof !

Well ! hail to Old Cato ! the hero of scenes
 May Astley or age ne'er his comforts abridge ;—
Oh, long may he munch Amphitheatre beans,
 Well "pent up in Utica" over the Bridge !

And to you, Mr. Dymoke, Cribb's rival, I keep
   Wishing all country pleasures, the bravest and best !
And oh ! when you come to the Hummums to sleep,
   May you lie "like a warrior taking his rest !"

ODE TO JOSEPH GRIMALDI, SENIOR.

"This fellow's wise enough to play the fool,
And to do that well craves a kind of wit."
                       Twelfth Night.

JOSEPH ! they say thou'st left the stage,
To toddle down the hill of life,
And taste the flannell'd ease of age,
Apart from pantomimic strife—
"Retired—[for Young would call it so]—
The world shut out"—in Pleasant Row !

And hast thou really wash'd at last
From each white cheek the red half-moon !
And all thy public Clownship cast,
To play the private Pantaloon ?
All youth—all ages yet to be
Shall have a heavy miss of thee !

Thou didst not preach to make us wise—
Thou hadst no finger in our schooling—
Thou didst not "lure us to the skies"—
Thy simple, simple trade was—Fooling !
And yet, Heav'n knows ! we could—we can
Much "better spare a better man !"

Oh, had it pleased the gout to take
The reverend Croly from the stage,
Or Southey, for our quiet's sake,

Or Mr. Fletcher, Cupid's sage,
Or damme! namby pamby Pool,—
Or any other clown or fool!

Go, Dibdin—all that bear the name,
Go Byeway Highway man! go! go!
Go, Skeffy—man of painted fame,
But leave thy partner, painted Joe!
I could bear Kirby on the wane,
Or Signor Paulo with a sprain!

Had Joseph Wilfred Parkins made
His grey hairs scarce in private peace—
Had Waithman sought a rural shade—
Or Cobbett ta'en a turnpike lease—
Or Lisle Bowles gone to *Balaam* Hill—
I think I could be cheerful still!

Had Medwin left off, to his praise,
Dead lion kicking, like—a friend!—
Had long, long Irving gone his ways
To muse on death at *Ponder's End*—
Or Lady Morgan taken leave
Of Letters—still I might not grieve!

But, Joseph—everybody's Jo!—
Is gone—and grieve I will and must!
As Hamlet did for Yorick, so
Will I for thee (though not yet dust),
And talk as he did when he miss'd
The kissing-crust that he had kiss'd!

Ah, where is now thy rolling head!
Thy winking, reeling, *drunken* eyes,

(As old Catullus would have said,)
Thy oven-mouth, that swallow'd pies—
Enormous hunger—monstrous drowth !—
Thy pockets greedy as thy mouth !

Ah, where thy ears, so often cuff'd !—
Thy funny, flapping, filching hands !—
Thy partridge body, always stuff'd
With waifs, and strays, and contrabands !—
Thy foot—like Berkeley's *Foote*—for why ?
'Twas often made to wipe an eye !

Ah, where thy legs—that witty pair !
For " great wits jump "—and so did they !
Lord ! how they leap'd in lamplight air !
Caper'd—and bounced—and strode away !—
That years should tame the legs—alack !
I've seen spring through an Almanack !

But bounds will have their bound—the shocks
Of Time will cramp the nimblest toes ;
And those that frisk'd in silken clocks
May look to limp in fleecy hose—
One only—(Champion of the ring)
Could ever make his Winter,—Spring !

And gout, that owns no odds between
The toe of Czar and toe of Clown,
Will visit—but I did not mean
To moralize, though I am grown
Thus sad,—Thy going seem'd to beat
A muffled drum for Fun's retreat !

And, may be—'tis no time to smother
A sigh, when two prime wags of London

Are gone—thou, Joseph, one,—the other,
A Joe!—"sic transit gloria *Munden!*"
A third departure some insist on,—
Stage-apoplexy threatens Liston!—

Nay, then, let Sleeping Beauty sleep
With ancient "*Dozey*" to the dregs—
Let Mother Goose wear mourning deep,
And put a hatchment o'er her eggs!
Let Farley weep—for Magic's man
Is gone—his Christmas Caliban!

Let Kemble, Forbes, and Willet rain,
As though they walk'd behind thy bier,—
For since thou wilt not play again,
What matters,—if in heav'n or here!
Or in thy grave, or in thy bed!—
There's *Quick** might just as well be dead!

Oh, how will thy departure cloud
The lamplight of the little breast!
The Christmas child will grieve aloud
To miss his broadest friend and best,—
Poor urchin! what avails to him
The cold New Monthly's *Ghost of Grimm?*

For who like thee could ever stride!
Some dozen paces to the mile!—
The motley, medley coach provide—
Or like Joe Frankenstein compile
The *vegetable man* complete!—
A proper *Covent Garden* feat!

* One of the old actors—still a performer (but in private) of Old Rapid.
—*Note to original edition.*

Oh, who like thee could ever drink,
Or eat,—swill—swallow—bolt—and choke!
Nod, weep, and hiccup—sneeze and wink?—
Thy very yawn was quite a joke!
Though Joseph, Junior, acts not ill,
"There's no Fool like the old Fool" still!

Joseph, farewell! dear funny Joe!
We met with mirth,—we part in pain!
For many a long, long year must go
Ere Fun can see thy like again—
For Nature does not keep great stores
Of perfect Clowns—that are not *Boors!*

TO SYLVANUS URBAN, ESQ.,

EDITOR OF THE "GENTLEMAN'S MAGAZINE."

"Dost thou not suspect my years?"
Much Ado about Nothing.

OH! Mr. Urban! never must *thou* lurch
    A sober age made serious drunk by thee;
Hop in thy pleasant way from church to church,
    And nurse thy little bald Biography.

Oh, my Sylvanus! what a heart is thine!
    And what a page attends thee! Long may I
Hang in demure confusion o'er each line
    That asks thy little questions with a sigh!

Old tottering years have nodded to their falls,
    Like pensioners that creep about and die;—
But thou, Old Parr of periodicals,
    Livest in monthly immortality!

How sweet !—as Byron of *his* infant said,—
    "Knowledge of objects" in thine eye to trace;
To see the mild no-meanings of thy head,
    Taking a quiet nap upon thy face !

How dear through thy Obituary to roam,
    And not a name of any name to catch !
To meet thy Criticism walking home
    Averse from rows, and never calling "Watch !"

Rich is thy page in soporific things,—
    Composing compositions,—lulling men,—
Faded old posies of unburied rings,—
    Confessions dozing from an opiate pen :—

Lives of Right Reverends that have never lived,—
    Deaths of good people that have really died,—
Parishioners,—hatch'd,—husbanded,—and wived,—
    Bankrupts and Abbots breaking side by side !

The sacred query,—the remote response,—
    The march of serious mind, extremely slow,—
The graver's cut at some right agèd sconce,
    Famous for nothing many years ago !

B. asks of C. if Milton e'er did write
    "Comus," obscured beneath some Ludlow lid ;—
And C., next month, an answer doth indite,
    Informing B. that Mr. Milton did !

X. sends the portrait of a genuine flea,
    Caught upon Martin Luther years agone ;—
And Mr. Parkes, of Shrewsbury, draws a bee,
    Long dead, that gather'd honey for King John.

There is no end of thee,—there is no end,
    Sylvanus, of thy A, B, C, D-merits!
Thou dost, with alphabets, old walls attend,
    And poke the letters into holes, like ferrets.

Go on, Sylvanus!—Bear a wary eye,
    The churches cannot yet be quite run out!
Some parishes must yet have been pass'd by,—
    There's Bullock-Smithy has a church no doubt!

Go on—and close the eyes of distant ages!
    Nourish the names of the undoubted dead!
So Epicures shall pick thy lobster-pages,
    Heavy and lively, though but seldom *red*.

Go on! and thrive! Demurest of odd fellows?
    Bottling up dulness in an ancient binn!
Still live! still prose!—continue still to tell us
    Old truths! no strangers, though we take them in!

AN ADDRESS TO THE STEAM WASHING
COMPANY.

"ARCHER. How many are there, *Scrub?*
    SCRUB. Five-and-forty, sir."—*Beaux Stratagem.*

' For shame—let the linen alone !"—*Merry Wives of Windsor.*

MR. SCRUB—Mr. Slop—or whoever you be!
The Cock of Steam Laundries,—the head Patentee
Of Associate Cleansers,—Chief founder and prime
Of the firm for the wholesale distilling of grime—
Co-partners and dealers, in linen's propriety—
That make washing public—and wash in society—
O lend me your ear! if that ear can forego
For a moment the music that bubbles below,

From your new Surrey Geysers* all foaming and hot,—
That soft "*simmer's* sang " so endear'd to the Scot—
If your hands may stand still, or your steam without
    danger—
If your suds will not cool, and a mere simple stranger,
Both to you and to washing, may put in a rub,—
O wipe out your Amazon arms from the tub,—
And lend me your ear,—Let me modestly plead
For a race that your labours may soon supersede—
For a race that, now washing no living affords—
Like Grimaldi must leave their aquatic old boards,
Not with pence in their pockets to keep them at ease,
Not with bread in the funds—or investments of cheese,
But to droop like sad willows that lived by a stream,
Which the sun has suck'd up into vapour and steam.
Ah, look at the laundress, before you begrudge
Her hard daily bread to that laudable drudge—
When chanticleer singeth his earliest matins,
She slips her amphibious feet in her pattens,
And beginneth her toil while the morn is still grey,
As if she was washing the night into day—
Not with sleeker or rosier fingers Aurora
Beginneth to scatter the dewdrops before her;
· Not Venus that rose from the billow so early,
Look'd down on the foam with a forehead more
    pearly†
Her head is involved in an aërial mist,
And a bright-beaded bracelet encircles her wrist;
Her visage glows warm with the ardour of duty;
She's Industry's moral—she's all moral beauty!
Growing brighter and brighter at every rub—

---

   * Geysers :—the boiling springs in Iceland.
   † Query, *purly ?*—Printer's Devil.

Would any man ruin her?—No, Mr. Scrub!
No man that is manly would work her mishap—
No man that is manly would covet her cap—
Nor her apron—her hose—nor her gown made of
    stuff—
Nor her gin—nor her tea—nor her wet pinch of snuff!
Alas! so *she* thought—but that slippery hope
Has betray'd her—as though she had trod on her soap!
And she,—whose support,—like the fishes that fly,
Was to have her fins wet, must now drop from her
    sky—
She whose living it was, and a part of her fare,
To be damp'd once a day, like the great white sea bear,
With her hands like a sponge, and her head like a
    mop—
Quite a living absorbent that revell'd in slop—
She that paddled in water, must walk upon sand,
And sigh for her deeps like a turtle on land!

Lo, then, the poor laundress, all wretched she stands,
Instead of a counterpane, wringing her hands!
All haggard and pinch'd, going down in life's vale,
With no faggot for burning, like Allan-a-Dale!
No smoke from her flue—and no steam from her pane,
Where once she watch'd heaven, fearing God and the
    rain—
Or gazed o'er her bleach-field so fairly engross'd,
Till the lines wander'd idle from pillar to post!
Ah, where are the playful young pinners—ah, where
The harlequin quilts that cut capers in air—
The brisk waltzing stockings—the white and the black,
That danced on the tight-rope, or swung on the slack—
The light sylph-like garments, so tenderly pinn'd,

L

That blew into shape, and embodied the wind!
There was white on the grass—there was white on the
    spray—
Her garden—it look'd like a garden of May!
But now all is dark—not a shirt's on a shrub—
You've ruin'd her prospects in life, Mr. Scrub!
You've ruin'd her custom—now families drop her—
From her silver reduced—nay, reduced from her
    copper!
The last of her washing is done at her eye,
One poor little kerchief that never gets dry!
From mere lack of linen she can't lay a cloth,
And boils neither barley nor alkaline broth,—
But her children come round her as victuals grow
    scant,
And recal, with foul faces, the source of their want—
When she thinks of their poor little mouths to be fed,
And then thinks of her trade that is utterly dead,
And even its pearlashes laid in the grave—
Whilst her tub is a-dry-rotting, stave after stave,
And the greatest of Coopers, ev'n he that they dub
Sir Astley, can't bind up her heart or her tub,—
Need you wonder she curses your bones, Mr. Scrub!
Need you wonder, when steam has deprived her of
    bread,
If she prays that the evil may visit *your* head—
Nay, scald all the heads of your Washing Committee,—
If she wishes you all the soot blacks of the City—
In short, not to mention all plagues without number,
If she wishes you all in the *Wash* at the Humber!

    Ah, perhaps, in some moment of drowth and despair,
When her linen got scarce, and her washing grew rare—

When the sum of her suds might be summ'd in a bowl,
And the rusty cold iron quite enter'd her soul—
When, perhaps, the last glance of her wandering eye
Had caught " the Cock Laundresses' Coach" going by,
Or her lines that hung idle, to waste the fine weather,
And she thought of her wrongs and her rights both
    together,
In a lather of passion that froth'd as it rose
Too angry for grammar, too lofty for prose,
On her sheet—if a sheet were still left her—to write,
Some remonstrance like this then, perchance, saw the
    light—

LETTER OF REMONSTRANCE

FROM BRIDGET JONES TO THE NOBLEMEN AND GENTLEMEN FORMING THE WASHING COMMITTEE.

It's a shame, so it is—men can't Let alone
Jobs as is Woman's right to do—and go about there
    Own—
Theirs Reforms enuff Alreddy without your new schools
For washing to sit Up,—and push the Old Tubs from
    their stools !
But your just like the Raddicals,—for upsetting of
    the Sudds
When the world wagg'd well enuff—and Wommen
    wash'd your old dirty duds,
I'm Certain sure Enuff your Ann Sisters had no steam
    Indins, that's Flat,—
But I Warrant your Four Fathers went as Tidy and
    gentlemanny for all that—
I suppose your the Family as lived in the Great Kittle
I see on Clapham Commun, some times a very con-
    siderable period back when I were little,

And they Said it went with Steem,—But that was a
joke!

For I never see none come of. it,—that's out of it—
but only sum Smoak—

And for All your Power of Horses about your Indians
you never had but Two

In my time to draw you About to Fairs—and hang
you, you know that's true!

And for All your fine Perspectuses,—howsomever you
bewhich 'em,

Theirs as Pretty ones off Primerows Hill, as ever a
one at Mitchum,

Thof I cant sea What Prospectives and washing has
with one another to Do—

It ant as if a Bird'seye Hankicher can take a Birds-
high view!

But Thats your look-out—I've not much to do with
that—But pleas God to hold up fine,

Id show you caps and pinners and small things as
lillywhit as Ever crosst the Line

Without going any Father off then Little Parodies
Place,

And Thats more than you Can—and Ill say it behind
your face—

But when Folks talks of washing, it ant for you too
Speak,—

As kept Dockter Pattyson out of his Shirt for a Weak!

Thinks I, when I heard it—Well thear's a Pretty
go!

That comes o' not marking of things or washing out
the marks, and Huddling 'em up so!

Till Their frends comes and owns them, like drownded
corpeses in a Vault,

But may Hap you havint Larn'd to spel—and That
  ant your Fault,
Only you ought to leafe the Linnins to them as has
  Larn'd—
For if it warnt for Washing,—and whare Bills is con-
  carnd,
What's the Yuse, of all the world, for a Wommans
  Headication,
And Their Being maid Schollards of Sundays—fit for
  any Cityation?

  Well, what I says is this—when every Kittle has its
  spout,
Theirs no nead for Companys to puff steam about!
To be sure its very Well, when Their ant enuff Wind
For blowing up Boats with,—but not to hurt human
  kind,
Like that Pearkins with his Blunderbush, that's loaded
  with hot water,
Thof a xSherrif might know Better, than make things
  for slaughtter,
As if War warnt Cruel enuff—wherever it befalls,
Without shooting poor sogers, with sich scalding hot
  washing* balls,—
But thats not so Bad as a Sett of Bear Faced Scrubbs
As joins their Sopes together, and sits up Steam
  rubbing Clubs,
For washing Dirt Cheap,— and eating other Peple's
  grubs!
Which is all verry Fine for you and your Patent Tea,
But I wonders How Poor Wommen is to get Their
  Beau-He!

---

* This word is omitted in the later edition.

They must drink Hunt wash (the only wash God nose
　　there will be !)
And their Little drop of Somethings as they takes for
　　their Goods,
When you and your Steam has ruined (G—d forgive
　　mee) their lively Hoods,
Poor Women as was born to Washing in their youth !
And now must go and Larn other Buisnesses Four
　　Sooth !
But if so be They leave their Lines what are they to
　　go at—
They won't do for Angell's—nor any Trade like That,-
Nor we cant Sow Babby Work,—for that's all Be
　　spoke,—
For the Queakers in Bridle ! and a vast of the confind
　　Folk
Do their own of Themselves—even the bettermost of
　　em—aye, and evn them of middling degrees—
Why—Lauk help you—Babby Linen ant Bread and
　　Cheese !
Nor we can't go a hammering the roads into Dust,
But we must all go and be Bankers, Like Mr. Marshes
　　and Mr. Chamber, and that's what we must !
God nose you oght to have more Concern for our Sects,
When you nose you have suck'd us and hanged round
　　our Mutherly necks,
And remembers what you Owes to Wommen Besides
　　washing—
You ant, blame you, like Men to go a slushing and
　　sloshing
In mob caps, and pattins, adoing of Females Labers
And prettily jear'd At, you great Horse God-meril
　　things, ant you now by your next door nayhbours—

Lawk, I thinks I see you with your Sleaves tuckt up
No more like Washing than is drownding of a Pupp—
And for all Your Fine Water Works going round and
    round   ʹ
They'll scruntch your Bones some day—I'll be bound
And no more nor be a gudgement,—for it cant come
    to good
To sit up agin Providince, which your a doing,—nor
    not fit It should,
For man warnt maid for Wommens starvation,
Nor to do away Laundrisses as is Links of Creation—
And cant be dun without in any Country But a naked
    Hot-tinpot Nation.
Ah, I wish our Minister would take one of your Tubbs
And preach a Sermon in it, and give you some good
    rubs—
ʹ But I warrants you reads (for you cant spel we nose)
    nyther Bybills or Good Tracks,
Or youd no better than Taking the Close off one's
    Backs—
And let your neighbours Oxin and Asses alone,—
And every Thing thats hern,—and give every one
    their Hone!

    Well, its God for us All, and every Washer Wommen
    for herself,
And so you might, without shoving any on us off the
    shelf,
But if you warnt Noddis youd Let wommen a-be
And pull off your Pattins,—and leave the washing to we
That nose what's what—Or mark what I say,
Youl make a fine Kittle of fish of Your Close some
    Day—

When the Aulder men wants Their Bibs and their
    ant nun at all,
And Crismass cum—and never a Cloth to lay in Gild
    Hall,
Or send a damp shirt to his Woship the Mare
Till hes rumatiz Poor Man, and cant set uprite to do
    good in his Harm Charc—
Besides Miss-Matching Larned Ladys Hose, as is sent
    for you not to wash (for you dont wash) but to
    stew
And make Peples Stockins yeller as oght to be Blew,
With a vast more like That,—and all along of Steem
Which warnt meand by Nater for any sich skeam—
But thats your Losses and youl have to make It Good,
And I cant say I'm sorry, afore God, if you shoud,
For men mought Get their Bread a great many ways
Without taking ourn,—aye, and Moor to your Prays,*
If You Was even to Turn Dust Men a dry sifting
    Dirt,
But you oughtint to Hurt Them as never Did You no
    Hurt!

Yourn with Anymocity,
Bridget Jones.

* The following additional lines were inserted in the third edition :—

"You might go and skim the creme off Mr. Mack-Adam's milky ways—
    that's what you might,
Or bete Carpets—or get into Parleamint,—or drive crabrolays from morn-
    ing to night,
Or, if you must be of your sects, be Watchemen, and slepe upon a poste !
(Which is an od way of sleping, I must say,—and a very hard pillow at
    most,)
Or you might be any trade, as we are not on that I'm awares,
Or be Watermen now, (not Water wommen) and roe people up and down
    Hungerford stares."

ODE TO CAPTAIN PARRY.

"By the North Pole I do challenge thee!"
Love's Labour's Lost.

PARRY, my man! has thy brave leg
Yet struck its foot against the peg
   On which the world is spun?
Or hast thou found No Thoroughfare
Writ by the hand of Nature there
   Where man has never run?

Hast thou yet traced the Great Unknown
Of channels in the Frozen Zone
   Or held at Icy Bay,
Hast thou still miss'd the proper track
For homeward Indian men that lack
   A bracing by the way?

Still hast thou wasted toil and trouble
On nothing but the North-Sea Bubble
   Of geographic scholar?
Or found new ways for ships to shape,
Instead of winding round the Cape,
   A short cut through the collar!

Hast found the ways that sighs were sent to *
The Pole—though God knows whom they went to!
   That track reveal'd to Pope—
Or if the Arctic waters sally,
Or terminate in some blind alley,
   A chilly path to grope?

Alas! though Ross, in love with snows,
Has painted them *couleur de rose,*

* "And waft a sigh from Indus to the Pole."—*Eloisa to Abelard.*

It is a dismal doom,
As Claudio saith, to Winter thrice,
" In regions of thick-ribbèd ice "—
All bright,—and yet all gloom !

'Tis well for Gheber souls that sit
Before the fire and worship it
    With pecks of Wallsend coals,
With feet upon the fender's front,
Roasting their corns—like Mr. Hunt—
    To speculate on poles.

'Tis easy for our Naval Board—
'Tis easy for our Civic Lord
    Of London and of ease,
That lies in ninety feet of down,
With fur on his nocturnal gown,
    To talk of Frozen Seas !

'Tis fine for Monsieur Ude to sit,
And prate about the mundane spit,
    And babble of *Cook's* track—
He'd roast the leather off his toes,
Ere he would trudge through polar snows,
    To plant a British *Jack !*

Oh, not the proud licentious great,
That travel on a carpet skate,
    Can value oils like thine !
What 'tis to take a Hecla range,
Through ice unknown to Mrs. Grange,
    And alpine lumps of brine !

But we, that mount the Hill o' Rhyme,
Can tell how hard it is to climb

The lofty slippery steep.
Ah ! there are more Snow Hills than that
Which doth black Newgate, like a hat,
   Upon its forehead, keep.

Perchance thou'rt now—while I am writing—
Feeling a bear's wet grinder biting
   About thy frozen spine !
Or thou thyself art eating whale,
Oily, and underdone, and stale,
   That, haply, cross'd thy line !

But I'll not dream such dreams of ill—
Rather will I believe thee still
   Safe cellar'd in the snow,—
Reciting many a gallant story
Of British kings and British glory,
   To crony Esquimaux—

Cheering that dismal game where Night
Makes one slow move from black to white
   Through all the tedious year,—
Or smitten by some fond frost fair,
That comb'd out crystals from her hair,
   Wooing a seal-skin dear !

So much a long communion tends,
As Byron says, to make us friends
   With what we daily view—
God knows the daintiest taste may come
To love a nose that's like a plum
   In marble, cold and blue !

To dote on hair, an oily fleece !
As though it hung from Helen o' Greece—

They say that love prevails
Ev'n in the veriest polar land—
And surely she may steal thy hand
    That used to steal thy nails !

But ah, ere thou art fixt to marry,
And take a polar Mrs. Parry,
    Think of a six months' gloom—
Think of the wintry waste, and hers,
Each furnish'd with a dozen *furs*,
    Think of thine icy *dome !*

Think of the children born to *blubber !*
Ah me ! hast thou an Indian rubber
    Inside !—to hold a meal
For months,—about a stone and half
Of whale, and part of a sea calf—
    A fillet of salt veal !—

Some walrus ham—no trifle but
A decent steak—a solid cut
    Of seal—no wafer slice !
A reindeer's tongue and drink beside !
Gallons of sperm—not rectified !
    And pails of water-ice !

Oh, canst thou fast and then feast thus ?
Still come away, and teach to us
    Those blessed alternations—
To-day, to run our dinners fine,
To feed on air and then to dine
    With Civic Corporations—

To save th' Old Bailey daily shilling,
And then to take a half-year's filling

In P. N.'s pious Row—
When ask'd to hock and haunch o' ven'son,
Through something we have worn our pens on
   For Longman and his Co.

O come and tell us what the Pole is—
Whether it singular and sole is,—
   Or straight, or crooked bent,—
If very thick or very thin,—
Made of what wood—and if akin
   To those there be in Kent?

There's Combe, there's Spurzheim, and there's Gall,
Have talk'd of poles—yet, after all,
   What has the public learn'd?
And Hunt's account must still defer,—
He sought the *poll* at Westminster—
   And is not yet *return'd!*

Alvanly asks if whist, dear soul,
Is play'd in snow towns near the Pole,
   And how the fur-man deals?
And Eldon doubts if it be true,
That icy Chancellors really do
   Exist upon the *seals?*

Barrow, by well-fed office-grates,
Talks of his own bechristen'd Straits,
   And longs that he were there;
And Croker, in his cabriolet,
Sighs o'er his brown horse, at his Bay,
   And pants to cross the *mer!*

O come away, and set us right,
And, haply, throw a northern light

On questions such as these :—
Whether, when this drown'd world was lost,
The surflux waves were lock'd in frost,
    And turn'd to Icy Seas?

Is Ursa Major white or black?
Or do the Polar tribes attack
    Their neighbours—and what for?
Whether they ever play at cuffs,
And then, if they take off their muffs
    In pugilistic war?

Tell us, is *Winter* champion there,
As in our milder fighting air?
    Say, what are *Chilly* loans?
What cures they have for rheums beside,
And if their hearts get ossified
    From eating bread of bones?

Whether they are such dwarfs—the quicker
To circulate the vital liquor,—*
    And then, from head to heel—
How short the Methodists must choose
Their dumpy envoys not to lose
    Their toes in spite of zeal?

Whether 'twill soften or sublime it
To preach of Hell in such a climate—
    Whether may Wesley hope
To win their souls—or that old function
Of seals—with the extreme of unction—
    Bespeaks them for the Pope?

---

* Buffon.

Whether the lamps will e'er be "learn'd"
Where six months' "midnight oil" is burn'd,
   Or letters must defer
With people that have never conn'd
An A. B. C, but live beyond
   The *Sound* of *Lancaster !*

O come away at any rate—
Well hast thou earn'd a downier state,
   With all thȳ hardy peers—
Good lack, thou must be glad to smell dock,
And rub thy feet with opodeldoc,
   After such frosty years.

Mayhap, some gentle dame at last,
Smit by the perils thou hast pass'd,
   However coy before,
Shall bid thee now set up thy rest
In that *Brest Harbour*, woman's breast,
   And tempt the Fates no more !

ODE TO R. W. ELLISTON, ESQ.,

• THE GREAT LESSEE !

"ROVER. Do you know, you villain, that I am this moment the greatest
man living ?"—*Wild Oats.*

OH ! Great Lessee ! Great Manager ! Great Man !
Oh, Lord High Elliston ! Immortal Pan
Of all the pipes that play in Drury Lane !
Macready's master ! Westminster's high *Dane*
(As Galway Martin, in the House's walls,
Hamlet and Doctor Ireland justly calls)
Friend to the sweet and ever-smiling Spring !
Magician of the lamp and prompter's ring !

Drury's Aladdin! Whipper-in of actors!
Kicker of rebel preface-malefactors!
Glass-blowers' corrector! King of the cheque-taker!
At once Great Leamington and Winston-Maker!
Dramatic Bolter of plain Bunns and cakes!
In silken *hose* the most reform'd of *Rakes!*
Oh, Lord High Elliston! lend me an ear!
(Poole is away, and Williams shall keep clear)
While I, in little slips of prose, not verse,
Thy splendid course, as pattern-work, rehearse!

Bright was thy youth—thy manhood brighter still!—
The greatest Romeo upon Holborn Hill—
Lightest comedian of the pleasant day,
When Jordan threw a sunshine o'er a play!*
But these, though happy, were but subject times,
And no man cares for bottom-steps, that climbs—
Far from my wish it is to stifle down
The hours that saw thee snatch the Surrey crown!
Though now thy hand a mightier sceptre wields,
Fair was thy reign in sweet St. George's Fields.
Dibdin was *Premier*—and a Golden *Age*
For a short time enrich'd the subject stage.
Thou hadst, than other Kings, more peace-and-plenty
Ours but one Bench could boast, but thou hadst twenty;
But the times changed—and Booth-acting no more
Drew Rulers' shillings to the gallery door.
Thou didst, with bag and baggage, wander thence,
Repentant, like thy neighbour Magdalens!

---

* Additional lines in third edition :—

" When fair Thalia held a merry reign,
  And Wit was at her Court in Drury Lane,
  Before the day when Authors wrote, of course,
  The Entertainment *not* for Man but Horse."

Next, the Olympic Games were tried, each feat
Practised the most bewitching in Wych Street.
Charles had his royal ribaldry restored,
And in a downright neighbourhood drank and whored;
Rochester there in dirty ways again
Revell'd—and lived once more in Drury Lane:
But thou, R. W.! kept thy moral ways,
Pit-lecturing 'twixt the farces and the plays,
A lamplight Irving to the butcher-boys
That soil'd the benches and that made a noise :—*
" You,—in the back !—can scarcely hear a line !
Down from those benches—butchers—they are MINE !"

Lastly—and thou wert built for it by nature !—
Crown'd was thy head in Drury Lane *Theatre* !
Gentle George Robins saw that it was good,
And renters cluck'd around thee in a brood.
King thou wert made of Drury and of Kean !
Of many a lady and of many a Quean !
With Poole and Larpent was thy reign begun—
But now thou turnest from the Dead and Dun,
Hook's in thine eye, to write thy plays, no doubt,
And Colman lives to cut the damnlets out !

Oh, worthy of the house ! the King's commission !
Isn't thy condition "a most bless'd condition ?"
Thou reignest over Winston, Kean, and all
The very lofty and the very small—

* Additional lines in third edition :—
    " Rebuking—half a Robert, half a Charles,—
    The well-bill'd man that call'd for promised Carles.
    ' Sir—have you yet to know !   Hush—hear me out !
    A man—pray silence—may be down with gout,
    Or want—or, sir—aw !—listen !—may be fated,
    Being in debt, to be incarcerated !' "

M

Showest the plumbless Bunn the way to kick—
Keepest a Williams for thy veriest stick—
Seest a Vestris in her sweetest moments,
Without the danger of newspaper comments—
Tellest Macready, as none dared before,
Thine open mind from the half-open door !—
(Alas ! I fear he has left Melpomene's crown,
To be a Boniface in Buxton town !)—
Thou holdst the watch, as half-price people know,
And callest to them, to a moment,—" Go ?"
Teachest the sapient Sapio how to sing—
Hangest a cat most oddly by the wing—*
Hast known the length of a Cubitt-foot—and kiss'd
The pearly whiteness of a Stephen's wrist—
Kissing and pitying—tender and humane !
" By heaven she loves me ! Oh, it is too plain !"
A sigh like this thy trembling passion slips,
Dimpling the warm Madeira at thy lips !

Go on, Lessee ! Go on, and prosper well !
Fear not, though forty glass-blowers should rebel—
Show them how thou hast long befriended them,
And teach Dubois *their* treason to condemn !
Go on ! addressing pits in prose and worse !
Be long, be slow, be anything but terse—
Kiss to the gallery the hand that's gloved—
Make Bunn the Great, and Winston the Beloved,†

* Additional lines in third edition :—

> "(To prove, no doubt, the endless free-list ended,
> And all, except the public press, suspended.)"

† Additional lines in third edition :—

> Ask the two-shilling gods for leave to dun
> With words the cheaper deities in the *One!*
> Kick Mr. Poole unseen from scene to scene,
> Cane Williams still, and stick to Mr. Kean,
> Warn from the benches all the rabble rout ;
> Say 'those are *mine*—in parliament or out !'—

Go on—and but in this reverse the thing,
Walk backward with wax lights before the King—
Go on! Spring ever in thine eye! Go on!
Hope's favourite child! ethereal Elliston!

ADDRESS TO MARIA DARLINGTON

ON HER RETURN TO THE STAGE.

"It was Maria!—
And better fate did Maria deserve than to have her banns forbid—
She had, since that, she told me, strayed as far as Rome, and walked
round St. Peter's once—and returned back—."
                    See the whole story in Sterne and the Newspapers.

THOU art come back again to the stage
    Quite as blooming as when thou didst leave it;
And 'tis well for this fortunate age
    That thou didst not, by going off, grieve it!
It is pleasant to see thee again—
    Right pleasant to see thee, by Herclé,
Unmolested by pea-colour'd Hayne!
    And free from that thou-and-thee Berkeley!

Thy sweet foot, my Foote, is as light
    (Not *my* Foote—I speak by correction
As the snow on some mountain at night,
    Or the snow that has long on thy neck shone.
The Pit is in raptures to free thee,
    The Boxes impatient to greet thee,
The Galleries quite clam'rous to see thee,
    And thy scenic relations to meet thee!

Swing cats, for in this house there's surely space,
Oh, Beasley for such pastime plann'd the place!
Do anything!—Thy frame, thy fortune, nourish!
Laugh and grow fat! be eloquent and flourish!"

Ah, where was thy sacred retreat?
    Maria! ah, where hast thou been,
With thy two little wandering Feet,
    Far away from all peace and pea-green!
'Far away from Fitzhardinge the bold,
    Far away from himself and his lot!
I envy the place thou hast stroll'd,
    If a stroller thou art—which thou'rt not!

Sterne met thee, poor wandering thing,
    Methinks, at the close of the day—
When thy Billy had just slipp'd his string,
    And thy little dog quite gone astray—
He bade thee to sorrow no more—
    He wish'd thee to lull thy distress
In his bosom—he couldn't do more,
    And a Christian could hardly do less!

Ah, me! for thy small plaintive pipe,
    I fear we must look at thine eye—
That eye—forced so often to wipe
    That the handkerchief never got dry!*
Oh sure 'tis a barbarous deed
    To give pain to the feminine mind—
But the wooer that left thee to bleed
    Was a creature more killing than kind!

The man that could tread on a worm
    Is a brute—and inhuman to boot;
But he merits a much harsher term
    That can wantonly tread on a Foote!

* In the third edition:—
      "I would it were my luck to wipe
      That hazel orb thoroughly dry!"

Soft mercy and gentleness blend
　　To make up a Quaker—but he
That spurn'd thee could scarce be a *Friend*,
　　Though he dealt in that Thou-ing of thee!

They that loved thee, Maria, have flown!
　　The friends of the midsummer hour!
But those friends now in anguish atone,
　　And mourn o'er thy desolate bow'r.
Friend Hayne, the Green man, is quite out,
　　Yea, utterly out of his bias;
And the faithful Fitzhardinge, no doubt,
　　Is counting his Ave Marias!

Ah, where wast thou driven away,
　　To feast on thy desolate woe?
We have witness'd thy weeping in play,
　　But none saw the earnest tears flow—
Perchance thou wert truly forlorn,—
　　Though none but the fairies could mark
Where they hung upon some Berkeley thorn,
　　Or the thistles in Burderop Park!

Ah, perhaps, when old age's white snow
　　Has silver'd the crown of Hayne's nob—
For even the greenest will grow
　　As hoary as "White-headed Bob—"
He'll wish, in the days of his prime,
　　He had been rather kinder to one
He hath left to the malice of Time—
　　A woman—so weak and undone!

ODE TO W. KITCHENER, M.D

AUTHOR OF "THE COOK'S ORACLE," "OBSERVATIONS ON VOCAL MUSIC," "THE ART OF INVIGORATING AND PROLONGING LIFE," "PRACTICAL OBSERVATIONS ON TELESCOPES, OPERA-GLASSES, AND SPECTACLES," "THE HOUSEKEEPER'S LEDGER," AND "THE PLEASURE OF MAKING A WILL."

"I rule the roast, as Milton says!"—*Caleb Quotem.*

HAIL! multifarious man!
Thou Wondrous, Admirable Kitchen Crichton!
Born to enlighten
The laws of Optics, Peptics, Music, Cooking—
Master of the Piano—and the Pan—
As busy with the kitchen as the skies!
Now looking
At some rich stew through Galileo's eyes,—
Or boiling eggs—timed to a metronome—
As much at home
In spectacles as in mere isinglass—
In the art of frying brown—as a digression
On music and poetical expression,—
Whereas, how few, of all our cooks, alas!
Could tell Calliope from "Calipee!"
How few there be
Could cleave the lowest for the highest stories,
(Observatories,)
And turn, like thee, Diana's calculator,
However *cook's* synonymous with *Kater**!
Alas! still let me say,
How few could lay
The carving knife beside the tuning fork,
Like the proverbial *Jack* ready for any work!

* Captain Kater, the moon's surveyor.

Oh, to behold thy features in thy book !
Thy proper head and shoulders in a plate,
How it would look !
With one raised eye watching the dial's date,
And one upon the roast, gently cast down—
Thy chops—done nicely brown—
The garnish'd brow—with "a few leaves of bay"—
The hair—"done Wiggy's way !"
And still one studious finger near thy brains,
As if thou wert just come
From editing of some
New soup—or hashing Dibdin's cold remains !
Or, Orpheus-like,—fresh from thy dying strains
Of music,—Epping luxuries of sound,
As Milton says, "in many a bout
Of linkèd sweetness long drawn out,"
While all thy tame stuff'd leopards listen'd round !

Oh, rather thy whole proper length reveal,
Standing like Fortune,—on the jack—thy wheel.
(Thou art, like Fortune, full of chops and changes,
Thou hast a fillet too before thine eye !)
Scanning our kitchen, and our vocal ranges,
As though it were the same to sing or fry—
Nay, so it is—hear how Miss Paton's throat
Makes "fritters" of a note !*
And is not reading near akin to feeding,
Or why should Oxford Sausages be fit
Receptacles for wit ?

---

* Additional lines in third edition :—

"And how Tom Cook (Fryer and Singer born
By name and nature) oh ! how night and morn
He for the nicest public taste doth dish up
The good things from that Pan of music—Bishop !"

Or why should Cambridge put its little, smart,
    Minced brains into a Tart?
Nay, then, thou wert but wise to frame receipts,
    Book-treats,
Equally to instruct the Cook and cram her—
    Receipts to be devour'd, as well as read,
      The Culinary Art in gingerbread—
    The Kitchen's *Eaten* Grammar!

Oh, very pleasant is thy motley page—
    Aye, very pleasant in its chatty vein—
So—in a kitchen—would have talk'd Montaigne,
That merry Gascon—humourist, and sage!
Let slender minds with single themes engage,
    Like Mr. Bowles with his eternal Pope,*—
Or Lovelass upon Wills,—Thou goest on
Plaiting ten topics, like Tate Wilkinson!
    Thy brain is like a rich Kaleidoscope,
Stuff'd with a brilliant medley of odd bits,
    And ever shifting on from change to change,
Saucepans—old Songs—Pills—Spectacles—and Spits!
    Thy range is wider than a Rumford range!
Thy grasp a miracle!—till I recall
'Th' indubitable cause of thy variety—
Thou art, of course, th' Epitome of all
That spying—frying—singing—mix'd Society
Of Scientific Friends, who used to meet
Welsh Rabbits—and thyself—in Warren Street!

Oh, hast thou still those Conversazioni,
Where learnèd visitors discoursed—and fed?

---

* Additional lines in third edition :—
        "Or Haydon on perpetual Haydon,—or
        Hume on—'Twice three make four.'"

There came Belzoni,
Fresh from the ashes of Egyptian dead—
    And gentle Poki—and that Royal Pair,
    Of whom thou didst declare—
" Thanks to the greatest *Cooke* we ever read—
They were—what *Sandwiches* should be—half *bred !*"
There famed M'Adam from his manual toil
Relax'd—and freely own'd he took thy hints
    On " making *Broth* with *Flints* "—
There Parry came, and show'd thee polar oil
For melted butter—Combe with his medullary
    Notions about the *Skullery,*
And Mr. Poole, too partial to a broil—
There witty Rogers came, that punning elf!
    Who used to swear thy book
    Would really look
A *Delphic* " Oracle," if laid on *Delf*—
There, once a month, came Campbell and discuss'd
His own—and thy own—" *Magazine* of *Taste* "—
    There Wilberforce the Just
Came, in his old black suit, till once he traced
    Thy sly advice to *Poachers* of Black Folks,—
    That " do not break their *yolks,*"—
Which huff'd him home, in grave disgust and haste !

There came John Clare, the poet, nor forbore
Thy *Patties*—thou wert hand-and-glove with Moore,
Who call'd thee " *Kitchen Addison* "—for why?
Thou givest rules for Health and Peptic Pills,
Forms for made dishes, and receipts for Wills,
" *Teaching us how to live and how to die !*"
There came thy Cousin-Cook, good Mrs. Fry—
There Trench, the Thames Projector, first brought on
    His sine *Quay* non,—

There Martin would drop in on Monday eves,
Or Fridays, from the pens, and raise his breath
         'Gainst cattle days and death,—
Answer'd by Mellish, feeder of fat beeves,
   Who swore that Frenchmen never could be eager
         For fighting on soup meagre—
" And yet (as thou wouldst add) the French have seen
   A Marshal *Tureen !*"

Great was thy Evening Cluster !—often graced
With Dollond—Burgess—and Sir Humphry Davy !
'Twas there M'Dermot first inclined to Taste,—
There Colburn learn'd the art of making paste
For puffs—and Accum analysed a gravy.
Colman—the Cutter of Coleman Street, 'tis said
Came there,—and Parkins with his Ex-wise-head,
(His claim to letters)—Kater, too, the Moon's
Crony,—and Graham, lofty on balloons,—
There Croly stalk'd with holy humour heated,
(Who wrote a light-horse play, which Yates com
         pleted)—
   And Lady Morgan, that grinding organ,
And Brasbridge telling anecdotes of spoons,—
Madame Valbrèque thrice honour'd thee, and came
With great Rossini, his own bow and fiddle,—*
And even Irving spared a night from fame,
And talk'd—till thou didst stop him in the middle,
         To serve round *Tewah-diddle !*†

Then all the guests rose up, and sighed good-bye !
So let them :—thou thyself art still a *Host !*

* Additional lines in third edition :—
         " The Dibdins,—Tom, Charles, Frognall, came with tuns
         Of poor old books, old puns !"
† The Doctor's composition for a *nightcap.*

Dibdin—Cornaro—Newton—Mrs Fry !
Mrs. Glasse, Mr. Spec !—Lovelass and Weber, ·   ·
Mathews in Quot'em — Moore's fire-worshipping
    Gheber—
Thrice-worthy Worthy ! seem by thee engross'd !
Howbeit the Peptic Cook still rules the roast,
Potent to hush all ventriloquial snarling,—
And ease the bosom pangs of indigestion !
        Thou art, sans question,
The Corporation's love—its Doctor *Darling!*
Look at the Civic Palate—nay, the Bed
    Which set dear Mrs. Opie on supplying
      " Illustrations of *Lying !*"
Ninety square feet of down from heel to head
      It measured, and I dread
Was haunted by a terrible night *Mare,*
A monstrous burthen on the corporation !—
Look at the Bill of Fare for one day's share,
Sea-turtles by the score—oxen by droves.
Geese, turkeys, by the flock—fishes and loaves
    Countless, as when the Lilliputian nation
Was making up the huge man-mountain's ration !

Oh ! worthy Doctor ! surely thou hast driven
The squatting Demon from great Garratt's breast—
      (His honour seems to rest !—)
And what is thy reward ?—Hath London given
Thee public thanks for thy important service ?
      Alas ! not even
The tokens it bestow'd on Howe and Jervis !—
Yet could I speak as Orators should·speak
Before the Worshipful the Common Council
(Utter my bold bad grammar and pronounce ill,)

Thou shouldst not miss thy Freedom for a week,
Richly engross'd on vellum :—Reason urges
That he who rules our cookery—that he
Who edits soups and gravies, ought to be
A *Citizen*, where sauce can make a *Burgess !*

AN ADDRESS TO THE VERY REVEREND
JOHN IRELAND, D.D.,

CHARLES FYNES CLINTON, LL.D.	WM. HARRY ED. BENTINCK, M.A,
THOMAS CAUSTON, D.D.	JAMES WEBBER, B.D.
HOWEL HOLLAND EDWARDS, M.A.	WILLIAM SHORT, D.D.
JOSEPH ALLEN, M.A.	JAMES TOURNAY, D.D.
LORD HENRY FITZROY, M.A.	ANDREW BELL, D.D.
THE BISHOP OF EXETER.	GEORGE HOLCOMBE, D.D.

THE DEAN AND CHAPTER OF WESTMINSTER.

" Sure the Guardians of the Temple can never think they get enough."
Citizen of the World.

OH, very reverend Dean and Chapter,
  Exhibitors of giant men,
Hail to each surplice-back'd adapter
  Of England's dead, in her stone den !
Ye teach us properly to prize
  Two-shilling Grays, and Gays, and Handels,
And, to throw light upon our eyes,
  Deal in Wax Queens like old wax candles.

Oh, reverend showmen, rank and file,
  Call in your shillings, two and two ;
March with them up the middle aisle,
  And cloister them from public view.
Yours surely are the dusty dead,
  Gladly ye look from bust to bust,
And set a price on each great head,
  And make it come down with the dust.

Oh, as I see you walk along
  In ample sleeves and ample back,
A pursy and well-order'd throng,
  Thoroughly fed, thoroughly black !
In vain I strive me to be dumb,—
  You keep each bard like fatted kid,
Grind bones for bread like Fee-faw-fum !
  And drink from skulls as Byron did !

The profitable Abbey is
  A sacred 'Change for stony stock,
Not that a speculation 'tis—
  The profit's founded on a rock.
Death and the Doctors in each nave
  Bony investments have inurn'd,
And hard 'twould be to find a grave
  From which "no money is return'd !"

Here many a pensive pilgrim, brought
  By reverence for those learnèd bones,
Shall often come and walk your short
  Two-shilling fare upon the stones.—*
Ye have that talisman of Wealth
  Which puddling chemists sought of old
Till ruin'd out of hope and health—
  The Tomb's the stone that turns to gold !

Oh, licensed cannibals, ye eat
  Your dinners from your own dead race, ·
Think Gray, preserved—a " funeral meat,"
  And Dryden, devil'd—after grace,

---

* " Since this poem was written, Doctor Ireland and those in authority under him have reduced the fares. It is gratifying to the English people to know that while butcher's meat is rising tombs are falling."—*Note in third Edition.*

A relish ;—and you take your meal
   From Rare Ben Jonson underdone,
Or, whet your holy knives on Steele,
   To cut away at Addison !

Oh say, of all this famous age,
   Whose learnëd bones your hopes expect,
Oh have ye number'd Rydal's sage,
   Or Moore among your Ghosts elect ?
Lord Byron was not doom'd to make
   You richer by his final sleep—
Why don't ye warn the Great to take
   Their ashes to no other heap !

Southey's reversion have ye got ?
   With Coleridge, for his body, made
A bargain ?—has Sir Walter Scott,
   Like Peter Schlemihl, sold his shade ?
Has Rogers haggled hard, or sold
   His features for your marble shows,
Or Campbell barter'd, ere he's cold,
   All interest in his "*bone* repose ?"

Rare is your show, ye righteous men !
   Priestly Politos,—rare, I ween ;
But should ye not outside the Den
   Paint up what in it may be seen ?
A long green Shakspeare, with a deer
   Grasp'd in the many folds it died in,—
A Butler stuff'd from ear to ear,
   Wet White Bears weeping o'er a Dryden !

Paint Garrick up like Mr. Paap,
   A Giant of some inches high ;

Paint Handel up, that organ chap,
    With you, as grinders, in his eye;
Depict some plaintive antique thing,
    And say th' original may be seen :—
Blind Milton with a dog and string
    May be the Beggar o' Bethnal Green!

Put up in Poet's Corner, near
    The little door, a platform small;
Get there a monkey—never fear,
    You'll catch the gapers, one and all!
Stand each of ye a Body Guard,
    A Trumpet under either fin,
And yell away in Palace Yard
    "All dead? All dead! Walk in! Walk in!"

(But when the people are inside,
    Their money paid—I pray you, bid
The keepers not to mount and ride
    A race around each coffin lid.—
Poor Mrs. Bodkin thought, last year,
    That it was hard—the woman clacks—
To have so little in her ear—
    And be so hurried through the Wax!—)

"Walk in! two shillings only! come!
    Be not by country grumblers funk'd!—
Walk in, and see th' illustrious dumb,
    The Cheapest House for the defunct!"
Write up, 'twill breed some just reflection,
    And every rude surmise 'twill stop—
Write up, that you have no connection
    (In large)—with any other shop!

And still, to catch the Clowns the more,
  With samples of your shows in Wax,
Set some old Harry near the door
  To answer queries with his *axe.*—
Put up some general begging-trunk—
  Since the last broke by some mishap,
You've all a bit of General Monk,
  From the respect you bore his Cap !

ODE TO H. BODKIN, ESQ.,

SECRETARY TO THE SOCIETY FOR THE SUPPRESSION OF MENDICITY.

" This is your cnarge—you shall comprehend all vagrom men."
                                        Much Ado about Nothing

HAIL, King of Shreds and Patches, hail,
  Disperser of the Poor !
Thou Dog in office, set to bark
  All beggars from the door !

Great overseer of overseers,
  And Dealer in old rags !
Thy public duty never fails,
  Thy ardour never flags !

" Oh, when I take my walks abroad,
  How many Poor "—I *miss !*
Had Doctor Watts walk'd now-a-days
  He would have written this !

So well thy Vagrant-catchers prowl,
  So clear thy caution keeps
The path—O, Bodkin, sure thou hast
  The eye that never sleeps !

No Belisarius pleads for alms,
  No Benbow, lacking legs;
The pious man in black is now
  The only man that begs!

Street-Handels are disorganized,
  Disbanded every band!—
The silent *scraper* at the door
  Is scarce allow'd to stand!

The Sweeper brushes with his broom,
  The Carstairs with his chalk
Retires,—the Cripple leaves his stand,
  But cannot sell his walk.

The old Wall-blind resigns the wall,
  The Camels hide their humps,
The Witherington without a leg
  Mayn't beg upon his stumps!

Poor Jack is gone, that used to doff
  His batter'd tatter'd hat,
And show his dangling sleeve, alas!
  There seem'd no 'arm in that!

Oh! was it such a sin to air
  His true blue naval rags,
Glory's own trophy, like St. Paul,
  Hung round with holy flags!

Thou knowest best. I meditate,
  My Bodkin, no offence!
Let us, henceforth, but nurse our pounds,
  Thou dost protect our pence!

Well art thou pointed 'gainst the Poor,
　For, when the Beggar Crew
Bring their petitions, thou art paid,
　Of course, to "run them through."

Of course thou art, what Hamlet meant—
　To wretches the last friend ;
What ills can mortals have,they can't
　With a bare *Bodkin* end ?

PLAYING AT SOLDIERS.
" WHO'LL SERVE THE KING ?'
AN ILLUSTRATION.

WHAT little urchin is there never
Hath had that early scarlet fever,
　Of martial trappings caught ?
Trappings well call'd—because they trap
And catch full many a country chap
　To go where fields are fought !

What little urchin with a rag
Hath never made a little flag,
　(Our plate will show the manner,)
And wooed each tiny neighbour still,
Tommy, or Harry, Dick or Will,
　To come beneath the banner !

Just like that ancient shape of mist
In Hamlet, crying, "'List, O 'list !"
　Come, who will serve the king,
And strike frog-eating Frenchmen dead
And cut off Boneyparty's head ?—
　And all that sort of thing.

So used I, when I was a boy,
To march with military toy,
   And ape the soldier-life ;—
And with a whistle or a hum,
I thought myself a Duke of Drum
   At least, or Earl of Fife.

With gun of tin and sword of lath,
Lord ! how I walk'd in glory's path
   With regimental mates,
By sound of trump and rub-a-dubs, ·
To 'siege the washhouse—charge the tubs—
   Or storm the garden gates !

Ah me ! my retrospective soul !
As over memory's muster-roll
   I cast my eyes anew,
My former comrades all the while
Rise up before me, rank and file
   And form in dim review.

Ay, there they stand, and dress in line,
Lubbock, and Fenn, and David Vine,
   And dark " Jamakey Forde !"
And limping Wood, and " Cocky Hawes,"
Our captain always made, because
   He had a *real* sword !

Long Lawrence, Natty Smart, and Soame,
Who said he had a gun at home,
   But that was all a brag ;
Ned Ryder, too, that used to snam
A prancing horse, and big Sam Lamb
   That *would* hold up the flag !

Tom Anderson, and " Dunny White,"
Who never right-abouted right,
  For he was deaf and dumb;
Jack Pike, Jem Crack, and Sandy Gray,
And Dicky Bird, that wouldn't play
  Unless he had the drum.

And Peter Holt, and Charley Jepp,
A chap that never kept the step—
  No more did "Surly Hugh;"
Bob Harrington, and " Fighting Jim"—
We often had to halt for him,
  To let him tie his shoe.

" Quarrelsome Scott," and Martin Dick,
That kill'd the bantam cock, to stick
  The plumes within his hat;
Bill Hook, and little Tommy Grout
That got so thump'd for calling out
  " Eyes right !" to " Squinting Matt."

Dan Simpson, that, with Peter Dodd,
Was always in the awkward squad,
  And those two greedy Blakes,
That took our money to the fair
To buy the corps a trumpet there,
  And laid it out in cakes.

Where are they now?—an open war
With open mouth declaring for?—
  Or fall'n in bloody fray?
Compell'd to tell the truth I am,
Their fights all ended with the sham,—
  Their soldiership in play.

Brave Soame sends cheeses out in trucks,
And Martin sells the cock he plucks,
   And Jepp now deals in wine;
Harrington bears a lawyer's bag,
And warlike Lamb retains his flag,
   But on a tavern sign.

They tell me Cocky Hawes's sword
Is seen upon a broker's board;
   And as for "Fighting Jim,"
In Bishopsgate, last Whitsuntide,
His unresisting cheek I spied
   Beneath a quaker brim!

Quarrelsome Scott is in the church,
For Ryder now your eye must search
   The marts of silk and lace—
Bird's drums are fill'd with figs, and mute,
And I—I've got a substitute
   To soldier in my place!

THE DEATH BED.

WE watch'd her breathing through the night,
   Her breathing soft and low,
As in her breast the wave of life
   Kept heaving to and fro.

So silently we seem'd to speak,
   So slowly moved about,
As we had lent her half our powers
   To eke her living out.

Our very hopes belied our fears,
    Our fears our hopes belied—
We thought her dying when she slept,
    And sleeping when she died.

For when the morn came dim and sad,
    And chill with early showers,
Her quiet eyelids closed—she had
    Another morn than ours.

TO MY WIFE.

STILL glides the gentle streamlet on,
With shifting current new and strange
The water, that was here, is gone,
But those green shadows never change.

Serene or ruffled by the storm,
On present waves, as on the past,
The mirror'd grove retains its form,
The self-same trees their semblance cast.

The hue each fleeting globule wears,
That drop bequeaths it to the next;
One picture still the surface bears,
To illustrate the murmur'd text.

So, love, however time may flow,
Fresh hours pursuing those that flee,
One constant image still shall show
My tide of life is true to thee.

SONG.

THERE is dew for the flow'ret
  And honey for the bee,
And bowers for the wild bird,
  And love for you and me.

There are tears for the many
  And pleasures for the few;
But let the world pass on, dear,
  There's love for me and you.

There is care that will not leave us,
  And pain that will not flee;
But on our hearth unalter'd
  Sits Love—'tween you and me.

Our love it ne'er was reckon'd,
  Yet good it is and true,
It's *half* the world to me, dear,
  It's *all* the world to you.

VERSES IN AN ALBUM.

FAR above the hollow
Tempest, and its moan,
Singing bright Apollo
In his golden zone,—
Cloud doth never shade him,
Nor a storm invade him,
On his joyous throne.

So when I behold me
In an orb as bright,

How thy soul doth fold me
In its throne of light !
Sorrow never paineth,
Nor a care attaineth,
To that blessed height.

THE WATER LADY.*

ALAS, the moon should ever beam
To show what man should never see !—
I saw a maiden on a stream,
And fair was she !

I staid awhile, to see her throw
Her tresses back, that all beset
The fair horizon of her brow
With clouds of jet.

I staid a little while to view
Her cheek, that wore in place of red
The bloom of water, tender blue,†
Daintily spread.

I staid to watch, a little space,
Her parted lips if she would sing;
The waters closed above her face
With many a ring.

And still I staid a little more,
Alas ! she never comes again !
I throw my flowers from the shore,
And watch in vain.

* From the " Forget-me-not " for 1826.
† A little water-colour sketch by Severn (given to my mother by Keats)
probably suggested these lines. The nymph's complexion is of a pale blue
(instead of ordinary flesh tint), as here described.

I know my life will fade away,
I know that I must vainly pine,
For I am made of mortal clay,
But she's divine!

AUTUMN.*

THE Autumn is old,
The sere leaves are flying;
He hath gather'd up gold,
And now he is dying;—
Old Age, begin sighing!

The vintage is ripe,
The harvest is heaping;—
But some that have sow'd
Have no riches for reaping;—
Poor wretch, fall a-weeping!

The year's in the wane,
There is nothing adorning,
The night has no eve,
And the day has no morning;— ˎ
Cold winter gives warning.

The rivers run chill,
The red sun is sinking,
And I am grown old,
And life is fast shrinking;—
Here's enow for sad thinking!

I REMEMBER, I REMEMBER.*

I REMEMBER, I remember,
The house where I was born,

* From "Friendship's Offering," 1826.

The little window where the sun
Came peeping in at morn;
He never came a wink too soon,
Nor brought too long a day,
But now, I often wish the night
Had borne my breath away!

I remember, I remember,
The roses, red and white,
The violets, and the lily-cups,
Those flowers made of light!
The lilacs where the robin built,
And where my brother set
The laburnum on his birth-day,—
The tree is living yet!

I remember, I remember,
Where I was used to swing,
And thought the air must rush as fresh
To swallows on the wing;
My spirit flew in feathers then,
That is so heavy now,
And summer pools could hardly cool
The fever on my brow!

I remember, I remember,
The fir trees dark and high;
I used to think their slender tops
Were close against the sky:
It was a childish ignorance.
But now 'tis little joy
To know I'm farther off from Heav'n
Than when I was a boy.

ADDRESS TO MR CROSS, OF EXETER CHANGE,

ON THE DEATH OF THE ELEPHANT.

"'Tis Greece, but living Greece no more."

OH, Mr. Cross,
Permit a sorry stranger to draw near,
And shed a tear
(I've shed my shilling) for thy recent loss !
I've been a visitor
Of old—a sort of a Buffon inquisitor
Of thy menagerie, and knew the beast,
That is deceased.
I was the Damon of the gentle giant,
And oft have been,
Like Mr. Kean,
Tenderly fondled by his trunk compliant.
Whenever I approached, the kindly brute
Flapped his prodigious ears, and bent his knees—
It makes me freeze
To think of it.   No chums could better suit,
Exchanging grateful looks for grateful fruit,—
For so our former dearness was begun,—
I bribed him with an apple, and beguiled
The beast of his affection like a child ;
And well he loved me till his life was done
(Except when he was wild).
It makes me blush for human friends—but none
I have so truly kept or cheaply won.

Here is his pen !
The casket—but the jewel is away ;
The den is rifled of its denizen,—
Ah, well a day !

This fresh free air breathes nothing of his grossness,
And sets me sighing even for its closeness.
                    This light one-story,
Where like a cloud I used to feast my eyes on
The grandeur of his Titan-like horizon,
Tells a dark tale of its departed glory;—
The very beasts lament the change like me.
                    The shaggy Bison
Leaneth his head dejected on his knee;
The Hyæna's laugh is hushed; the Monkeys pout;
The Wild Cat frets in a complaining whine;
The panther paces restlessly about,
                    To walk her sorrow out;
The lions in a deeper bass repine;
The Kang'roo wrings its sorry short forepaws;
                    Shrieks come from the Macaws;
The old bald Vulture shakes his naked head,
                    And pineth for the dead;
The Boa writhes into a double knot;
                    The Keeper groans,
                    Whilst sawing bones,
And looks askance at the deserted spot;
Brutal and rational lament his loss,
The flower of the beastly family;—
                    Poor Mrs. Cross
Sheds frequent tears into her daily tea,
                    And weakens her Bohea.

Oh, Mr. Cross, how little it gives birth
To grief when human greatness goes to earth;
                    How few lament for Czars,—
But, oh, the universal heart o'erflowed
                    At his "high mass,"
                    Lighted by gas,

When like Mark Antony the keeper showed
            The Elephantine scars.
            Reporters' eyes
            Were of an egg-like size;
Men that had never wept for murdered Marrs,*
Hard-hearted editors with iron faces,
            Their sluices all unclosed,—
            And discomposed
Compositors went fretting to their cases,
            That grief has left its traces;
The poor old Beef-eater has gone much greyer,
            With sheer regret;
            And the Gazette
Seems the least trouble of the beasts' Purveyor.

And I too weep! a dozen of great men
I could have spared without a single tear;
            But, then,
They are renewable from year to year.
Fresh gents would rise though Gent resigned the pen;
            I should not wholly
Despair for six months of another C****,†
Nor, though F********* lay on his small bier,
            Be melancholy.
But when will such an elephant appear?
Though Penley were destroyed at Drury-lane,
            His like might come again;
            Fate might supply,
A second Powell if the first should die;
Another Bennet if the sire were snatched;
            Barnes—might be matched;
            And Time fill up the gap

* The Marr family murdered by Williams. See De Quincy's "Murder as a Fine Art."
† Probably "Croly"—the "F." I am at a loss to discover.

Were Parsloe laid upon the green earth's lap;
Even Claremont might be equalled,—I could hope
(All human greatness is, alas, so puny!)
For other Egertons—another Pope,
   But not another Chunee!

Well! he is dead!
And there's a gap in Nature of eleven
   Feet high by seven—
Five living tons!—and I remain nine stone
   Of skin and bone!
It is enough to make me shake my head
   And dream of the grave's brink—
   'Tis worse to think
How like the Beast's the sorry life *I've* led!—
   A sort of show
Of my poor public self and my sagacity,
   To profit the rapacity
Of certain folks in Paternoster Row,
A slavish toil to win an upper story—
   And a hard glory
Of wooden beams about my weary brow!
   Oh, Mr. C.!
If ever you behold me twirl my pen
To earn a public supper, that is, eat
   In the bare street,—
Or turn about their literary den—
   Shoot *me!*

THE POET'S PORTION.

WHAT is a mine—a treasury—a dower—
A magic talisman of mighty power?

A poet's wide possession of the earth.
He has th' enjoyment of a flower's birth
Before its budding—ere the first red streaks,
And Winter cannot rob him of their cheeks.

Look—if his dawn be not as other men's!
Twenty bright flushes—ere another kens
The first of sunlight is abroad—he sees
Its golden 'lection of the topmost trees,
And opes the splendid fissures of the morn.

When do his fruits delay, when doth his corn
Linger for harvesting? Before the leaf
Is commonly abroad, in his pil'd sheaf
The flagging poppies lose their ancient flame.

No sweet there is, no pleasure I can name,
But he will sip it first—before the lees.
'Tis his to taste rich honey,—ere the bees
Are busy with the brooms. He may forestall
June's rosy advent for his coronal;
Before th' expectant buds upon the bough,
Twining his thoughts to bloom upon his brow.

Oh! blest to see the flower in its seed,
Before its leafy presence; for indeed
Leaves are but wings on which the summer flies,
And each thing perishable fades and dies,
Escap'd in thought; but his rich thinkings be
Like overflows of immortality:
So that what there is steep'd shall perish never,
But live and bloom, and be a joy for ever.

ODE TO THE LATE LORD MAYOR,

ON THE PUBLICATION OF HIS "VISIT TO OXFORD." *

> "Now, Night descending, the proud scene is o'er,
> But lives in Settle's numbers one day more."
> POPE—*On the Lord Mayor's Show.*

O WORTHY MAYOR !—I mean to say Ex-Mayor !
Chief Luddite of the ancient town of Lud !
Incumbent of the City's easy chair !—
Conservator of Thames from mud to mud !
  Great river-bank director !
  And dam-inspector !
Great guardian of small sprats that swim the flood !
Lord of the scarlet gown and furry cap
  King of Mogg's map !
Keeper of Gates that long have "gone their gait !"
Warder of London stone and London Log !
Thou first and greatest of the civic great,
  Magog or Gog !—

  O Honorable Ven——
(Forgive this little liberty between us),
Augusta's first Augustus !—Friend of men
  Who wield the pen !
  Dillon's Mæcenas !
Patron of learning where she ne'er did dwell,
Where literature seldom finds abettors,
Where few—except the postman and his bell—
  Encourage the *bell-lettres !*—

* See the published work of the Rev. Mr. Dillon, the Lord Mayor's Chaplain, who, in his zealous endeavour to stamp immortality upon the civic expedition to Oxford, has outrun every production in the annals of burlesque, even the long renowned "Voyage from Paris to St. Cloud." It was entitled "The Lord Mayor's Visit to Oxford in the month of July 1826, written by the desire of the party by the Chaplain to the Mayoralty."

Well hast thou done, Right Honorable Sir—
Seeing that years are such devouring ogresses,
And thou hast made some little journeying stir,—
To get a Nichols to record thy Progresses !

Wordsworth once wrote a trifle of the sort;
  But for diversion,
For truth—for nature—everything in short—
I own I do prefer thy own " Excursion."
  The stately story
  Of Oxford glory—
The Thames romance—yet nothing of a fiction—
Like thine own stream it flows along the page—
  "Strong, without rage,"
In diction worthy of thy jurisdiction !
To future ages thou wilt seem to be
  A second Parry;
  For thou didst carry
Thy navigation to a fellow crisis.
He penetrated to a Frozen Sea,
And thou—to where the Thames is turned to *Isis !**

  I like thy setting out !
Thy coachman and thy coachmaid boxed together !†
I like thy Jarvey's serious face—in doubt
Of " four fine animals "—no Cobbetts either !‡

* The Chaplain doubts the correctness of the Thames being *turned into*
the Isis at Oxford: of course he is right—according to the course of the
river, it must be the Isis that is turned into the Thames.
 † " As soon as the female attendant of the Lady Mayoress had taken her
seat, dressed with becoming neatness, at the side of the well-looking coachman, the carriage drove away."—*Visit.*
 ‡ The coachman's countenance was reserved and thoughtful, indicating
full consciousness of the test by which his equestrian skill would this day be
tried."—*Visit.*

        O

I like the slow state pace—the pace allowed
The best for dignity *—and for a crowd,
  And very July weather,
So hot that it let off the Hounslow powder !†
I like the She-Mayor's proffer of a seat
To poor Miss Magnay, fried to a white heat ;‡
'Tis well it didn't chance to be Miss *Crowder !*

I like the steeples with their weathercocks on,
Discerned about the hour of three, P. M. ;
I like thy party's entrance into Oxon,
For oxen soon to enter into *them !*
I like the ensuing banquet better far,
Although an act of cruelty began it ;—
For why—before the dinner at the *Star*—
Why was the poor Town-clerk sent off to *plan it ?*

I like your learned rambles not amiss,
Especially at Bodley's, where ye tarried
The longest—doubtless because Atkins carried
Letters (of course from Ignorance) to Bliss !§
The other Halls were scrambled through more hastily
  But I like this—

* "The carriage drove away ; not, however, with that violent and extreme rapidity which rather astounds than gratifies the beholders ; but at that steady and majestic pace, which is always an indication of real greatness."

† "On approaching Hounslow, there was seen at some distance a huge volume of dark smoke." The Chaplain thought it was only a blowing up for rain, but it turned out to be the spontaneous combustion of a powder-mill.

‡ "The Lady Mayoress, observing that they (the Magnays) must be somewhat crowded in the chaise, invited Miss Magnay to take the fourth seat."

§ "The Rev. Dr. Bliss, of St. John's College, the Registrar of the University, to whom Mr. Alderman Atkins had letters of introduction."—Page 32.

I like the Aldermen who stopped to drink
Of Maudlin's " classic water " very tastily,*
Although I think—what I am loth to think—
Except to Dillon, it has proved no Castaly!

I like to find thee finally afloat;
I like thy being barged and Water-bailiff'd,
 Who gave thee *a* lift
To thy state-galley in his own state-boat.
I like thy small sixpennyworths of largess
Thrown to the urchins at the City's charges;
I like the sun upon thy breezy fanners,
Ten splendid scarlet silken stately banners!
Thy gilded bark shines out quite transcendental !
 I like dear Dillon still,
 Who quotes from " Cooper's Hill,"
And Birch, the cookly Birch, grown sentimental; †
I like to note his civic mind expanding
And quoting Denham, in the watery dock
 Of Iffley lock—
Plainly no Locke upon the Understanding !
 I like thy civic deed
 At Runnymede,
Where ancient Britons came in arms to barter
Their lives for right—Ah, did not Waithman grow
 Half mad to show
Where his renowned forefathers came to bleed—
And freeborn *Magnay* triumph at his *Charter* ?
I like full well thy ceremonious setting

---

* " The buttery was next visited, in which some of the party tasted the classic water."—Page 57.
 † " Mr. Alderman Birch here called to the recollection of the party the beautiful lines of Sir John Denham on the river Thames :—'Tho' deep yet clear,' &c."—Page 90.

The justice-sword (no doubt it wanted whetting !)
On London Stone; but I don't like the waving
Thy banner over it,* for I must own
    Flag over stone
Reads like a most superfluous piece of paving !

I like thy Cliefden treat; but I'm not going
To run the civic story through and through,
But leave thy barge to Pater Noster Row-ing,
    My plaudit to renew.—
Well hast thou done, Right Honorable rover,
To leave this lasting record of thy reign,
A reign, alas ! that very soon is " over
And gone," according to the Rydal strain !
    'Tis piteous how a mayor
    Slips through his chair.
I say it with a meaning reverential
But let him be rich, lordly, wise, sentential,
Still he must seem a thing inconsequential—
A melancholy truth one cannot smother ;
    For why ? 'tis very clear
    He comes in at one *year*,
    To go out by the other !
This is their Lordships' universal order !—
But thou shalt teach them to preserve a name—
Make future Chaplains chroniclers of fame !
And every Lord Mayor his own Recorder !

---

* " It was also a part of the ceremony, which, though important, is
simple, thst the City banner should wave over the stone."—Page 144.

ELEGY ON DAVID LAING, ESQ.*

BLACKSMITH AND JOINER (WITHOUT LICENCE) AT GRETNA GREEN.

AH me! what causes such complaining breath,
　Such female moans, and flooding tears to flow?
It is to chide with stern, remorseless Death,
　　　For laying Laing low!
From Prospect House there comes a sound of woe—
A shrill and persevering loud lament,
Echoed by Mrs. J.'s Establishment
　　"For Six Young Ladies,
In a retired and healthy part of Kent."
　　All weeping, Mr. L—— gone down to Hades!
Thoughtful of grates, and convents, and the veil!
　　　Surrey takes up the tale,
And all the nineteen scholars of Miss Jones
With the two parlour-boarders and th' apprentice—
So universal this mis-timed event is—
　　　Are joining sobs and groans!
The shock confounds all hymeneal planners
　　And drives the sweetest from their sweet behaviours:
The girls at Manor House forget their manners,
　　　And utter sighs like paviours!
·Down—down through Devon and the distant shires
　Travels the news of Death's remorseless crime;
And in all hearts, at once, all hope expires
　　　Of *matches* against time!

* On the 3rd inst., died in Springfield, near Gretna Green, David Laing,
aged seventy-two, who had for thirty-five years officiated as high-priest at
Gretna Green.   He caught cold on his way to Lancaster, to give evidence
on the trial of the Wakefields, from the effects of which he never recovered.
—*Newspapers, July,* 1827.

Along the northern route
The road is water'd by postilions' eyes;
    The topboot paces pensively about,
And yellow jackets are all strained with sighs·
There is a sound of grieving at the Ship,
And sorry hands are ringing at the Bell.
        In aid of David's knell.
The postboy's heart is cracking—not his whip—
    To gaze upon those useless empty collars
His way-worn horses seem so glad to slip—
    And think upon the dollars
That used to urge his gallop—quicker! quicker!
        All hope is fled,
        For Laing is dead—
Vicar of Wakefield—Edward Gibbon's vicar!
        The barristers shed tears
Enough to feed a snipe (snipes live on suction),
        To think in after years
No suits will come of Gretna Green abduction,
        Nor knaves inveigle
Young heiresses in marriage scrapes or legal.
        The dull reporters
Look truly sad and seriously solemn
        To lose the future column
On Hymen-Smithy and its fond resorters!
    But grave Miss Daulby and the teaching brood
Rejoice at quenching the clandestine flambeau—
    That never real beau of flesh and blood
Will henceforth lure young ladies from their *Chambaud.*

Sleep—David Laing—sleep
In peace, though angry governesses spurn thee !
Over thy grave a thousand maidens weep,

And honest postboys mourn thee !
Sleep, David !—safely and serenely sleep,
  Be-wept of many a learnèd legal eye !
To see the mould above thee in a heap
  Drowns many a lid that heretofore was dry!—
Especially of those that, plunging deep
  In love, would "ride and tie !"—
Had I command, thou shouldst have gone thy ways
In chaise and pair—and lain in Père-la-Chaise !

SONNET.

WRITTEN IN A VOLUME OF SHAKSPEARE.

How bravely Autumn paints upon the sky
The gorgeous fame of Summer which is fled !
Hues of all flow'rs, that in their ashes lie,
Trophied in that fair light whereon they fed,—
Tulip, and hyacinth, and sweet rose red,—
Like exhalations from the leafy mould,
Look here how honour glorifies the dead,
And warms their scutcheons with a glance of gold !—
Such is the memory of poets old,
Who on Parnassus-hill have bloom'd elate ;
Now they are laid under their marbles cold,
And turn'd to clay, whereof they were create ;
But god Apollo hath them all enroll'd,
And blazon'd on the very clouds of Fate !

A RETROSPECTIVE REVIEW.

Oh, when I was a tiny boy,
My days and nights were full of joy,
  My mates were blithe and kind !—

No wonder that I sometimes sigh,
And dash the tear-drop from my eye,
　To cast a look behind!

A hoop was an eternal round
Of pleasure.　In those days I found
　A top a joyous thing;—
But now those past delights I drop,
My head, alas! is all my top,
　And careful thoughts the string!

My marbles—once my bag was stored,—
Now I must play with Elgin's lord,
　With Theseus for a taw!
My playful horse has slipt his string,
Forgotten all his capering,
　And harness'd to the law!

My kite—how fast and far it flew!
Whilst I, a sort of Franklin, drew
　My pleasure from the sky!
'Twas paper'd o'er with studious themes,
The tasks I wrote—my present dreams
　Will never soar so high!

My joys are wingless all and dead;
My dumps are made of more than lead;
　My flights soon find a fall;
My fears prevail, my fancies droop,
Joy never cometh with a hoop,
　And seldom with a call!

My football's laid upon the shelf;
I am a shuttlecock myself

The world knocks to and fro ;—
My archery is all unlearn'd,
And grief against myself has turn'd
 My arrows and my bow !

No more in noontide sun I bask ;
My authorship 's an endless task,
 My head 's ne'er out of school :
My heart is pain'd with scorn and slight,
I have too many foes to fight,
 And friends grown strangely cool !

The very chum that shared my cake
Holds out so cold a hand to shake,
 It makes me shrink and sigh :—
On this I will not dwell and hang,—
The changeling would not feel a pang
 Though these should meet his eye !

No skies so blue or so serene
As then ;—no leaves look half so green
 As clothed the playground tree !
All things I loved are alter'd so,
Nor does it ease my heart to know
 That change resides in me !

Oh for the garb that mark'd the boy,
The trousers made of corduroy,
 Well ink'd with black and red ;
The crownless hat, ne'er deem'd an ill—
It only let the sunshine still
 Repose upon my head !

Oh for the riband round the neck !
The careless dogs'-ears apt to deck

My book and collar both !
How can this formal man be styled
 Merely an Alexandrine child,
  A boy of larger growth ?

Oh for that small, small beer anew !
And (heaven's own type) that mild sky-blue
 That wash'd my sweet meals down ;
The master even !—and that small Turk
That fagg'd me !—worse is now my work—
 A fag for all the town !

Oh for the lessons learn'd by heart !
Ay, though the very birch's smart
 Should mark those hours again ;
I'd " kiss the rod," and be resign'd
Beneath the stroke, and even find
 Some sugar in the cane !

The Arabian Nights rehearsed in bed !
The Fairy Tales in school-time read,
 By stealth, 'twixt verb and noun !
The angel form that always walk'd
In all my dreams, and look'd and talk'd
 Exactly like Miss Brown !

The *omne bene*—Christmas come !
The prize of merit, won for home—
 Merit had prizes then !
But now I write for days and days,
For fame—a deal of empty praise,
 Without the silver pen !

Then " home, sweet home !" the crowded
  coach—
The joyous shout—the loud approach—

The winding horns like rams' !
The meeting sweet that made me thrill,
The sweetmeats, almost sweeter still,
　No 'satis' to the 'jams !'—

When that I was a tiny boy
My days and nights were full of joy,
　My mates were blithe and kind !
No wonder that I sometimes sigh,
And dash the tear-drop from my eye,
　To cast a look behind !

BALLAD.

IT was not in the Winter
　Our loving lot was cast ;
It was the Time of Roses,—
　We pluck'd them as we pass'd !

That churlish season never frown'd
　On early lovers yet :—
Oh, no—the world was newly crown'd
　With flowers when first we met !

'Twas twilight, and I bade you go,
　But still you held me fast ;
It was the Time of Roses,—
　We pluck'd them as we pass'd.—

What else could peer thy glowing cheek,
　That tears began to stud ?
And when I ask'd the like of Love,
　You snatch'd a damask bud ;

And oped it to the dainty core,
  Still glowing to the last.—
It was the Time of Roses,
  We pluck'd them as we pass'd !

STANZAS TO TOM WOODGATE,
OF HASTINGS.

Tom ;—are you still within this land
Of livers—still on Hastings' sand,
  Or roaming on the waves?
Or has some billow o'er you rolled,
Jealous that earth should lap so bold
  A seaman in her graves ?

On land the rushlight lives of men
Go out but slowly ; nine in ten,
  By tedious long decline—
Not so the jolly sailor sinks,
Who founders in the wave, and drinks
  The apoplectic brine !

Ay, while I write, mayhap your head
Is sleeping on an oyster-bed—
  I hope 'tis far from truth !—
With periwinkle eyes ;—your bone
Beset with mussels, not your own.
  And corals at your tooth !

Still does the Chance pursue the chance
The main affords—the Aidant dance
  In safety on the tide?
Still flies that sign of my good-will*
A little *bunting* thing—but still
  To thee a flag of pride?

* My father made Woodgate a present, in the shape of a small flag.

Does that hard, honest hand now clasp
The tiller in its careful grasp—
   With every summer breeze
When ladies sail, in lady-fear—
Or, tug the oar, a gondolier
   On smooth Macadam seas?

Or are you where the flounders keep,
Some dozen briny fathoms deep,
   Where sand and shells abound—
With some old Triton on your chest,
And twelve grave mermen for a 'quest,
   To find that you are—drown'd?

Swift is the wave, and apt to bring
A sudden doom—perchance I sing
   A mere funereal strain;
You have endured the utter strife—
And are—the same in death or life—
   A good man 'in the main'!

Oh, no—I hope the old brown eye
Still watches ebb, and flood, and sky;
   That still the brown old shoes
Are sucking brine up—pumps indeed!—
Your tooth still full of ocean weed,
   Or Indian—which you choose.

I like you, Tom! and in these lays
Give honest worth its honest praise,
   No puff at honour's cost;
For though you met these words of mine,
All letter-learning was a˜line
   You, somehow, never cross'd!

Mayhap we ne'er shall meet again,
Except on that Pacific main,
   Beyond this planet's brink;
Yet, as we erst have braved the weather,
Still may we float awhile together,
   As comrades on this ink!

Many a scudding gale we've had
Together, and, my gallant lad,
   Some perils we have pass'd;
When huge and black the wave career'd,
And oft the giant surge appear'd
   The master of our mast;—

'Twas thy example taught me how
To climb the billow's hoary brow,
   Or cleave the raging heap—
To bound along the ocean wild,
With danger—only as a child
   The waters rock'd to sleep.

Oh, who can tell that brave delight,
To see the hissing wave in might
   Come rampant like a snake!
To leap his horrid crest, and feast
One's eyes upon the briny beast,
   Left couchant in the wake!

The simple shepherd's love is still
To bask upon a sunny hill,
   The herdsman roams the vale—
With both their fancies I agree;
Be mine the swelling, scooping sea,
   That is both hill and dale!

I yearn for that brisk spray—I yearn
To feel the wave fiom stem to stern
   Uplift the plunging keel ;
That merry step we used to dance
On board the Aidant or the Chance,
   The ocean " toe and heel."

I long to feel the steady gale
That fills the broad distended sail—
   The seas on either hand !
My thought, like any hollow shell,
Keeps mocking at my ear the swell
   Of waves against the land.

It is no fable—that old strain
Of syrens !—so the witching main
   Is singing—and I sigh !
My heart is all at once inclined
To seaward—and I seem to find
   The waters in my eye !

Methinks I see the shining beach ;
The merry waves, each after each,
   Rebounding o'er the flints ;
I spy the grim preventive spy !
The jolly boatmen standing nigh !
   The maids in morning chintz!

And there they float—the sailing craft!
The sail is up—the wind abaft—
   The ballast trim and neat.
Alas ! 'tis all a dream—a lie !
A printer's imp is standing by,
   To haul my mizen sheet !

My tiller dwindles to a pen—
My craft is that of bookish men—
  My sail—let Longman tell!
Adieu, the wave, the wind, the spray!
Men—maidens—chintzes—fade away!
  Tom Woodgate, fare thee well!

TIME, HOPE, AND MEMORY.

I HEARD a gentle maiden, in the spring,
Set her sweet sighs to music, and thus sing:
" Fly through the world, and I will follow thee,
Only for looks that may turn back on me;

" Only for roses that your chance may throw—
Though wither'd—I will wear them on my brow,
To be a thoughtful fragrance to my brain,—
Warm'd with such love, that they will bloom again.

" Thy love before thee, I must tread behind,
Kissing thy foot-prints, though to me unkind;
But trust not all her fondness, though it seem,
Lest thy true love should rest on a false dream.

" Her face is smiling, and her voice is sweet;
But smiles betray, and music sings deceit;
And words speak false;—yet, if they welcome prove,
I'll be their echo, and repeat their love.

" Only if waken'd to sad truth, at last,
The bitterness to come, and sweetness past;
When thou art vext, then turn again, and see
Thou hast loved Hope, but Memory loved thee."

FLOWERS.

I WILL not have the mad Clytie
Whose head is turn'd by the sun;
The tulip is a courtly quean,
Whom, therefore, I will shun;
The cowslip is a country wench,
The violet is a nun;—
But I will woo the dainty rose,
The queen of every one.

The pea is but a wanton witch,
In too much haste to wed,
And clasps her rings on every hand;
The wolfsbane I should dread;
Nor will I dreary rosemarye,
That always mourns the dead;—
But I will woo the dainty rose,
With her cheeks of tender red.

The lily is all in white, like a saint,
And so is no mate for me—
And the daisy's cheek is tipp'd with a blush,
She is of such low degree;
Jasmine is sweet, and has many loves,
And the broom's betroth'd to the bee;—
But I will plight with the dainty rose,
For fairest of all is she.

BALLAD.

SHE'S up and gone, the graceless girl,
And robb'd my failing years!

P

My blood before was thin and cold
    But now 'tis turn'd to tears;—
My shadow falls upon my grave,
    So near the brink I stand,
She might have stay'd a little yet,
    And led me by the hand!

Aye, call her on the barren moor,
    And call her on the hill:
'Tis nothing but the heron's cry,
    And plover's answer shrill;
My child is flown on wilder wings
    Than they have ever spread,
And I may even walk a waste
    That widen'd when she fled.

Full many a thankless child has been,
    But never one like mine;
Her meat was served on plates of gold,
    Her drink was rosy wine;
But now she'll share the robin's food,
    And sup the common rill,
Before her feet will turn again
    To meet her father's will!

RUTH.

SHE stood breast high amid the corn
Clasp'd by the golden light of morn,
Like the sweetheart of the sun,
Who many a glowing kiss had won.

On her cheek an autumn flush,
Deeply ripen'd;—such a blush

In the midst of brown was born,
Like red poppies grown with corn.

Round her eyes her tresses fell,
Which were blackest none could tell,
But long lashes veil'd a light,
That had else been all too bright,

And her hat, with shady brim,
Made her tressy forehead dim ;—
Thus she stood amid the stooks,
Praising God with sweetest looks :—

Sure, I said, Heav'n did not mean,
Where I reap thou shouldst but glean,
Lay thy sheaf adown and come,
Share my harvest and my home.

A SENTIMENTAL JOURNEY

FROM ISLINGTON TO WATERLOO BRIDGE, IN MARCH, 1821.

"The son of Cornelius shall make his own legs his compasses ; with those he shall measure continents, islands, capes, bays, straits, and isthmuses."— *Memoirs of Martinus Scriblerus.*

" I SHOULD very much like to travel," said a young cockney, with his feet on the fender. " London is a vast place ; but the world is ten times bigger, and no doubt a many strange things are to be seen in it."

" And pray, young man," said an old gentleman, whom he called the philosopher, "pray, are you so familiar with the features of your own country ; are you so well acquainted with its men and manners, that you must go out of it for matter of investigation and speculation."

"As for men," replied the cockney, "we may see them anywhere. I've seen Cribb and Spring, and the *best good ones* that ever peel'd ; and as for manners, I learned them at the dancing-school. I have not been all over England, to be sure, like my father's riders ; but I've been to Margate, Brighton, and Moulsey Hurst ; so that what I have not seen by sack I have seen by sample. Besides, London is the very focus of England ; and sure I am, that I know it from Wapping to Hyde Park Corner, and have seen all that is instructive in it. I've been up the Monument, and down St. Paul's, over the Bridges, and under the Tunnel. I've seen the King and Court, Mrs. Salmon's royal waxwork too, and the wild beasts at Exeter 'Change ;—I've seen Drury Lane and Covent Garden play-houses, besides the Houses of Lords and Commons—the Soho Bazaar, and both Bartlemy Fair and the Brighton Pavilion. I never missed a Lord Mayor's show, nor anything that is worth seeing ; and I know by sight Lord Castlereagh, Jack Ketch, Sir William Curtis, Billy Waters, and many other public and distinguished characters."

"If you have seen no more than you say," said the philosopher," you have seen a great deal more than is English ; and if you only wish to study mankind, it is at least a reason against your leaving the country. England, has, to be sure, its national character ; but it gives birth to many mongrels, who belong rather to the Spanish, Dutch, or other breeds : there are foreigners born here, as well as others who visit us ; and why should we go abroad to study them, when we have them all in epitome at home ? Different nations, like different men, are only compounds of the same ingredients, but in different proportions. We shall find knaves and honest men in every state, and a large proportion of fools and dunces in them all. We shall find every where the same passions, the same virtues and vices, but altered in their proportions by the influences of education, laws, and religion; which in some parts tend to improve, and, in others, to pervert the common nature of mankind.

" It is in their civil and religious institutions that we are to look for the grand causes effecting those distinctions which constitute national character; but before we go to investigate them, we should at least understand a little of our own."

"Pshaw!" said the cockney, who began to grow tired of this harangue; " there are sights to be seen abroad which can't be brought over here, and as for men being the same all the world over, it's all my eye,—a'nt there the Hottentots that have noses like your pug's, and heads as black and woolly as my poodle's? A'nt the Frenchmen all skinny, and haven't the Spaniards large whiskers? There are the Patagonians, too, that are as big as the Irish giant, and Laplanders no bigger than Miss What's-her-name, the dwarf?"

"Pshaw," said the philosopher, in his turn; "all these are minor distinctions, and shrink, as it were, to nothing when compared with the immeasurable distances between the minds of men: whether I be Englishman or Hottentot, a Laplander or a Patagonian,—

> If I could stretch from pole to pole,
>   And grasp the ocean in a span,
> I must be measur'd by my soul:
>   The mind's the standard of the man.

" There is, no doubt, a considerable difference

between a Hottentot's nose and my own, which, as you observe, is a fine Roman one, and very like Cæsar's; but there is, I flatter myself, a much greater difference between our understandings. The first is only a difference in the conformation of matter, but the last is a gradation in mind, which, to speak in common language, is the most material matter of the two."

Here the Cockney was quite out of patience; "he did not care," he said, "about mind and matter; and as to the difference of men's minds, why men would differ, but he meant to be of his own mind, and the philosopher might be of his," and so they parted.

As I was present at this conversation, it occurred to me that if men were so much alike everywhere, or rather, if every soil produced the same varieties, I could see as much of them in a walk through the populous streets of London as in a hasty journey all over the Continent. Oh! I will not travel, said I, for, in the first place, it's unnecessary; and second' . I do not feel equal to its fatigues and dangers; and lastly, said I (for we always get to the true reason at last), I can't afford it. Besides, I had not seen Waterloo Bridge; and we ought to see our own bridges before we go to see the bridges of others. A traveller, said I, should have all his wits about him, and so will I. He should let nothing escape him, no more will I. He should extract reflections out of a cabbage stump, like sun-beams squeezed out of cucumbers; so will I, if I can; and he should converse with every and any one, even a fish-woman. Perhaps I will, and perhaps I will not, said I. Who knows but I may make a sentimental journey, as good as

Sterne's; but at any rate I can write it, and send it to the London Magazine.

I had hardly left the threshold of my door, ere I met, as I thought, with an adventure. I had just reached that ancient and grotesque house which is said to have been a summer seat of Queen Elizabeth, though now in the centre of the village, or rather town of Islington, when I observed that the steps which led down to the door had become the seat, or rather the couch, of an unfortunate female. She had, like Sterne's Maria, her *dog*, and her *pipe*, and like her, too, she was evidently beside herself. "Poor unfortunate and interesting Maria," said I, as she came into my mind, exactly as Sterne had drawn her. I had touched a string—at the name of Maria, the female for the first time raised her head, and I caught a glance at her uncommon countenance. The rose had not fled from it, nor the bloom, for this was damson, and that was damask; there was a fixedness in her gaze, and although she quickly turned her head away, she could not hide from me that she had a drop in her eye. "It won't do," said I, shaking my head, "Maria found Sterne's handkerchief, and washed it with tears, and dried it in her bosom; but if I lose mine here, it's ten to one if I see it again; and if this Maria should wet it with her eyes,' methinks it would dry best again at her nose. There is nothing to sympathise with in her bewilderment—she's rather bewitched than bewitching—she's a dry subject," and so I left her. My eyes, however, were full charged with the tears, and my bosom with the sighs, which I had expected to mingle with those of the supposed unfortunate. Some sentimentalists would have vented them upon the first dead dog or lame chicken they might meet with; but I held them too valuable to be wasted upon such objects. I hate the weeping-willow set, who will cry over their pug dogs and canaries, till they have no tears to spare for the real children of misfortune and misery; but sensibility is too scarce, and too valuable, not to be often imitated; and these, therefore, are the ways in which they advertise their counterfeit drops. They should be punished like any other impostors, and they might be made of some use to society at the same time; for a: other convicts are set to beat hemp, and pick oakum, so I would set these to perform funerals, and to chop onions. These reflections, and the incidents which gave rise to them, I resolved to treasure up, for they would perhaps have their use in some part of my journey.

They will warn me against being too sentimental, said I. In the first place it is ridiculous; secondly, it's useless; and lastly, it's inconvenient; for I just recollect that there's a very large hole in my pocket handkerchief. These reflections brought me into Colebrook Row, or rather into a heap of mud that stood at the end of it, for street reveries are very subject to such sudden terminations. They say that Englishmen have a rusticity about them that only rubs off by a little travel; but that must certainly be erroneous, for I had hardly gone a quarter of a mile, ere I lost, in the mudding of my boots, the little all of polish that I wore about me. Barring the first agony of mortification, I bore it, however, with uncommon fortitude, for I knew that travellers must expect to meet, as I did, with sad and serious accidents. There passed however a young gentleman in very tight *trotter-cases*, but whilst his feet gave evident signs of suffering, I observed that his countenance was calm, vacant, and stoical. Pshaw! said I, if he can bear his pinches so well, I may surely put up with my splashes; this pain of mine exists only in imagination, whereas his poor feet, like Shakspeare's stricken deer, " distend their leathern coats almost to bursting." What a felicity there is in a happy application of words! I was so pleased with the resemblance which I had discovered between the foot of a dandy and a stricken deer, that I quite forgot my vexation, and its cause. I found, as I thought, that I had a genius for apt quotations, and resolved not to be sparing of them; they would give to my travels an air of great learning ; and if learning be better than riches, there would be no more harm in showing it thus than in pulling out a large purse, as some do, to give a poor beggar a halfpenny.

"Give a poor beggar a halfpenny," said a man, as if he had heard and echoed the last part of my thought.

The City Road was excessively dirty, but he had swept a cleaner passage over it, and as I trod across his little track of Terra Firma, I dropped the merited coin into his hat, for I saw he had only half-a-crown in it. "Thank your honour," said he, looking full in my face, and then looking down upon my boots, he thanked me again, and still more emphatically. "It is very true," said I, entering into his feeling—" it's very true—and if I too had looked upon my boots, you probably had not had it."

He thought, no doubt, with certain philosophers,

that man's main-spring is selfishness, and perhaps he
was not quite wrong; but at all events to decide it, I
resolved to watch his customers and analyze his
profits. "A plague take the fellow!" said an old
gentleman, whom he had hunted fifty paces for a halfpenny, "you ought to be reported to the Mendicity
Society." He gave it to him, to get rid of his impor-
tunity, thought I. He would have kept his halfpenny
by walking a little faster, but he walks very lame,
poor old gentleman, and that perhaps makes him
pettish. The next halfpenny he got from a lady, who
had walked a long way down the road to avail herself
of his labour. It was rather for her upper leathers
than for her soul's sake, said I; and as for that old
lady that followed her, I can read in his face that she
has given him a pocket-piece; but they all go in
charity, as it is called, and I have learned, by the bye,
what to do with a forged or flash note. As nobody
else seemed inclined to give him anything, I summed
up my calculations: one third had given from incon-
venience, and one third for convenience, and the rest,
or the pocket-piece, was the gift of pure charity.
We may say of charity, as Hamlet Travestied, does
of death—that it's truly a fine thing to talk of. We
all preach it—we all praise and admire, but when we
come to the practice of it, we "leave that to men of
more learning;" and are as careful of our pence as of
our lives, when we find they've no chance of return-
ing. I had hardly ended these uncharitable reflections, when I was obliged to retract and repent them.
I had begun to read a very conspicuous hand-bill
which was posted on some palings near Sadler's Wells,
and invited the admirers of fisty-cuffs to a grand spar-

ring benefit at Five's Court. But I had hardly got farther than the noble science of self-defence, than it was for the most part eclipsed by a new hand-bill, fresh from the pole of the bill-sticker; and altogether, they then appeared as follows :—To the Fancy—on such a day—a Sermon will be preached by such a Bishop at such a Church, for the benefit of such a charity—and as a little piece of the other bill expressed at the bottom that *real good ones* were expected, I applied it of course to the exclusion of pocket-pieces. I had a fresh subject besides in this piece of waggery of the bill-sticker's, which had afforded me no little entertainment. Shakspeare was right, and so was the philosopher, in my estimation ; for I saw that what they had represented was correct, that certain characters are confined to no class, condition, nor country. We may meet with dull pedagogues and authors, and with sensible clowns and with witty bill-stickers; and I doubt not that we as readily meet with blunt Frenchmen, with shuffling Englishmen, and honest and brave Italians. I met with no other incident worth relating or reflecting upon, till I came to a public house near Lady Huntingdon's Chapel, and there I met with matter of interest and amusement, inasmuch as it involved a question upon national and domestic government.

It was no less than a quarrel between a man and his wife, who had just ejected him from his seat in the parlour ; and the argument was, not whether he should go there at all, but whether he should go there without her permission first sought and obtained. There were not wanting auxiliaries and allies upon each side, and there were as many advocates for the

rights of women, as there were supporters of the doc-
trine of the free will of man.   There was, besides, a
third party, composed chiefly of young persons, perhaps spinsters and bachelors, who by siding, sometimes with one and sometimes with the other, seemed
inclined to provoke the opposing parties to a general
combat.   It was evident from the clamour of the
females, and from the swearing of the men, that the
argument, if such it might be called, would never
arrive at any legitimate conclusion; and taking advantage therefore of a general pause, the effect of
exhausted rage, I was induced to offer my aid as a
mediator between the two sexes.   Now, it so happens,
that when persons are angry or ridiculous, they like
to make parties of all the spectators; and as I had
taken no part in the fray, but had been strictly neutral,
the proposal was generally agreed to ; especially as I
had the appearance of one of the meek among men.
Getting therefore upon one of the benches, I stretched
forth my hand, and proceeded as follows :—

" Ladies and gentlemen, the question which you
have referred to me is one of the greatest importance,
not only to me, but to you,—not only to you, but to
all the world.

" It requires to know which of the sexes was born
for dominion—whether woman should rule ('or man
should be ruled,' said an Irishman).   It not only
questions whether wife should rule husband, or husband rule wife—but also if Queens should ascend the
throne, or if Kings should sit upon it; for whichever
may be unfit to command a family must be equally
unqualified to rule a nation."   The conclusion of this
sentence was followed by shouts of applause from

both parties, each applying to the other the unfitness to which I alluded. "If," said I, "we may judge from a law which exists and has existed, I should say that the softer sex are unqualified for the thrones, from which by that very law they stand excluded." Here I was obliged to bow to the applause of my male hearers, and also to the ladies, in order to avoid the force of a flying patten.

"But there is one circumstance," I continued, "and it certainly goes strongly against such a conclusion;—I mean that in that instance the men were the law makers." Here again I had to bow to the ladies, and duck to the gentlemen. "I will say, moreover, that if we refer to the history of a nation where that law was unknown, we shall find that the reigns of two thirds of her Queens have been happy and glorious. (Loud applause from the females.)

"This fact, however, goes no further in support of this side of the question, than the Salic law on the other; for allowing that the sway of those Queens was so sweet and splendid, yet we must remember, that they governed by their ministers, and conquered by their generals and admirals. (Cheers from the men.) If we trace still further back in history, even unto the days of Saul and David, and if we find a frequent mention of Kings, and of their being anointed, what then shall we say of this question, if we find in the whole course of that history, no instance of an anointed Queen! (Hisses and groans from the ladies.) If such be the fact, what shall we infer from it, but that there were no priestesses? (Shouts and laughter from the ladies.) But why had they no priestesses? I must confess that I am unable to answer. (Cheers from the males.) I will now consider the other branch of the subject; for although it is evident, that those who are unfit to rule families, must be unqualified to rule kingdoms, yet it does not follow, therefore, that those who are unable to govern kingdoms, are unequal to the lighter task of governing a family. There are very many worthy women whom I should be loth to trust with a sceptre, but they sway the domestic rod with vigour and success—(hear! from the men); and there are also many men of a different stamp, of indolent and profligate characters, whose affairs thrive best, or would thrive better under the guidance of their wives. (Hear! from the women.) We know, too, that there are others who have willingly resigned to their wives the control of their purse, and the direction of their affairs; convinced, by experience, that they were the best merchants, the best accountants, and the best orators. (Hear, hear! from the ladies.) Upon these grounds we may assign the right of dominion to the female sex (screams of applause from the women, and groans from the men; I say, upon these grounds we may assign the right of dominion to the female sex (the same tumult repeated); I say (said I, raising my voice), I say that upon these groans we may assign the right of dominion to the female sex, provided that the whole, or greater portion of men, may be supposed idle, profligate, or the most ignorant. But I must confess, and I do it with all sincerity, that this would appear to me to be a most unhandsome, most uncharitable, and unjust estimate. (Shouts from the men, and hisses from the ladies.)

"How then shall we decide this great question,

seeing that the trial by battle is by parliament abolished? It may be ruled by precedent, or rather the want of it, that the female sex be excluded from the sovereignty and the priesthood, but their claims to domestic dominion are as yet uncontroverted (cheers from the ladies); and as yet unestablished. (Cheers from the gentlemen. There only remains, in my opinion, a middle course to pursue.

> Let all agree,—let none engross the sway,
> But each command by turns, and each obey.

Let the lady be paramount in the kitchen and the nursery, and absolute in the garrets. Let the gentleman be king in his parlour, and emperor in his study; and as for the drawing room and the garden, let their sway there be divided. Let her be a judge in fashions, in novels, and in all fancy articles; and let him decide on politics, on liquors, and on horseflesh. As for all other matters of argument, let them be considered as drawn battles at draughts; and finally let each sex consider itself as bound to the other, by an alliance offensive and defensive." The conclusion of this my oration was followed by very general cries of applause, which were the more gratifying, when I considered the difficulty of pleasing all parties in a concern of so much interest to each. Nor was that my only reward, for I received I know not how many invitations to partake of porter, gin, and punch, all of which I declined, alleging that I wished to go straightway to Waterloo Bridge—at least, as far as it was possible to do so by Gray's Inn Lane, Chancery Lane, and the Strand. I had just reached the middle of Elm Street, when I was alarmed by loud and piercing screams, and as a carriage had rapidly turned the corner, I feared that some unfortunate human being had been run over. There is something in the shrill cry of a female in distress, that irresistibly impels, and wings one to her succour; I flew up the hill—turned the corner, and beheld at my feet a poor swine, which was screaming under the repeated lashes of a ruffian drover. She had sunk down, apparently from exhaustion, in the middle of the kennel, and as she started and kicked under the blood-thirsty thong, her struggles and splashings were truly shocking. Aged—and a female —exposed to insult, cruelty, and indignity; her grunts so like groans, and her squeaks so like screams, it was impossible for humanity to look on and be passive. I straddled over the unfortunate sow, and interposed my body betwixt her and her tormentor; and had it been at the risk of immola-tion, my feelings could not have allowed me to shrink from it. I should have died a glorious martyr to humanity! I protected the innocent, and I did more, for I threatened to chastise her oppressor; and I should certainly have done so with his own whip, if I could only have wrested it from him. However, I accepted the brute's challenge to fight; and here I must say, that upon any other occasion, I should have deemed it disgraceful and ungentlemanly; but in such a cause, as the champion of humanity, the guardian of the brute creation, I thought it not only gentlemanly, but angelic; and I felt that I was quite in my duty when I folded up my new coat, and con-fided it to the care of a decent shopkeeper. We exchanged only a few blows, and if I did not thrash him heartily, he owed it to my humanity; for it was merely from a reluctance to end in blood what I.had begun in tears, that I so speedily declined the combat. The spectators indeed did not seem to enter into my feeling; but whip me the man who would not prefer the praise of mercy to the meed of victory! Besides, I considered it a sin, a kind of profanation, to mar and disfigure "the human face divine," and one of us at least, was handsome.

I did not however resign the cause and interests of the poor sow, but slipping a crown into the hand of the drover, I recommended her to his mercy as a man and a Christian: "coax her," said I, "call her, or run before her, and entice her with a cabbage leaf—do anything but whip her so cruelly. And now," I continued, addressing myself to the bystanders, amongst whom were some very well dressed ladies and gentlemen, "now let me impress one very great error as regards pig driving. A pig will run this way and that, and any way, perhaps, but the right one; but it is uncharitable and cruel to attribute to *obstinacy* what may only originate in an over anxiety to please. I have seen a pig run backward, and forward, and sideways, and if it had been possible to run a dozen ways at once, I verily believe it would have done it."

The sow got up, the crowd dispersed, and I pursued my journey. It afterwards struck me that I heard at a distance the same shrill, humanlike, and persevering screams; but it might be fancy, for I believe they will ring in my ears as often as I pass the corner of Elm Street, Gray's Inn Lane. Gray's Inn Lane, by the bye, is not, as I conjecture, the true name of it; the ancient appellation must have been anything but what it now bears—perhaps *Grazing Lane*, because ere it was built upon, the cattle used to graze in it.

Be that as it may, there is nothing farther to remark of Gray's Inn Lane, but that it brings one into Holborn.

Hence, and through Chancery Lane, I amused myself by speculating on the faces of the passengers. It's a study I am very fond of, and if I am in any way superstitious, it is in the signs and forebodings of the countenance. Who cannot trace in the face of a dandy the circulation of his two ideas,—his opinion of himself and others ; and who is there that mistakes the keen eye of a genius?

But it is Temper that writes the most legible hand in the countenance ; and it is easy therefore to distinguish, amongst a crowd, the pet lamb of his mother; the tyrant of his family; and the humble servant of his wife. There's that man, said I, looking at a gentleman who was standing on the edge of the pavement—his curled lip indicates his pride ; but I know by the very restlessness of his eye, that he's afraid of bailiffs. As for that man who has just passed, I would not live with such a temper for my board and lodging. That lady's mask is handsome ; but I must say with the fox, " cerebrum non habet;" and her little girl's doll has more wit in her one eye than she has in two. My judgments, however, were not always fortunate; the man with restless eyes was only looking for his poodle dog; and as the cross-looking man went soon afterwards into a cook shop, I supposed that he had been rather hungered than ill-natured. As for the lady and the child, I don't know whether I set them down rightly or not, but in the meantime I will suppose so, and cling to my study. I was now in the Strand, close to Temple Bar; and from hence to Waterloo Bridge, I calculated would be the journey of an hour. Who is there that can walk along this, or any of the principal City streets, without admiring the number of elegant shops, and the still more elegant and wonderful productions which they contain? they are to me the sources of the greatest pleasure, and when time will permit me to do so, I inspect them from the goldsmith's and jeweller's, down to the humbler repositories of the tinman and brazier. Nay I have been caught, and rallied by my acquaintance for looking in lovingly at the haberdasher's and milliner's.

It is not that I am merely smitten with the beauty of their articles that I look into them with such admiration and delight, but it is because I can there trace an evident and progressive improvement in the arts and manufactures of my country. *This* affords me a delight in which all ought to sympathise, and *that* calls forth an admiration in which all must participate. Whether we examine those paintings and prints, which are more strictly termed works of art; whether we examine those fabrics which have been produced by the most complicated machinery, or those minor articles which are the work of the handicraftsman, we shall find that there prevails in all a degree of taste which can only be the result of a general cultivation of mind. It is this that has led to so many ingenious inventions, and has tended above all to promote the general alliance between elegance and utility; and when we contemplate the mighty

effects of its progress hitherto, who can calculate its
future attainments? Long may it continue its mighty
march, to the honour and happiness of my country-
men; and may they, in better days, obtain for their
industry and ingenuity those rewards which hitherto
have not kept pace with their merits. May they still
travel onwards in the path of improvement, and
surmounting all obstacles which a meaner ambition
would plant in their way, reach that point of excel-
lence and perfection to which man in this world may
be destined to attain! Here a bookseller's shop gave
a new turn to my speculations. We are certainly a
reading people, I thought, as I looked in at the
window; but I would fain know if this cultivation of
the mind conduces to happiness. I was inclined to
decide in the affirmative; for the collection before
me suggested the names of Shakspeare, Addison,
Milton, and a host of other authors, linked with a
thousand delightful reminiscences—much must de-
pend upon one's course of reading, said I, while
running over the titles:—*A Sermon to Sinne—The
Foole's Jest Book—Dialogues of the Dead—Life in
London—Tomline's Sea Worthies—The Newgate Cal-
endar—Cato's Letter to the Country—The King's Reply
to his People—Wordes to the Wyse—Witte's Chronykill
—a New Spelling Book.* But what have we here?
It happened very strangely, I might almost say
miraculously, that I read a solution of my speculation
in a book before me. It was called *The Prayse of
Ignorance;* and in the two grave-looking brown
complexioned pages that lay open, I read as follows:—

" Hee was made to bee happye but not learned:

for eating of the Tree of Knowledge hee was caste out of Paradyse. Hys was the Blisse of Ignorance ; but We being born to bee learned, and unhappye withal, have noght but the Ignorance of Blisse. Soe we aske not which bee the most happye; but which bee the leeste unhappye ; and trulye hee hath leeste Paines that hath not most Bokes. Hee is your Berkshire or Hampshire manne with a harde Head and a long Stomach—which is a Hogge among Wittes, not a Witte among Hogges ; and when hee sleepes you wot not which can grunte loudeste. For why? Hee beares no care on hys Head, excepte hys Hatte, and that hee hath not much care withal except a-Sundayes. One maye rede in hys Vysage that he wots not to write : but he maketh hys Marke and soe hath one to ten chances against the Gallowes. Hys Haire is unkempte ; and so is hys Intellecte ; but betwixt both hee saveth a World of Trouble. Hys Head itches : it doth not ake. It is as emptye as a drye Bowle ; but hys Belly is crammede to the fulle—for hee is no author.

You may write him downe a Manne with an Idea : but hee is more blessede than anye with two ; for hee hath nonne of their feverish Deliriums. How can hys Minde wandere?

Now look you to your Schollar. He cryes in hys very Birthe, for hee is stryped into his A B C ; most of hys Wordes doe end in O, and hys Whyppinges have many Syllables. Hee hateth his Boke fulle sore : and noe Marvel ! For he wotteth to the Sorrowe of hys Bottom, that Learning is at the Bottom of hys Sorrowe. There is a naturall Hyphen betwixt them. A connexion of Minde and Matter. One cometh not without the other, and hee curseth them both in his Waye. Hys Grammar bringes him fresh annoye : for hee onlye weepeth in another Sense. But hee gets the Interjections by Harte. Figures are a great Greefe unto him ; and onlye multiplie hys Paines. The dead Tongues doe bringe him a lively sorrowe : hee gets them at hys Fingers endes. And soe hee waxeth in Growth ; into a Quarto or Folio, as maye bee ; a greater Bulke of Learning and Heavinesse ; and belike hee goeth madde with Study overmuch. Alsoe hee betaketh him to write ; and letts hys Braines be sukede forthe through a Quill. If hee seeke to get Monnye hys Boke is unsolde ; and if hee wolde have of the Worlde's Fame hee is praysde of those that studye not hys Rimes : or is scornde and mockede of those that will not understande hys Conceites, which is a greate Sorrowe ; for Poesie hath made hys Harte tender, and a little Worde is a greate Paine. Soe hee gets no Substance, but looses Fleshe. Lastlye hee dyeth a pitifull Death ; the kindly Creditour of an unkindlye Worlde ; and then hee is weepede for ; and it is askde, ' Why will hee not write again ?'

And the Parishe Clarke hys witte sufficeth to hys Epitaph, which runnes :—

> Alake ! alake ! that Studye colde not save
> Soe great a Witte out of so small a grave.
> But Learning must decaye, and Letters both,
> And Studye too. Death is a dreadful Goth,
> Which spareth nonne."——

Unfortunately, I could neither read further, nor turn over the leaf through the glass ; and still more unfortunately, I did not go in and purchase the book. However, I had read enough to lead me to a decision, that the ignorant are the most happy; and as I walked away from the window I repeated the lines :—

> " No more : where ignorance is bliss,
> 'Tis folly to be wise."

As this was the second great question that I had decided, I walked onward to Waterloo Bridge, without any doubt of being able to determine the third, viz. : as to the merits and demerits of the bridge and its architect. But here an unforeseen difficulty presented itself; for owing to the lateness of my arrival, and the sudden fall of a very dense fog, I was unable to do anything more than determine to come again.

I accordingly walked back into the Strand, and finding a stage at Somerset House, I took my seat in it, and turned towards home. I had three travelling companions, two males and one female; and after we had discussed the usual topics, and paid the usual compliments, the conversation dwindled away into a profound silence ; I therefore employed myself in the arrangement of my travels, and in recollecting the various incidents and reflections to which they had given rise.

I must request, Mr. Editor, your utmost indulgence towards one, so inexperienced as a traveller, and if you should find that the style of my narration is rugged and uneven, and that the incidents and reflections are abrupt and unconnected, I beg that you will attribute it to the unpleasant jolting of the stage, and the frequent interruptions and stoppages that it met with.

EXTRACTS FROM THE LION'S HEAD.

IF I. E. L. had written her "Stanzas" before the appearance of Lord Byron's, their merit would have been unquestionable.

G.'s Muse should use Steer's Opodeldoc, which is allow to be excellent for "strains."

To Y. and Y.—No; a word to the Y's.

L.—sends us a "Scene from Memory, from the French." We suppose L.'s memory is in French.

A. B. F.—"Hymn; in Imitation of Wordsworth." Lion's Head is unfortunately obliged to decline giving it the opportunity of being "said or sung" by the readers of the "London."

A Correspondent has sent us some lines "On Winter," which with much gravity he informs us are meant for burlesque. The following are certainly serious :

> "Riding on the storm, he shies
> Hail and snowballs from the skies :
> And the earth, all over white,
> Is very bad for a weak sight ;
> But spectacles made of green glass
> Will make it look again like grass,
> And you shall dream of making hay
> In the middle of Christmas-day,
> And think you spy green gooseberries budding
> In all the eyes of a raisin pudding."

W.'s " Night " is too long, for the moon rises twice in it.

We are happy to learn from L. that he has " descended from his poetic flights into another *walk;*" perhaps he has a prose essay on foot for our next number.

G. R.'s diction would inflate a balloon. He should

remember that "a power of fine words" is not "poetic power."

T. says that his tale is out of his own head; is he a tadpole?

B. conjures us to tell him "whether he may ever hope to produce anything he need not blush at?" No, never; if he continues to write such poetry as he now submits to our perusal. To be serious, let our correspondent take a hint from Dr. Watts: ,

> "How doth the little busy *b*
> *Improve* each shining hour."

Sam Sparkle's Anacreontic (from Queen Street, Cheapside—hush!) is too far gone : the Conduits in Chepe do not run wine now-a-days. The Muse is often agreeable in her cups; but when she stammers in her grammar and stumbles in her metaphors, it is high time she should be seen home. Sam's Muse has not a *foot* to stand upon. Can he send us something soberer, or was his Muse born with a claret-mark?

Minor's "Conflagration" exhibits some power. Sometimes indeed his "words that burn" go a step on the other side of the sublime.

> "Uprose the curling flames, and writhed amain,
>   As they had burned themselves, and roar'd with pain ;
> *   *   *   *
> And flocks of glowing fragments, forced on high,
>   Like red flamingos soar'd along the sky."

We really did not know that "Juvenile was handed down to posterity as an author much read by the Romans." For this information we are indebted to B., and not less so for his candour in pointing out one fault in our Magazine—that "the London is too full of literature." We are glad it is no worse, and have no doubt that with B.'s assistance we shall be able, when necessary, to render it quite otherwise.

Centaur on "Riding" seems to have been inspired by the King's Mews. If he had as much of it as Charles at Charing Cross, he would be glad to feel his own feet again. Riding, however—we do not mean C.'s paper—is a good exercise.

H.'s "Captivity" is in some parts pathetic; but in others he has allowed himself to be tempted into a strain that accords but ill with its melancholy.

> " Ah me, it is the worst of wretched things
> When men are pinion'd and have got no wings;
> They watch regretfully the sparrows small,
> And gaze with envy on a *free*stone wall.
> Night brought me hither, and relieved my pains
> Awhile, because she hid me from my chains;
> The morning came, and she was *mist*, and I
> Was left," &c.

"It is pleasant to be immortal," says a correspondent signed S., "if it be only for a season." Marry, here is a fellow that discounts eternity.

Anacreon, in his foolish Greek manner, entreated one of the Royal Academy of Antiquity (some Sir Thomas Lawrence of Teos) to paint his mistress; and though he desired effects which were sufficient to pose the acutest brush, he still did not (to use Mr. Egan's fanciful phraseology) "render the features perfectly unintelligible." A Chelsea Anacreon submits the following directions to the R. A.'s of this age. Whether they are capable of execution we leave to the painters to determine; but the lines have an originality about them which seems to hold out its own protection. We should like to see Mr. Shee or Mr. Phillips working to this pattern.

" Come, take thy pencil—paint my love
More tender than most tender dove ;
Suffuse her cheeks with that warm glow
Would fain on lover hope bestow ;
And make it frequent *go and come*
Back to and from its sighful home.
Lay on her *tongue the tone of truth,*
The Vesper Hymn of virgin youth.
She loves each eve, in pious praise,
To lisp to Sol's declining rays ;
And hide that song from vulgar men
Within its own most hallow'd pen,
By double row of pillars, chaste
As Dian in the *moral waste* [&c.]
From those lips *let odours breathe ;*
Round them *all my kisses wreathe.*
In her fond voluptuous chin
Mould a dimple, hearts to *gin ;*
And make thy magic art uprear
A heartsease smile behind each tear [&c.]
Give to her feet the airy motion
Of sunbeams trembling on the ocean ;
Lay her white fingers on a harp
Of gold, the power of gloom to warp.
And *if thou canst*, in its warm nest
Paint, paint the heart beneath the breast ;
Make visible its million springs,
Nor snap one of its thousand strings ;
Depict it in a tear-wove guise
Floating upon a sea of sighs,
Its hundred ears inclined to one
Sweet tale of love," &c., &c.

We suspect H. B.'s "Sonnet to the Rising Sun" was written for a lark.

Thersites is left "to be reclaimed," as he desires ; of which there is much need, and perchance but little hope.

We should be loth to make Mr. Christie angry by printing Athenæus's "Ode to Fonthill Abbey," now that it is advertised for sale. The poem opens bravely, but sneaks off miserably at the conclusion— or, to speak in our own style, takes up at *The Lion*, and sets down at *The Lamb*. Caliph Vathek is not "that simple Eastern tale of Turkish hearts" which the bard describes. Why cannot our correspondent get his ode inserted among the sundries in the catalogue. It would sound well. "Three saucepans, four sets of fire-irons, two grates, one ode, and a coal-scuttle." There is a way of getting these things smuggled in.

The following verses are selected from an ode written in fear of the new Marriage Act:

"FARE THEE WELL.

"Before our banns be published like a tax,
Ask'd on the portals of St. Mary Axe,
If thou wilt marry me—then prythee tell—
Oh now—or fare thee well !

"Think of old maids of seventy—fourscore,
Fourscore old women at the temple's door,
Those that can read, and those that learn to spell—
Oh now—or fare thee well !

"Suppose our names a history—suppose
Our love forepicked to pieces, like a rose
Shed blushing all abroad—my Isabel !
Oh now—or fare thee well !"—Theodosius.

L. F., who dates himself under sixteen years of age, will do well to remember that youth may excuse, but not recommend, bad poetry. The "Night Thoughts" are not admired because the author was Young.

A. R.'s poem has been burnt, as he requested, with a multitude of others. "It looked indifferent well," as Sir Andrew Aguecheek has it, "in a flame-coloured stock."

The Elegy on Dr. Hutton is well written —— by Mr. Carstairs.

M.'s Ode on the Martyrs who were burnt in the *rain* of Queen Mary is original, but wants fire.

"The Sketch of a Plan for abolishing Beggars"— by making them Gentlemen—is humane but Utopian.

A LETTER FROM AN EMIGRANT.

SQUAMPASH FLATTS, *9th November*, 1827.

DEAR BROTHER,

Here we are, thank Providence, safe and well, and in the finest country you ever saw. At this moment I have before me the sublime expanse of Squampash Flatts—the majestic Mudiboo winding through the midst—with the magnificent range of the Squab mountains in the distance. But the prospect is impossible to describe in a letter! I might as well attempt a Panorama in a pill-box!

We have fixed our Settlement on the left bank of the river. In crossing the rapids we lost most of our heavy baggage and all our iron work, but by great good fortune we saved Mrs. Paisley's grand piano and the children's toys. Our infant city consists of three log huts and one of clay, which however, on the second day, fell in to the ground landlords. We have now built it up again;—and, all things considered, are as comfortable as we could expect—and have christened our settlement New London, in compliment to the Old Metropolis. We have one of the log houses to ourselves—or at least shall have when we have built a new hog-stye. We burnt down the first one in making a bonfire to keep off the wild beasts, and for the present the pigs are in the parlour. As yet our rooms are rather usefully than elegantly furnished. We have gutted the Grand Upright, and it makes a convenient cupboard,—the chairs were obliged to blaze at our bivouacs, but thank Heaven we have never leisure to sit down, and so do not miss them. My boys are contented, and will be well when they have got over some awkward accidents in lopping and felling. Mrs. P. grumbles a little, but it is her custom to lament most when she is in the midst of comforts. She complains of solitude, and says she could enjoy the very stiffest of stiff visits.

The first time we lighted a fire in our new abode, a large serpent came down the chimney, which I looked upon as a good omen. However, as Mrs. P. is not partial to snakes, and the heat is supposed to attract those reptiles, we have dispensed with fires ever since. As for wild beasts, we hear them howling and roaring round the fence every night from dusk till daylight, but we have only been inconvenienced by one Lion. The first time he came, in order to get rid of the brute peaceably, we turned out an old ewe, with which he was well satisfied;—but ever since he comes to us as regular as clock-work for his mutton; and if we do not soon contrive to cut his acquaintance, we shall hardly have a sheep in the flock. It would have been easy to shoot him, being well provided with muskets, but Barnaby mistook our remnant of gunpowder for onion seed, and sowed it all in the kitchen garden. We did try to trap him into a pitfall; but after twice catching Mrs. P., and every one of the children in turn, it was given up. They are now, however, perfectly at ease about the animal, for they never stir out of doors at all, and to make them quite comfortable, I have blocked up all the windows and barricaded the door.

We have lost only one of our number since we came; namely, Diggory, the market gardener, from Glasgow, who went out one morning to botanise, and never came back. I am much surprised at his absconding, as he had nothing but a spade to go off with. Chippendale, the carpenter, was sent after him, but did not return ; and Gregory, the smith, has been out after them these two days. I have just despatched Mudge, the Herdsman, to look for all three, and hope he will soon give a good account of them, as they are the most useful men in the whole settlement, and, in fact, indispensable to its existence.

The river Mudiboo is deep, and rapid, and said to swarm with alligators, though I have heard but of three being seen at one time, and none of those above eighteen feet long ; this, however, is immaterial, as we do not use the river fluid, which is thick and dirty, but draw all our water from natural wells and tanks. Poisonous springs are rather common, but are easily distinguished by containing no fish or living animal. Those, however, which swarm with frogs, toads, newts, efts, etc., are harmless, and may be safely used for culinary purposes.

In short, I know of no drawback but one, which, I am sanguine, may be got over hereafter, and do earnestly hope and advise, if things are no better in England than when I left, you, and as many as you can persuade, will sell off all, and come over to this African Paradise.

The drawback I speak of is this : although I have never seen any one of the creatures, it is too certain that the mountains are inhabited by a race of Monkeys, whose cunning and mischievous talents exceed even the most incredible stories of their tribe. No human art or vigilance seems of avail; we have planned ambuscades, and watched night after night, but no attempt has been made ; yet the moment the guard was relaxed, we were stripped without mercy.   I am convinced they must have had spies night and day on our motions, yet so secretly and cautiously, that no glimpse of one has yet been seen by any of our people.   Our last crop was cut and carried off, with the precision of an English Harvesting.   Our spirit stores—(you will be amazed to hear that these creatures pick locks with the dexterity of London burglars)—have been broken open and ransacked, though half the establishment were on the watch ; and the brutes have been off to their mountains, five miles distant, without even the dogs giving an alarm. I could almost pesuade myself at times, such are their supernatural knowledge, swiftness, and invisibility, that we have to contend with evil spirit.   I long for your advice, to refer to on this subject, and am, Dear Philip, Your loving brother,   AMBROSE MAWE.

P.S. Since writing the above, you will be concerned to hear the body of poor Diggory has been found, horribly mangled by wild beasts.   The fate of Chippendale, Gregory, and Mudge, is no longer doubtful.   The old Lion has brought the Lioness, and the sheep being all gone, they have made a joint attack upon the Bullock-house.   The Mudiboo has overflowed, and Squampash Flatts are a swamp.   I have just discovered that the Monkeys are my own rascals, that I brought out from England.   We are coming back as fast as we can.

ODE TO M. BRUNEL.

"Well, said, old Mole! canst work i' the dark so fast? a worthy pioneer!"
—Hamlet.

WELL!——Monsieur Brunel,
How prospers now thy mighty undertaking,
To join by a hollow way the Bankside friends
Of Rotherhithe, and Wapping,—
     Never be stopping,
But poking, groping, in the dark keep making
An archway, underneath the Dabs and Gudgeons,
For Collier men and pitchy old Curmudgeons,
To cross the water in inverse proportion,
Walk under steam-boats under the keel's ridge,
To keep down all extortion,
And without sculls to diddle London Bridge!
In a fresh hunt, a new Great Bore to worry,
Thou didst to earth thy human terriers follow,
Hopeful at last from Middlesex to Surrey,
    To give us the "View hollow."
In short it was thy aim, right north and south,
To put a pipe into old Thames's mouth;
Alas! half-way thou hadst proceeded, when
Old Thames, through roof, not water-proof,
Came, like "a tide in the affairs of men;"
And with a mighty stormy kind of roar,
     Reproachful of thy wrong,
     Burst out in that old song
Of Incledon's, beginning "Cease, rude Bore"—
Sad is it, worthy of one's tears,
   Just when one seems the most successful,
To find one's self o'er head and ears
   In difficulties most distressful!
Other great speculations have been nursed,

R

Till want of proceeds laid them on a shelf;
But thy concern was at the worst,
　　When it began to *liquidate* itself!
But now Dame Fortune has her false face hidden,
And languishes thy Tunnel,—so to paint,
Under a slow incurable complaint,
　　　　Bed-ridden!
Why, when thus Thames—bed-bother'd—why repine!
Do try a spare bed at the Serpentine!
Yet let none think thee daz'd, or craz'd, or stupid;
　　And sunk beneath thy own and Thames's craft;
Let them not style thee some Mechanic Cupid
　　Pining and pouting o'er a broken shaft!
I'll tell thee with thy tunnel what to do;
Light up thy boxes, build a bin or two,
The wine does better than such water trades:
　　Stick up a sign—the sign of the Bore's Head;
　　I've drawn it ready for thee in black lead,
And make thy cellar subterrane,—Thy Shades?

ANACREONTIC.

FOR THE NEW YEAR.

COME, fill up tne Bowl, for if ever the glass
　　Found a proper excuse or fit season,
For toasts to be honour'd, or pledges to pass,
　　Sure, this hour brings an exquisite reason:
For hark! the last chime of the dial has ceased,
　　And Old Time, who his leisure to cozen,
Had finish'd the Months, like the flasks at a feast,
　　Is preparing to tap a fresh dozen!
　　　　　　Hip! Hip! and Hurrah!

Then fill, all ye Happy and Free, unto whom
   The past Year has been pleasant and sunny;
Its months each as sweet as if made of the bloom
   Of the *thyme* whence the bee gathers honey—
Days usher'd by dew-drops, instead of the tears,
   May be wrung from some wretcheder cousin—
Then fill, and with gratitude join in the cheers
   That triumphantly hail a fresh dozen!
             Hip! Hip! and Hurrah!

And ye, who have met with Adversity's blast,
   And been bow'd to the earth by its fury;
To whom the Twelve Months, that have recently
     pass'd,
   Were as harsh as a prejudiced jury,—
Still, fill to the Future! and join in our chime,
   The regrets of remembrance to cozen,
And having obtained a New Trial of Time,
   Shout in hopes of a kindlier dozen!
             Hip! Hip! and Hurrah!

A WATERLOO BALLAD.

To Waterloo, with sad ado,
   And many a sigh and groan,
Amongst the dead, came Patty Head,
   To look for Peter Stone.

"O prithee tell, good sentinel,
   If I shall find him here?
I'm come to weep upon his corse,
   My Ninety-Second dear!

"Into our town a sergeant came
  With ribands all so fine,
A-flaunting in his cap—alas
  His bow enlisted mine!

"They taught him how to turn his toes,
  And stand as stiff as starch;
I thought that it was love and May,
  But it was love and March!

"A sorry March indeed to leave
  The friends he might have kep',—
No March of Intellect it was,
  But quite a foolish step.

"O prithee tell, good sentinel,
  If hereabout he lies?
I want a corpse with reddish hair,
  And very sweet blue eyes."

Her sorrow on the sentinel
  Appear'd to deeply strike :—
"Walk in," he said, "among the dead,
  And pick out which you like."

And soon she pick'd out Peter Stone,
  Half turned into a corse;
A cannon was his bolster, and
  His mattrass was a horse.

"O Peter Stone, O Peter Stone,
  Lord here has been a skrimmage!
What have they done to your poor breast,
  That used to hold my image?"

"O Patty Head, O Patty Head,
   You're come to my last kissing;
Before I'm set in the Gazette
   As wounded, dead, and missing!

"Alas! a splinter of a shell
   Right in my stomach sticks;
French mortars don't agree so well
   With stomachs as French bricks.

"This very night a merry dance
   At Brussels was to be;—
Instead of opening a ball,
   A ball has opened me.

"Its billet every bullet has,
   And well it does fulfil it;—
I wish mine hadn't come so straight,
   But been a 'crooked billet.'

"And then there came a cuirassier
   And cut me on the chest;—
He had no pity in his heart,
   For he had *steel'd his breast.*

"Next thing a lancer, with his lance,
   Began to thrust away;
I call'd for quarter, but, alas!
   It was not Quarter-day.

"He ran his spear right through my arm,
   Just here above the joint:—
O Patty dear, it was no joke,
   Although it had a point.

"With loss of blood I fainted off,
  As dead as women do—
But soon by charging over me,
  The *Coldstream* brought me to.

"With kicks and cuts, and balls and blows,
  I throb and ache all over;
I'm quite convinc'd the field of Mars
  Is not a field of clover!

"O why did I a soldier turn
  For any royal Guelph?
I might have been a butcher, and
  In business for myself!

"O why did I the bounty take
  (And here he gasp'd for breath)
My shillingsworth of 'list is nail'd
  Upon the door of death!

"Without a coffin I shall lie
  And sleep my sleep eternal:
Not ev'n a *shell*—my only chance
  Of being made a *Kernel!*

"O Patty dear, our wedding bells
  Will never ring at Chester!
Here I must lie in Honour's bed,
  That isn't worth a *tester!*

"Farewell, my regimental mates,
  With whom I used to dress!
My corps is changed, and I am now,
  In quite another mess.

" Farewell, my Patty dear, I have
 No dying consolations,
Except, when I am dead, you 'll go
And see th' Illuminations."

COCKLE *v.* CACKLE.

THOSE who much read advertisements and bills,
 Must have seen puffs of Cockle's Pills,
  Call'd Anti-bilious—
Which some Physicians sneer at, supercilious,
But which we are assured, if timely taken,
 May save your liver and bacon ;
Whether or not they really give one ease,
  I, who have never tried,
  Will not decide ;
But no two things in union go like these —
Viz.—Quacks and Pills—save Ducks and Pease.
Now Mrs. W. was getting sallow,
Her lilies not of the white kind, but yellow,
And friends portended was preparing for
  A human Pâté Périgord ;
She was, indeed, so very far from well,
Her Son, in filial fear, procured a box
Of those said pellets to resist Bile's shocks,
And—tho' upon the ear it strangely knocks—
To save her by a Cockle from a shell !
But Mrs. W., just like Macbeth,
Who very vehemently bids us " throw
Bark to the Bow-wows," hated physic so,

It seem'd to share "the bitterness of Death :"
Rhubarb—Magnesia—Jalap, and the kind—
Senna—Steel—Assa-fœtida, and Squills—
Powder or Draught—but least her throat inclined
To give a course to Boluses or Pills ;
No—not to save her life, in lung or lobe,
For all her lights' or all her liver's sake,
Would her convulsive thorax undertake,
Only one little uncelestial globe !

'Tis not to wonder at, in such a case,
If she put by the pill-box in a place
For linen rather than for drugs intended—
Yet for the credit of the pills let's say
  After they thus were stow'd away,
  Some of the linen mended ;
But Mrs. W. by disease's dint,
Kept getting still more yellow in her tint,
When lo ! her second son, like elder brother,
Marking the hue on the parental gills,
Brought a new charge of Anti-tumeric Pills,
To bleach the jaundiced visage of his Mother—
Who took them—in her cupboard—like the other.

  "Deeper and deeper, still," of course,
   The fatal colour daily grew in force ;
Till daughter W. newly come from Rome,
Acting the self-same filial, pillial, part,
To cure Mamma, another dose brought home
Of Cockles ;—not the Cockles of her heart !
  These going where the others went before,
  Of course she had a very pretty store ;

And then—-some hue of health her chee adorning,
    The Medicine so good must be,
    They brought her dose on dose, which she
Gave to the up-stairs cupboard, "night and morn-
    ing."
Till wanting room at last, for other stocks,
Out of the window one fine day she pitch'd
The pillage of each box, and quite enrich'd
The feed of Mister Burrell's hens and cocks,—
    A little Barber of a by-gone day,
        Over the way
Whose stock in trade, to keep the least of shops,
Was one great head of Kemble,—that is, John,
Staring in plaster, with a *Brutus* on,
And twenty little Bantam fowls—with *crops.*
Little Dame W. thought when through the sash
    She gave the physic wings,
    To find the very things
So good for bile, so bad for chicken rash,
For thoughtless cock, and unreflecting pullet!
But while they gathered up the nauseous nubbles,
Each peck'd itself into a peck of troubles,
And brought the hand of Death upon its gullet.
They might as well have addled been, or ratted,
For long before the night—ah woe betide
The 'Pills! each suicidal Bantam died
        Unfatted!

    Think of poor Burrel's shock,
Of Nature's debt to see his hens all payers,
And laid in death as Everlasting Layers,
With Bantam's small Ex-Emperor, the Cock,

In ruffled plumage and funereal hackle,
Giving, undone by Cockle, a last Cackle!
To see as stiff as stone, his un'live stock,
It really was enough to move his block.
Down on the floor he dash'd, with horror big,
Mr. Bell's third wife's mother's coachman's wig;
And with a tragic stare like his own Kemble,
Burst out with natural emphasis enough,
  And voice that grief made tremble,
Into that very speech of sad Macduff—
"What!—all my pretty chickens and their dam,
  At one fell swoop!—
  Just when I'd bought a coop
To see the poor lamented creatures cram!"

  After a little of this mood,
  And brooding over the departed brood,
With razor he began to ope each craw,
Already turning black, as black as coals;
When lo! the undigested cause he saw—
  "Pison'd by goles!"

To Mrs. W.'s luck a contradiction,
Her window still stood open to conviction;
And by short course of circumstantial labour,
He fix'd the guilt upon his adverse neighbour;—
Lord! how he rail'd at her: declaring now,
He'd bring an action ere next Term of Hilary,
Then, in another moment, swore a vow,
He'd make her do pill-penance in the pillory!
She, meanwhile distant from the dimmest dream
Of combating with guilt, yard-arm or arm-yard,

Lapp'd in a paradise of tea and cream;
When up ran Betty with a dismal scream—
"Here's Mr. Burrell, ma'am, with all his farm-
        yard!"
Straight in he came, unbowing and unbending,
        With all the warmth that iron and a barbe
                Can harbour;
To dress the head and front of her offending,
The fuming phial of his wrath uncorking;
In short, he made her pay him altogether,
In hard cash, very *hard*, for ev'ry feather,
Charging of course, each Bantam as a Dorking;
Nothing could move him, nothing make him
        supple,
So the sad dame unpocketing her loss,
Had nothing left but to sit hands across,
And see her poultry "going down ten couple,"

Now birds by poison slain,
· As venom'd dart from Indian's hollow cane,
Are edible; and Mrs. W.'s thrift,—
She had a thrifty vein,—
Destined one pair for supper to make shift,—
Supper as usual at the hour of ten:
But ten o'clock arrived and quickly pass'd,
Eleven—twelve—and one o'clock at last,
Without a sign of supper even then!
At length the speed of cookery to quicken,
Betty was called, and with reluctant feet,
        Came up at a white heat—
"Well, never I see chicken like them chicken!
My saucepans, they have been a pretty while in 'em!

Enough to stew them, if it comes to that,
To flesh and bones, and perfect rags ; but drat
Those Anti-biling Pills ! there is no bile in 'em !"

HALFPENNY HATCH.

THE END.

E. Moxon, Son, & Co., Dover Street, W.